# Praise for Alice Clayton's laugh-out-loud sexy Cocktail Series

## *MAI TAI'D UP*

"Alice Clayton is a genius! *Mai Tai'd Up* is sexy, steamy, and totally hilarious! A must read that I didn't want to end."

—*New York Times* and *USA Today* bestselling author Emma Chase

## *SCREWDRIVERED*

"Cheers to Alice Clayton! *Screwdrivered* is a hilarious cocktail of crackling banter, heady sexual tension, and pop-your-cork love scenes. The heroine is brisk and lively (can we be friends, Viv?) and the hot librarian hero seduced me with his barely-restrained sensuality. I've never wanted a nerd more."

—*New York Times* and *USA Today* bestselling author Kresley Cole

## *RUSTY NAILED*

"We want to bask in the afterglow: giddy, blushing, and utterly in love with this book."

—*New York Times* and *USA Today* bestselling author Christina Lauren

"Clayton's trademark wit and general zaniness shine through in abundance as readers get an intimate view of the insecurities one faces while in a serious relationship. Steamy playful sex scenes and incorrigible friends make this a wonderful continuation of Wallbanger and Nightie Girl's journey to their happily ever after."

—*RT Book Reviews*

"For fun, sex, and strudel, make sure to spend some time with these wallbangers."

—*Heroes and Heartbreakers*

"A great follow-up to *Wallbanger* . . . just as funny and HOT as the first!"

—*Schmexy Girl Book Blog*

"Humorous, sizzling hot, romantic, and not missing dramatics. If you weren't a fan before, you certainly will be after reading *Rusty Nailed*."

—*Love Between the Sheets*

"Excuse me, I need to catch my breath. Either from panting or cracking up. Because I was always doing one of the two while reading *Rusty Nailed*. Alice Clayton, you never disappoint."

—*Book Bumblings*

"Simon and Caroline are as adorable, funny, and sexy as ever."

—*The Rock Stars of Romance*

"Witty dialogue, a quirky and lovable cast, and a whirlwind of a romance. . . ."

—*Peace Love Books*

"A great summer read, fantastic for lazing about and having fun with."

—*Under the Covers Book Blog*

"A story that is sure to please."

—*The Reading Café*

"I fell in wholehearted book-love! Fantastic voice, amazing characters!"

—*Teacups and Book Love*

"An entertaining romantic story overflowing with hilarity, passion, and emotion."

—*Sensual Reads*

## WALLBANGER

"Sultry, seXXXy, super-awesome . . . we LOVE it!"

—Perez Hilton

"An instant classic, with plenty of laugh-out-loud moments and riveting characters."

—Jennifer Probst,
*New York Times* bestselling author of *Searching for Perfect*

"Fun and frothy, with a bawdy undercurrent and a hero guaranteed to make your knees wobbly . . . The perfect blend of sex, romance, and baked goods."

—Ruthie Knox, bestselling author of *About Last Night*

"Alice Clayton strikes again, seducing me with her real woman sex appeal, unparalleled wit, and addicting snark; leaving me laughing, blushing, and craving knock all the paintings off the wall sex of my very own."

—Humor blogger Brittany Gibbons

"From the brilliantly fun characters to the hilarious, sexy, heartwarming storyline, *Wallbanger* is one that shouldn't be missed. I laughed. I sighed. Mostly, I grinned like an idiot."

—*Tangled up in Books*

"Finally a woman who knows her way around a man and a KitchenAid Mixer. She had us at zucchini bread!"

—*Curvy Girl Guide*

"A funny, madcap, smexy romantic contemporary. . . . Fast pacing and a smooth flowing storyline will keep you in stitches. . . ."

—*Smexy Books*

## And for her acclaimed Redhead series

"Zany and smoking-hot romance [that] will keep readers in stitches . . ."

—*RT Book Reviews*

"Alice Clayton makes me laugh, cringe, yell at the characters and cry."

—*Harlequin Junkie*

"I adore Grace and Jack. They have such amazing chemistry. The love that flows between them scorches the pages."

—*Smexy Books*

"Steamy romance, witty characters and a barrel full of laughs. . . ."
—*The Book Vixen*

"Laugh out loud funny."

—*Smokin Hot Books*

# also by alice clayton

## The Redhead Series

*The Unidentified Redhead*

*The Redhead Revealed*

*The Redhead Plays Her Hand*

## The Cocktail Series

*Wallbanger*

*Rusty Nailed*

*Screwdrivered*

# MAI TAI'D UP

alice clayton

G

GALLERY BOOKS

NEW YORK   LONDON   TORONTO   SYDNEY   NEW DELHI

# G

Gallery Books
A Division of Simon & Schuster, Inc.
1230 Avenue of the Americas
New York, NY 10020

First Gallery Books trade paperback edition December 2014

GALLERY BOOKS and colophon are registered trademarks
of Simon & Schuster, Inc.

For information about special discounts for bulk purchases,
please contact Simon & Schuster Special Sales at 1-866-506-1949
or business@simonandschuster.com.

The Simon & Schuster Speakers Bureau can bring authors to your live event.
For more information or to book an event contact the Simon & Schuster Speakers
Bureau at 1–866–248–3049 or visit our website at www.simonspeakers.com.

Manufactured in the United States of America

10   9   8   7   6   5   4   3   2   1

Library of Congress Cataloging-in-Publication Data is available.

ISBN 978-1-4767-6671-3
ISBN 978-1-4767-6674-4 (ebook)

*I've never been lucky enough to own a pit bull,*
*but I've always been a tiny bit in love with them.*
*This one's for all those gorgeous doggy grins.*

# acknowledgments

I've got the best job in the entire world. Scratch that. I've got the second best job in the entire world. The actual best job in the entire world is Robert Pattinson's massage therapist . . . but that's a story for a different day. Today I'm calling out the people in my life that help me keep this amazing story going. Especially on the days when the words aren't coming, even though the main characters want to be. See what I did there? Thanks to everyone who helped make *Mai Tai'd Up,* and the entire Cocktail Series, happen.

Here's that special hit list. I may have been watching too much *Sons of Anarchy* . . .

## team gallery
Nuding
Bergstrom
Dwyer
Horbachevsky
Psaltis
Burke

*team author*

Cole
Probst
Reisz
Proby
Evans
Chase

*team comma*

Royer

*team sanity*

Hogrebe

*team sanctuary*

Bocci
Hobbs
Billings

*team fam*

Struble
Struble
Osterloh
Tolpa

*team heart*

Peter

You stay classy, San Diego
Alice
xoxo

# MAI TAI'D UP

# prologue

I grinned as I watched the two of them circle each other without leaving their chairs. Perched backward on hers, she pointed aggressively in response to something he said. He pointed back just as hard, which made her . . . unbutton another button on her shirt?

These two. I'd never heard my cousin Clark complain so much about a girl, which made me 100 percent positive this girl was perfectly matched for him. Vivian this and Vivian that—that's literally all I'd heard from him in the last few weeks.

I leaned back against the bar and pondered the passion that was pinging back and forth between them. Their words were antagonistic, but their body language? They were already having the sex; they just didn't know it yet. He leaned; she leaned. He rolled his eyes; she all but rolled her hips. Words were heated; their skin even more so.

My skin was rarely heated. In fact, everything south of my ankles was getting decidedly cold. But that was normal for a bride, right?

I was getting married in a month. After spending the last

few weeks running around like crazy with wedding preparations, I was treating myself to a long weekend at my favorite B&B in Mendocino to see my favorite cousin. Coming up to visit him was the break I'd needed from my real life in San Diego. I'd spent the last few days walking on the beach, sitting by a crackling fire at night, and trying hard to see the forest for the trees in my life. And listening to Clark talk nonstop about this girl who had rocked his world. I was supposed to be working on my thank-you cards for gifts we'd already received, but getting distracted by my somewhat old-fashioned, hopelessly romantic cousin Clark and his obvious affection for this new girl in town was exactly what I really needed.

And now, watching these two dance around each other, watching his eyes being drawn again and again to the bosom she seemed to be deliberately using to her advantage, I realized that this was what it was *supposed* to be about. The dance. The back-and-forth, the spark, the excitement.

I'd never had that spark with anyone. And after watching Clark go toe-to-toe with this Vivian? I wanted to get sparked too. And I was no longer sure that I'd be getting sparked in San Diego . . .

# chapter one

"And so tonight, I raise a glass to the most beautiful girl in the world—my daughter, Chloe Patterson. And to her intended, I say: take care of her. Because I know people."

I could feel my blush rise as my father toasted me and my fiancé—the "intended" he'd just threatened in front of the fifty people attending our rehearsal dinner. Threatened in a perfectly acceptable way, of course, like a father of the bride would tease the man who's going to take away his little girl forever. And everyone laughed along with me, raising their glasses in our direction.

My intended, Charles Preston Sappington, rose to his feet, shaking my father's hand and clapping him on the back goodnaturedly. Was the clap a little harder than necessary? Yes. Was the threat as affable as my father made it sound? No.

I caught my dad's eye and he winked. I giggled loudly, earning an eye roll from my mother, who had the most audible eye roll in the room. In *any* room. And particularly any room my father was in.

Relieved that I could get back to my dinner, I felt Charles' hand on the back of my neck. He leaned over me, pressing an absentminded kiss onto the top of my head. "Going to go say hello to the Nickersons; I'll be right back," he whispered.

I kissed the air behind him as he sped off to press some more flesh, and turned to see my mother watching us.

"Don't you think you should go with him, dear?" she asked, watching as my fiancé schmoozed. Our rehearsal dinner, and he was schmoozing.

"Not particularly. Did you try the artichoke soufflé? It's delicious," I answered, forking up another bite.

"Don't you think you've had enough, dear? That wedding dress barely fits as it is." She signaled for a waiter to remove my plate.

I smiled resignedly, setting down my fork with a clatter that earned me an eyebrow raise. "Sorry," I mumbled, patting at my lips delicately with my napkin, which I refolded and placed squarely in the center of my lap.

"Oh, leave her alone, Marjorie, she's getting married! She should enjoy this night! You know, before the Big Fade," Dad teased.

A snort escaped me, and my mother's neck turned three shades of red.

"Honestly, Thomas, I hardly think it's appropriate to tease her like that, the night before she gets married. And what was that toast? *You know people?* For goodness' sake, who are these alleged people? Accountants? Pencil pushers?"

"Oh, lighten up! It was a joke, that's all," my father protested, clearly loving this.

Divorced for the last six years after twenty-two years of bickering, my father loved nothing in the world more than to get my mother's back up. And she never failed to take the bait.

But tonight, she surprised us both by pushing back from the table. "Chloe, go stand with Charles. He shouldn't have to chat up all these guests by himself," she chided, not giving my father a second glance as she sailed away. Tall and regal and every inch the mother of the bride, she slipped seamlessly into the background, making sure that the waiters were circling and everyone had everything they needed. She was the hostess with the mostest, a job that I supposed I should be doing. Truth? I wanted more of that sinful artichoke soufflé.

I glanced at my father's plate and he grinned, shoving it across the table toward me. I grinned back, then quickly ate the soufflé.

"So, you ready for tomorrow?" he asked as we watched the room.

Pleasantries, mingling, restrained and dignified laughter spilling around the room. Fifty of our very *very* closest friends and family. And this was only the rehearsal. Four hundred (four hundred!) people from all over Southern California had been invited to the wedding tomorrow, being held at one of San Diego's toniest country clubs. We'd been members for years, and when my parents' divorce was final, my mother made it clear that it was now her territory alone. But my father was required to pay the membership dues every year. Alimony.

"I suppose," I said, and sighed, wondering not for the first time why I sighed every time someone asked me about the wedding.

My father noticed. "Kiddo?" he asked, concern crossing his handsome face.

"I'd better go chat with the Nickersons," I answered, having just gotten the stink eye from my mother from across the room. She meant well. And it was my rehearsal dinner, after all; I *should* be enjoying hearing everyone's congratulations. I reminded myself of this several times in the time it took me to make my way from the corner table to the center of the restaurant, where my intended held his hand out for me. I pasted on the look of happiness and sincerity that had won me Miss Golden State nearly two years ago. Charles, the most handsome man I'd ever known, smiled down at me, my smile taking its cue from his as he slipped his arm around me and brought me effortlessly into the conversation.

Smile. Nod. Laugh. Smile. Nod. Laugh. Smile. Nod. Sigh.

I stole a moment later in the evening, after the coffee had been served and the endless toasts completed (how in the world would anyone have anything to say tomorrow if they blew their toast wad at the rehearsal dinner?), and guests were beginning to edge toward the door. My mother mingled like a pro, smiling and nodding at each one as they complimented her on what a lovely daughter, what a lovely couple, what a lovely evening . . . arghh. Smiling and nodding was what she did best.

It was a grace I didn't possess naturally, although I could fake it with the best of them. Case in point: my earlier smile and nod when a twenty-minute discussion was waged over which was the best lawn service in town. Have to keep those lawns as green as possible, even when there was a drought, you know. Or my smile and nod when Mrs. Snodgrass went on and on about a racy book that everyone was talking about but no one would admit to reading, when in fact I know every woman there had read it. I even smiled and nodded when Mr. Peterson lectured us about illegal immigration, when I knew for a fact that his nanny was undocumented. Honestly, I felt like a bobblehead at times. But that pageant training kicked in, and I could smile and nod for hours on end, always looking interested, always looking pleasant, always looking pretty.

But inside my head *wasn't* pretty. Inside my head, I was

wondering what would happen if I jumped onto a table and started screaming. What would the reaction be? Startlement? Horror? Amusement? How quickly would someone usher me off the table, and how quickly would everyone else go back to their coffee?

I was saved from my mental screaming by my mother, who was making a second pass around the restaurant. "Dear, the Snodgrasses are leaving. Be a good girl and go thank them for coming."

"Yes, Mother." I smiled and nodded. In particular at my handsome fiancé, who had already beaten me to the Mr. and Mrs. Snodgrass.

Finally, Charles and I found ourselves alone in front of the restaurant. Before Cinderella was packed off into her stretch limo coach, she was to say good night to her handsome prince.

"Are you excited about tomorrow?" he asked, encircling me with his strong arms. Arms he kept strong, along with every other part of his body, with hours of tennis, racquetball, swimming, jogging, and, of course, golf. Avid golfer. I'd been encouraged to take up the sport, so I did. Of course I did. Sigh.

"I'm very excited for tomorrow," I murmured into his chest, catching the scent of his cologne. Heady.

"I mentioned to Nancy Nickerson that you'd be interested in volunteering some time when we get back in town. She's chairing the committee for the new pediatric wing at the hospital. I signed you up."

"Well, okay. But I'm not sure how much time I'm going to have. They just got two new therapy dogs at the hospital, and they need some help with—"

"Chloe. Baby. We talked about this before. Working with your pageant platform is one thing; the therapy dog charity was great. But you're not doing pageants anymore, and we agreed it's time to start moving on, taking on some new projects, right?"

"But, Charles, I've worked with this organization since high school; it was never *just* because I was in pageants. They always need help, and I think that—"

"No."

"Um. What?" I asked, crinkling my nose and looking up at him.

Charles Preston Sappington was tall. Dark. Handsome. Perfect. My mother, who traded in perfect, had introduced us. He was an attorney. He argued for a living, which is why I never bothered to argue with him. Hard to go toe-to-toe with the toughest litigator in all of Southern California. I know this because he had it on a plaque above his desk. So I rarely bothered. However . . .

"Did you just tell me *no*?"

"Yes."

"Can you explain to me why?" I asked, pushing against his chest a bit when he tried to hold me tighter.

"Not right now."

"But—"

"Baby, it's late. We've got plenty of time to talk about stuff like this. But for now? Just concentrate on getting some sleep tonight so you can be beautiful for me tomorrow." His voice *sounded* soothing. "You know I can't wait for tomorrow, right? But then after that? The honeymoon, baby—the best part."

His hands slid up my back and succeeded in pulling me into him. I sighed, bit back my remark, and concentrated on the band that was tightening around my chest. His arms, I mean.

"Two weeks in Tahiti. Private bungalow. Bikini. Maybe even no bikini," he whispered, hands sliding down and giving my bum a grab.

"Charles! Someone could see!" I protested, looking around. He laughed, thinking this particular squall was over. After all, I was getting married tomorrow. Sigh.

"Baby, go to sleep. And then tomorrow, I'll be waiting at the end of that aisle. You'll be gorgeous. We'll say some words, slip on some rings, and then you're all mine. Sound good?" he crooned as he spun me around, then set me down to open the limo door.

"Mm-hmm," I managed, a bit dizzy from all the spinning.

"There you two are! Now, Charles, scoot. She's all yours tomorrow, but she's still mine tonight," my mother cried, appearing at my side with a grand smile.

"Yes, Mother Patterson," Charles replied, knowing how much she hated when he called her that.

I giggled in spite of myself, and my mother frowned at me.

"Say good night to Charles," she said primly, keeping any comments about Mother Patterson to herself for a change.

"Good night, Charles," I echoed, leaning in for a kiss on the forehead.

"Night, ladies. See you tomorrow," Charles said, packing us into the limo in a swish of silk and satin.

Sitting next to my mother, I listened to her chatter as we pulled away from the restaurant and headed toward our home. Where I'd lived since college.

Parents' house. Sorority house. Parents' house. Husband's house? Sigh.

An hour later, I was in the bedroom I'd been sleeping in since I was seven. Canopy bed. Pom-poms. Tiaras. Sashes. Trophies. Pageant girl, remember? Elbow elbow wrist wrist.

Curled up on top of the covers, I was hot, my heart beating

faster than normal. Nervous about tomorrow, I suppose. Marrying Charles. Becoming a Sappington and everything that meant.

I looked at the picture of us on my nightstand, taken the evening he'd proposed. The ring shone as brightly in the photo as it shone on my hand now. It was the largest diamond I'd ever seen, almost embarrassingly so. I slipped it off, setting next to the picture.

I'd met Charles eleven months ago. We were engaged five months to the day after we met. Whirlwind to say the least, and Charles was the most perfectly put-together whirlwind you've ever seen. Never a hair out of place, never a spot of food on his tie, or a piece of spinach in his teeth. The spinach would never dare.

But any piece of spinach would love to get the chance to lodge there. Charles Preston Sappington was *the* man about town, the bachelor every woman from San Diego to Santa Barbara had been trying to land for years. Any piece of spinach would count herself extremely lucky to be trapped between his pedigreed teeth; it was the dream tiny spinaches were told by their spinach mothers. Tall. Handsome. Rich. Good family. And if you do as you're told, you too can go for the brass ring.

I was Miss Golden State. He was my final tiara after a lifetime of pretty and prancing. Now I could go quietly into that beautifully manicured good night, my wedding veil firmly in place. And a silent scream in the back of my throat.

With that comforting thought—and if by comforting, I mean abject terror—I turned out my light.

Toss. Turn. Toss. Turn. Toss. Turn. Tears.


Looking back, I wish I could tell you there was one particular thing that tipped the scales and made me run away from my wedding. But all I know was that from the moment I set my feet on the floor that morning, I knew something was off. And not just my stomach, although that had been burbling and gurgling since 3 A.M. Too much artichoke soufflé? I'll never tell.

I ate oatmeal practically every morning of my life. Steel-cut oats, the slightest sprinkling of Splenda, fresh fruit (blueberries were my mother's preferred choice—antioxidants are our friends), with a splash of nonfat milk. But today when I shuffled into the kitchen, I saw something I had *never* seen there before.

Donuts.

Actual. Beautiful. Sugary. Fatty. Gorgeous. Donuts.

Like, with the sugar and the fat.

I looked around to make sure that, yes, I was still in my own house. My oatmeal bowl was set out, place mat and utensils laid with care, as it was every day. Slow cooker was plugged in, with my preportioned amount piping hot and ready for eating. The small pitcher of nonfat milk sat by my place setting, holding exactly a half cup of gray, watery, not-so-much milk.

But . . . did I mention there were donuts?

On reflection, I was wrong when I said I didn't know what tipped the scales that morning. Donuts were where I went off the rails.

Taking one more look around to make sure no one was there to witness this culinary mortal sin, I walked over toward the platter. And regarded the donuts, piled high and arranged with attention toward making a beautifully delicious display. These confectionary wonders, these puffy delights, these sugary and fatty diet cheats—I chose one toward the back, sticky with chocolate glaze and full of spite toward every diet I'd ever been put on.

I was a slim girl; genetics plus a Southern California lifestyle had made me so. Part of the reason I won Miss Golden State is due to the fact that I look exactly like every picture of the "Wish they all could be" variety of a California Girl. Long blond hair. Tan. Tall; not so much curves as there were hills and valleys; strong from running, tennis, Pilates, yoga, you name it. I'd nevertheless had it drilled into me from a young age that skinny was better, and to enforce that, nary a donut was ever brought into this home. Of course, I'd had them at friends' slumber parties occasionally. And when I turned sixteen, and realized that a driver's license and a little bit of baby-sitting money allowed me the freedom to eat anything and everything—which, to be fair, resulted in a weight gain of eleven pounds and a very stern lecture by my mother on health and wellness, and a ban on baby-sitting—I'd indulged occasionally when my mouth wasn't under supervision.

But again: never in my life had I seen a donut in my own home. And then in my hand. And then in my mouth. And then . . . perhaps a second?

Somewhere around the third donut, my mother walked in with my wedding planner, Terrance. By the screech that came out of her mouth, you'd have thought she'd found me holding a bloody knife, not an innocent cinnamon twist.

Then she said quietly, "Those donuts are for the help today, Chloe."

Frankly, I preferred the screech. Her quiet meant danger. She also failed to notice that Terrance flinched when she said "the help," but in that moment, I didn't care. It was every man for himself. Or herself.

Normal, chastised Chloe would have nodded, put down the donut in an apologetic fashion, and exited the room quietly, knowing that this indiscretion would be mentally catalogued and trotted out sometime in the future, typically when I least expected it. I was a twenty-four-year-old woman who still got a "talking to" when my mother thought it necessary. As the years went on I'd tolerated them with a sense of almost bemusement, but lately the control she exerted over my life—which I'd frankly allowed her to have—had worn thin.

I knew there'd be a critical remark later today, when I'd need to take a bigger-than-normal breath to be sewn into my wedding dress. And for whatever reason, I decided to draw a line in the sand—with my big, luscious donut.

I crammed four inches of heaven into my mouth, chewed, breathed through my nose, and took the other four inches, then grinned, calories and twenty-four years of silent "go fudge yourself, Mother" rioting through my bloodstream. It was a heady mix. Swallowing, I calmly licked my fingertips, never taking my eyes off my mother.

True to form, she remained cool. "Terrance, I wonder if you'd be so good as to set up in the living room? I imagine the hairdresser will be here any moment, and I want to make sure everything is as it should be," she said with a regal dip of her head.

Terrance shot a stifled grin my way, snagged a cinnamon twist of his own, and went where he was told.

I was alone with my mother.

"Now, Chloe, I'm sure you didn't mean to be as rude as you just were. What must our wedding planner think? A gorgeous bride, stuffing her face just hours before she'll be sewn into the wedding gown we've spent months preparing your body for. As it is, we'll be lucky if the buttons don't pop."

I let out a tiny but defiant burp.

My mother sighed and looked at the counter. And as she did, I realized it was the single most reliable expression she had on her face when it came to me. She was always sighing, if she wasn't pushing. She was always sighing, if she wasn't shushing.

She was always sighing, if she wasn't detailing exactly what I had done wrong.

I loved my mother, but it sure was hard to like her sometimes.

"Chloe?" I heard, and I realized the sighing was over.

"Yeah?"

"Is that how a young lady responds to a question from her mother?"

I straightened up automatically, tummy in, chest up and out, head balanced on a tiny cloud floating on top of my spine. Good posture is the calling card of good breeding, after all. "Mother, I'm sorry I was rude. I'm sure I'll fit into my beautiful gown."

She studied me carefully, her pretty face carefully composed, her pretty hair carefully composed, and finally nodded once. "Now go apologize to Terrance, dear, and please don't eat another thing until your new husband offers you some wedding cake. This is going to be a beautiful day—I'm so happy for you." As she turned to head outside, where the gardener was once again positively ruining her prize begonias, she called over her shoulder, "I'll put a water pill on your bedside table, dear; let's see what we can do about that puffiness around your ankles."

It took everything I had not to kick something with my allegedly puffy ankles. If I could manage to lift my giant elephant legs off the floor. I relaxed my posture, licked a traitorous bit of sugar from the corner of my mouth, and headed in to see Terrance and the rest of the "help."

"You know," Terrance said, "I have seen it *all*. Mothers of the bride getting in screaming matches with the mothers of the groom. Grooms getting drunk at the reception and falling into the wedding cake. Once I even saw a father of the bride trying to make out with a groomsman."

The glam squad was going full throttle. I had someone curling my hair, someone painting my nails, someone applying my makeup, and someone touching up my pedicure. In the background, happy music played and happy bridesmaids danced while sipping mimosas. The entire house was Happy Wedding Central, bursting with feminine giggles. Yet I, the one the frivolity was revolving around, was ready to burst into tears. Something that seemed to have escaped everyone's attention. My bridesmaids had been my friends for years—friends I once had something in common with, but from whom I'd been feeling more and more distant in the last few months as I was marched toward this wedding cliff. As I looked around at their perfect faces, I realized I didn't care a whit about any of them. No one was noticing my dark mood except my wedding planner.

"And I've seen my share of nervous brides and cold feet," Terrance continued, leaning down in front of me, between two nail techs and a makeup artist. "So you wanna tell me what's going on?"

Terrance was six feet six inches of fabulous stuffed into five feet two inches of tiny shoes. Which I was pretty sure were stacked. Caramel skin, tiny dreadlocks, and an enormous personality, he'd planned the weddings of every major socialite and debutante in Southern California for the last ten years. He alone had listened to what I wanted for my wedding, and even though I eventually gave in to what my mother wanted, he had fought for me all along. And seemed to see things that others didn't—or chose not to. And now he saw that the tears that were building in my eyes were not, in fact, due to the false lashes recently applied, as I had tried to spin it.

Since I'd gotten out of bed this morning, a ball of awful had been kicking in my stomach. And it wasn't nerves. I'd been in pageants since I was four years old and I knew how to deal with butterflies in my tummy. As each hour passed, that ball of awful was getting bigger and bigger, and it was starting to affect the rest of my body. There was a ringing in my ears. My fingers and toes felt buzzy. My tongue felt thick. And my eyes kept filling with tears. My pulse was racing, my hands were clammy, and words were thundering up my throat, literally begging to get out.

Scary words. Like *no*. And *stop*. And *seriously stop this*.

But it was just wedding nerves, right? The cold feet I'd been phantom feeling for a month or so? Not so phantom now. They were blocks of foot ice. But normal, right? It wasn't like my entire body was turning in on itself for protection, trying to manifest real doubt into some kind of action . . . right?

"I just need a little quiet time, I think," I managed to get out past the other words fighting to follow, fighting desperately for breath.

Choke. Breathe. Choke. Breathe. *Please* breathe. And . . . Crumple.

Terrance took one more look at me and told the glam squad to scram. Bridesmaids whooshed out in a wave of orange juice and champagne, my curls were quickly pinned to my head, and then I was all alone.

I put my head into my hands and just sobbed. As you do on your wedding day, right? Oh, so wrong. This *felt* wrong, all of this, just felt so very wrong. I was beyond nerves; I was into panic. Panic that needed space to move and give voice to what was raging inside.

My mother entered the room and asked, "Care to tell me why there are five bridesmaids, two nail technicians, and a makeup artist drinking mimosas on the patio right now?"

And as I sat there, surrounded by tufted crinoline and pretty,

I finally threw up the words that had been cooking all day. "I don't want to marry Charles." Oh. *Oh.*

Have you ever had those moments when words just seem to hang in the air? I could literally hear them echoing back to me in the stark silence. I lifted my head to see peep-toe pumps, one of them now tapping furiously against the dark teak wooden floor. I saw tanned and toned legs, knees that were *just* beginning to wrinkle, an off-white linen afternoon skirt, a peach silk wraparound blouse, a ruby, an emerald, a diamond, Chanel lipstick (Rouge Coco Shine, thank you very much), and wide green eyes accented by more than a touch of irritation.

"Pardon me, young lady?" she asked, concern crossing her features for the first time.

Concern over how I was feeling? Or concern that I might unravel her perfect day? I know which horse I was betting on.

"I don't want to marry Charles Preston Sappington." Oh, that felt pretty good.

Sigh. "Chloe, do you mind telling me what's going on?" she asked.

So I told her once more, with feeling: "I *don't* want to marry Charles Preston Sappington! Not today. Not any day." My body had an immediate reaction to saying those words out loud. My spine straightened as if a weight had been lifted, and my head was floating on a tiny string twelve inches above my body.

If I'd been in a factory, I'd have written it on a piece of cardboard and climbed on top of a table to wave it around Norma Rae style.

"Okay. I don't know exactly what has gotten into you today, but I'm beginning to get a little peeved."

Peeved? Here's some word vomit to go with your peeve.

"I *don't* want to marry Charles Preston Sappington. Not today. Not *any* day."

Fudge me, I was starting to feel *good*. My head was now floating a full two feet in the air, light as a feather. And oh boy, now I was smiling? Small, but it was there. Smiling.

The same could not be said for my mother. "Explain yourself," she commanded, and when my mouth opened she said, "and if you say that one more time I'll—"

I laughed out loud. With a saucy Latin rhythm I repeated, "*I* don't want to *marry. Charles* Preston *Sap*pington. Not *today*, not *any* day," finishing with a hip bump that shook my pinned-up curls.

"I've had just about enough of this nonsense!" my mother snapped. "Now straighten up and get it together. We've got a house full of people and I won't have them witnessing a breakdown."

"Breakdown?" I laughed again. "I think maybe I'd better go get some air. Yeah—air is good." I hiccup-giggled, my smile now wrapping across my entire face. "Bye, Mother." I whirled for the kitchen and grabbed my purse and the keys to my convertible. Convertibles were good for one thing only, something I needed desperately right now. Built in air. Let's go.

"You'll do no such thing, Chloe. Chloe, you listen to me!" she yelled after me as I raced out the front door, cackling. Wow, breakdowns happened fast. I slid behind the wheel of my BMW, turned the ignition, and was out of the driveway before she made it to the front door.

"I'm calling Charles!" she yelled as I waved madly at my glam squad peeking over the backyard gate.

"I'm not marrying Charles Preston Sappington. Not today. Not any day!" I yelled once more, this time in full opera voice to the tune of *Ode to Joy*.

I sped out of my neighborhood, took a few crazy turns, and headed out onto the highway, top down, music at full blast. Still in my nightgown and pinned curls.

Point: mother-fudging Chloe.

**M**y mother called my phone. Seventeen times in a row. Then Charles called. Fourteen times in a row. Then my father called. Once. I let them all go to voice mail. My text box was filling up by the minute. I didn't look once. After driving for a while, I ended up at the beach. I sat on the sand, picked the pins out of my hair, and let the sun shine down through my thin cotton nightgown. I ran my fingers through my curled hair, not caring that there was sand clinging to my fingertips.

I watched as a family of four headed down toward the water. Mom and Dad, Junior and Girl Junior. They splashed and played, Mom looked amazing in a bikini, and Dad was good looking too. They kissed once while the kids were busy building a sand castle. Dad's hand migrated south, grabbing a handful of buns and squeezing, making Mom laugh and pretend to slap his hand away. The kids saw them kissing and made a great show of pretending to be disgusted, but laughed the entire time. Then Mom and Dad grabbed the kidlets, and into the water they all went once more.

Good-looking couple. Good-looking kids. Happy family. Pretty didn't *have* to mean fake. It just did where I was concerned. My family had been pretty, and bickery. I knew full well how something could look pretty on the outside and be wasp-nasty on the inside. After my parents' divorce, the energy my mother had put into bickering with my father was channeled toward me, and making sure I was always on top of my game. Stage mother, not technically. But pushy, yes. Determined, yes.

She never remarried, she never even dated, and bitter she became. It didn't happen overnight, but it happened.

And a life with Charles would have become a Day in the Life of the Bickersons. Oh, not right away. First would be the pretty. I saw my life line up in front of my eyes as if it had already happened. Marriage to Charles would give me everything I'd been brought up to want. A handsome husband. A beautiful home. A new car every two years. A membership to the right country club. A position on all the correct social committees. Three children spaced exactly two years apart. Then the obligatory "mommy job" where I went in for my tummy tuck and boob lift to keep everything exactly the way it was "supposed" to be. With vacations every summer, Christmas, and spring break, who could ask for anything more?

But I wanted *less*. I wanted so very much less. And while there were tiny bubbles of "is this what you really want?" all along, I was in denial about it until about forty-five minutes ago. Pretty led to bicker, bicker led to divorce, and divorce led to bitter. I didn't want pretty, then separated. I didn't want bitter; I wanted forever. I wanted swoony, sparky, maddening, sexy love. And if we were going to fight, we'd fight, not bicker. Bickering's the worst.

My phone rang again. Charles. I stood up, dusted myself off, walked down to the water's edge, and heaved my phone as far into the Pacific as I could.

Then I got back in my car and drove to my father's house.

When my parents divorced, I was a freshman in college. I was old enough that I didn't have to pick a side. But in the small ways, which become bigger over time, I unofficially picked my father. Easygoing, nonpushy, quick to bear hug and even quicker to laugh—when I was with my dad, I was a different daughter. *Stop slouching, stand up straight, don't you think the fruit cup is a better option*—those were all statements my mother would murmur without a thought. With Dad I was more likely to hear: *you looked great up there, you'll get 'em next time, tiger; you can eat prunes when you're old—go ahead and get that Big Mac now.*

My dad loved me—and that was it. So in the middle of a breakdown and in need of a safe haven? Where else would I go?

He wasn't home when I arrived, so I pulled my car around back, then curled up in the hammock on the back porch, keeping my mind away from anything too major. I heard his car pull into the driveway, stopping short at the sight of my car.

He walked toward the porch with a concerned look on his face. And after taking in the nightgown and the sand still clinging to my bare feet, he quickly understood more than even I knew at that point.

"Oh, Chloe," he said quietly.

"Yeah," I answered, then gave a kick to get the hammock moving again.

He stood there for a moment, watching me swing. "Okay," he finally said, and took out his phone. I listened as he told my mother that yes, he'd found me, yes, I was fine, and no, I wasn't getting married that day. And that he'd bring me home when I was ready. And no, she couldn't come over right now. When I heard her screech about sending Charles over to collect me, he told her exactly what he thought about that idea. It may have involved an ass and a kick. Then he disappeared into the house, came back with two beers, and we sat next to each other in silence.

And they weren't even light beers. I seemed determined to ingest every calorie in California in one twenty-four-hour period.

Sounded pretty fudging great to me.

# chapter two

As a general rule, my family avoids conflict. I'm not talking about squabbling over the remote every night when our family unit was still intact but about the big stuff. The giant problems, the huge glaring mistakes human beings make, the actual issues behind the remote control—we avoid those conversations like the plague. If we ignore them, or if we only talk quietly about the "incident in question" for the shortest amount of time possible, maybe we can avoid anything unpleasant.

So when I saw my mother barreling up the driveway, I knew she was prepared to go to a very civilized war.

Having thrown my phone into the ocean, I was incommunicado. So my father's phones were ringing off the hook like command central. When he finally unplugged the house phone and turned off the ringer on his cell phone, it was only a matter of time. My mother pulled into the driveway just as I finished my second beer.

"Do you have any idea what you've done?" she whisper-yelled, ever aware of the neighbors.

"I am just beginning to understand what I've done, Mother.

How about you?" I replied, reaching down to the cooler at my feet. "Beer?" I offered, holding up a dripping bottle.

My father coughed. My mother? Quietly burned.

She looked around the yard, making sure our dysfunctional family unit was in fact alone, then lowered herself to the patio steps. Arranging herself in an elegantly casual way, she sat with her legs crossed at the ankle, hands nestled in her lap. She looked like she was sitting for a portrait at Olan Mills. I chanced a look at my father, who was struggling to contain his amusement.

"Okay, let's talk this out, since rational thought has clearly left the building," she began, making sure to glance in my father's direction when speaking of the lack of rational thought.

"I feel pretty rational," I explained, my nightgown perhaps giving away a small slice of credibility. "But I agree, we should talk about what's happened." Her face lit up in triumph, and I held up my hand. "But I'm not marrying Charles Preston Sappington. Not today. Not any—"

"Oh, would you stop saying that!" she snapped, finally showing some emotion. "You mind telling me why exactly you're feeling so dramatic about all of this?"

I unscrewed the cap on my third beer and took a long swallow. "I don't have the foggiest idea why I walked out on my wedding. Maybe I'll know why tomorrow. But today? I don't have any answers. Except what I've been saying all day. Do you really want me to say it again?"

"Well, *I'd* like to hear it."

Charles was here. Standing in the driveway. Cool, calm, collected, handsome.

My beer shattered as I threw it to the ground, then I stood up quickly and headed for the house.

"Chloe. Baby. Let's talk this out, shall we?" I heard over my shoulder as I struggled to get the sliding door open. My hands were slippery from the cold beer, and I couldn't get purchase on the handle. As I fumbled, I could hear my mother speaking to Charles under her breath, prompting him. Oh for fudge's sake, this *door*!

"Marjorie, I told you not to bring him over here. She obviously needs some space today. Don't you think that—"

"You stay out of this, Thomas. Is it any coincidence that she came here, of all places? She knew you'd coddle her. She knew you'd—"

"*Coddle* her? She knew I'd listen, for Christ's sake! When all you can do is—"

"Oh, please, like you'll know how to get her back on track after this? She doesn't know what she's doing, and your helping her isn't going to—"

Charles's voice broke through the fray. "Chloe, baby, come on. Let's go talk this out, okay? We can still make this happen today—you know you want to, don't you? You know it's the right thing—"

All of these conversations were happening at the same time while I was pawing at the glass door like a cat trying to get out of a window. "Oh, for fuck's sake, why won't this door *open*!"

Silence. Total silence. Even the birds had stopped chirping. My mother and father were frozen in their all-too-familiar antagonistic pose, while Charles stood in the driveway with his hands raised, looking like Jesus at the Last Supper.

The latch finally clicked, and the door slid open.

"I'm going inside. No one is following me. I'll talk about this tomorrow." I started to go in, when I caught Charles's eye. And saw his expression. Frustration, yes. Irritation, the beginnings of it, yes. Deep, profound anguish that the love of his life had just told him she wasn't marrying him? Not even the slightest hint. Still . . .

"I really am very sorry," I said, to him and only to him. And then I went inside.

And threw up donuts and beer.

I thought there was no way I'd sleep that night, but I slept like a baby. And when I woke up and saw a note from my father on the nightstand that he'd gone on a bagel run, I smiled, rolled over, and went back to sleep. And when I heard my dad whistling as he made coffee a half hour later, I got up and went downstairs with a smile on my face.

Which fell as soon as I saw a brand-new iPhone sitting at my place at the table. "What's this?" I asked, slumping into my chair.

"What does it look like?" he promptly replied from behind his newspaper.

"Dad. Come on, seriously."

"I stopped by the store this morning, got you a new phone. Is that what you're referring to?" The newspaper rustled.

I looked down at the phone, thinking hard. "But I threw my old one in—"

"—the ocean, I know. Try not to do that again, would you, kiddo? You have any idea how expensive these phones are?"

I pushed the phone, and my place mat, away. But then tugged it back to get to the orange juice. The newspaper rustled.

"I didn't want to talk to anybody . . ." I mumbled, and my father finally appeared from behind the paper.

"I realize that, but you made a decision yesterday that affects a lot of people. And you need to explain it, specifically to some of those people."

"But I thought *you* understood . . ." I began, my eyes filling with tears for the first time since I'd bolted yesterday.

"I understood that you didn't want to get married, and no

way was I going to force you into that. But I don't understand why, and neither does your mother," he said, laying down his paper and looking at me over the top of his glasses. "And neither does Charles."

I winced.

"You don't have to marry him, but you do need to explain your actions yesterday. You owe them both that much."

And with a rustle of paper, the voice of reason disappeared once more behind the financial section. Call Charles. Hmm. I could do this. I *could* do this. I picked up the phone, then put it down. Yikes. What was I going to say? What could I say? How could I tell him why, when I wasn't 100 percent sure myself? I picked up the phone again, then put it down again.

The third time I reached for it, the voice behind the paper said, "For goodness' sake, Chloe, I think you can have breakfast before you explain yourself. Go get a bagel and stop fidgeting."

Reprieved. I exhaled gratefully and headed for the toaster oven. I knew couldn't dodge those two much longer. But did you know that if you pick off every single sesame seed and every single garlic crispy thingie from an everything bagel before you eat it, it can take over an hour? Especially if you count the poppy seeds too . . .


By noon, I'd listened to all the messages that had poured in yesterday. Starting with the first, "Chloe, you turn right around and come back here, young lady," to "Now you listen to me, and listen good. I didn't spend the last two months killing myself on designing the perfect wedding for you, only to have you and your cold feet ruin everything," to, "Where in the world are you? Oh, I just can't believe you would *do* this to me, Chloe! Think of what everyone's going to say when they find out! We can still make it to the church on time; just tell me where you are and I'll come get you. We can still make this happen and no one will ever know," to finally, "I've called Charles. Maybe he can talk some sense into you."

Doubtful. I stalled for some more time by heading into my dad's office and jumping onto his home computer. I'd just check my email, clear it out before making those phone calls. One poppy seed, two poppy seeds . . .

Emails from two of my bridesmaids, wondering what in the world was going on in my head. I'm sure they *were* wondering— who ever walked away from the brass ring? I wonder if they'd be so interested in his brass if they knew how small his . . . Don't go there.

No. Actually, *do* go there.

Confession time. I'd only ever "been with" Charles, in the biblical sense. So technically, I had no basis for comparison on actual length and girth. But while I was technically a virgin, it's not like I hadn't been privy to a man's private bits before. I'd rounded a few bases (read handies in a dark backseat) with guys I'd dated in college (read two guys dated, so two peens seen). I had a computer. I had the Internet. I had girl talk. And it would seem to me, as peni went, that Charles was . . . less than average. But I was in love (read pretty sure I was in love) and ready to throw away my V card (read sooooo ready), and so BAM we had the sex a few weeks into dating. And BAM I saw the penis. And bam it was all up in there. And by *all up in there,* I mean . . . I thought this was supposed to hurt the first time?

Truth be told, our sex life was satisfactory. I had orgasms. He certainly had orgasms. Little tiny peashooter orgasms. Jesus, what an asshole I am. I was going to marry this guy yesterday, and now all I can do is disparage his manhood.

I thought, okay, this is how it is. And if I was on top, I could

eke out something pretty good there. But there was no screaming, there was no shrieking, there was no "Holy Mary mother of
God!" But that was okay, right?

Except twenty-four hours had given me the gift of clarity.
What I could see now was that *nothing* about our relationship
was "Holy Mary mother of God." It was smooth and beautiful
and covered in swirls of yummy on the outside, but the inside
was fat free and full of air and nothing. And if I was going to
have a life of air and nothing, I'd at least like a big fat dick to
bounce on.

*Chloe!* my crass meter chided, sounding frighteningly like
my mother.

I blushed at my naughty thoughts and finally picked up the
phone to call Charles, when an email from Lou Fiorello caught
my eye. Buried by wedding nonsense, it'd been sitting in my
in-box for several days.

Part of being named Miss Golden State—just one step behind Miss California, a title I'd literally worked my entire pageant career for—was being heavily involved in my charity of
choice. Since I'd always loved animals, my charitable platform
was an organization that worked with therapy dogs, Paws for
the Cause. Taking those dogs into nursing homes, working with
special-needs children, and sitting with patients suffering from
Alzheimer's, was wonderful. There was nothing I wanted to do
more; it was a program I'd love to work with long after I put my
crowns on a shelf and retired my butt glue.

SO THAT MY BATHING SUIT NEVER RODE UP.

But then one day I met Lou Fiorello, who pointed me in
a different direction. A potential option. Working at a nursing
home one day with a gorgeous golden retriever named Sparkle,
I saw a man and a dog come out of a patient's room. The man
was in his midfifties with long gray hair and a longer gray beard,

wearing a tie dyed T-shirt and beat-up camouflage pants. Tattered sneakers completed the aging hippie vibe, and when I looked at the dog next to him, he had a similar tattered look: a black pit bull wearing a red bandana and missing an ear. The two approached, and I held Sparkle's leash a bit tighter.

I'd seen the news reports; I'd heard the terrible stories. Even working with animals as long as I had, and knowing that it's usually the owner's behavior that dictates the dog's, I was still myself wary as the two walked toward us.

He stopped, taking notice of the tiara, the sash, the heels. During official appearances as Miss Golden State, the crown and the sash were required. He looked down at Sparkle, who was sniffing the other dog unconcernedly. The pit's tail wagged happily, the red bandana giving him a jaunty look.

"Therapy dog?" the man asked, nodding at Sparkle.

"Yes, we're here to spend some time with the patients; they really love it. You should see their eyes—"

"Light up? Yep, I know. Joe here's a therapy dog too, aren't you, boy?" he said, looking down at the pit bull. Joe looked up at Lou and his mouth split into a wide grin, tongue lolling out of the side of his mouth.

"He's a therapy dog?" I asked, surprise evident in my voice. Flushing a little, I bit back the obvious "but he's a pit bull" comment, although it was implied.

Lou let out a huff. "You know much about pit bulls, princess?"

"Just what I see on the news," I admitted, resisting the urge to straighten my crown.

"Mm-hmm. So nothing, really?" he asked.

"No?" I offered, and he grinned.

"Take Joe here. When I got him he was eight months old, and had never lived a day off a chain in the backyard. Starved half to death. Mixed it up with some other dogs, that's how I assume he lost the ear. But within three months of coming to stay with me? He was like the poster dog for Our Gang, weren't you, big guy?"

Tail wagged enthusiastically.

"Our Gang?" I asked, kneeling down to pet Joe. With one look at that big grin, I was in love. And as Lou told me more and more about his organization, I became more and more sure that it was something I wanted to become involved in. He operated a shelter in Long Beach for rescued and abandoned pit bulls. Think Cesar Millan, with less *sssssht*. Some of the dogs were rescued from fighting rings, and the more he told me, the more my heart broke. He used the name Our Gang to remind people that the dog from *The Little Rascals* was a pit bull. The breed's more recent history is all anyone ever remembered, either forgetting or never knowing that they were even used as baby-sitters a hundred years ago—something that I admit blew my mind.

I spent the next hour asking Lou everything I could think of about Our Gang, while Sparkle and Joe napped peacefully at our ankles. And I went straight home that night to tell my mother all about the new charity I wanted to support.

My mother had other ideas. She always has lots of ideas, as you can imagine. Is she a snob? If you consider a snob to be a blue-haired old woman who eats crustless cucumber sandwiches and complains about how hard it is to find good help, then no, she isn't a snob. But she does have very particular ideas about everything and everyone, and into *that* preordained, predestined, predetermined box we all must go. And for her daughter, who she expected to ride her tiara straight into a wealthy marriage, how things appeared was key. Appearances are everything, didn't you know?

So her daughter, she of the crown and sash, going to work with rescued pit bulls? Not. Going. To fly.

I'd tried to explain to Lou as best as I could why I couldn't work with his organization, and he told me he understood. All too well. But we bumped into each other occasionally when I was out with a therapy dog, and we emailed, and I followed his organization on Facebook. And whenever I clicked on one of those gorgeous faces, usually with that telltale pit bull grin, I'd think about what a wonderful opportunity it would be to work with dogs like that.

So when I saw Lou's name in my in-box now, it made me smile. And when the subject line read "Want to work for Our Gang North?" it made me sit up straight and forget all about calling Charles.

So the first important phone call I made was to Lou Fiorello. And after hanging up, I realized that for the first time in my life, I had options.

Scratch that. Options that I'd found *on my own.*

Emboldened, I decided to call my mother next. I sat back in the chair, drumming a pencil nervously on the legal pad I'd made notes all over during my call with Lou. After several rings, she answered. Had she deliberately let the phone ring? I'd seen her do that to other people. *"Always keep people wanting a little more, Chloe. Don't be rude, but don't be too eager either."* It had never had occurred to me to think she'd employed this technique on her own daughter.

"Hello?"

"Hi, Mom," I said, and she waited a beat.

"Oh, hello, Chloe dear," she replied, managing to sound unconcerned and somewhat surprised I'd called. She knew it was me; she had caller ID right there on the phone—but no matter. I'd be cool as well.

"I'd like to come by the house to talk to you, if that's okay."

"Yes, I think that's a good idea. Will it be soon? I'll put on some tea."

"I can come now. I'll just get changed and be right over."

"Still in your pajamas?"

Only four words, and yet oh so much judgment. I sidestepped the obvious trap. "I'll be there in twenty," I replied, clenching my hands.

"I'll be here," she said.

"Oh, and Mother?"

"Hmm?"

"If I see his car in the driveway, I'm turning around."

Silence. Sigh. And then finally, "I'll see you in twenty."

I'd won nothing in actuality. But I unclenched my hands, and that was good. I then texted Charles:

Hi.

He responded right away:

Hi.

I wasn't a robot. I could feel a bit of remorse beginning to poke through.

I'd like to call you later, talk
about some things?

He didn't respond right away, so I went to get changed. I was, in fact, still in my pajamas. But as I pushed my head through a San Diego State sweatshirt of my dad's, I heard my phone beep.

Talk about some things?
I'll say we need to talk
about some things. I'll
come by at 5 and pick
you up.

I didn't want to see him. Not yet.

No, no that's not a good
idea. I need some more
time. I'll call you, let's start
there.

Whatever you say . . .

I texted him bye, but for the first time, didn't add XOXO.

I pulled on some sweatpants and went downstairs. "I'm heading over to Mom's to talk; you need anything while I'm out?" I asked my father, who was reading another newspaper. Each Sunday he had the *New York Times*, the *LA Times*, the *Chicago Tribune*, and the *Wall Street Journal* delivered. He liked to "cover his bases." What he covered were his fingerprints with ink, as well as doorjambs and countertops.

"You want me to go with you?" he asked. "Nice outfit, by the way."

"Thanks. If I hold up the pants on the side I should be able to keep them on," I laughed. "And no, I'm good to go solo. If you hear a sonic boom coming from her side of town, you'll know how it's going."

"I'm familiar with that boom," he replied, one corner of his mouth turning up.

So I headed out the front door to explain to my mother why

I'd canceled her perfect wedding. Hopefully I'd be able to think up a good reason on the way over.

I walked into the house, my house, and saw that everything was still exactly as it was yesterday. Chairs were arranged in the living room in the semicircle I'd been in when I'd freaked out. There were still nail polish bottles on the coffee table. One thing was different, though. My wedding dress had been in my room but was now displayed in the entryway, hanging from the banister so you couldn't miss it.

Point: Mom.

"Hello?" I called, walking through the foyer and past the living room carnage.

"In the kitchen," she called back, and I headed for her voice. I found her sitting at the breakfast table. Teapot. Cups. Saucers. Milk. Sugar cubes. And holy fudge, she was wearing her Chanel. The suit she wore when she felt she needed something a little extra.

I hovered in the doorway. "Hi."

"Hello, dear," she said softly. Uh-oh. Softly again. Usually her default position. She rose, deposited a quick kiss on my cheek, then poured the tea. "One cube, or two?" she asked. She never encouraged me to have more than a solitary cube. Hmm . . .

"Three please," I volleyed, and sank into my usual chair.

Point: Chloe.

She clenched her jaw for just the scantest second, and then three sugar cubes were placed carefully into my teacup with silver tongs. We'd traveled to London when I was in sixth grade, and every afternoon we had tea at Fortnum & Mason. It was something we both enjoyed, and tried our best to replicate when we came home. I can remember the two of us giggling as we ate our crustless sandwiches and spoke in the poshest British accent we could muster.

Over the years, however, it started to feel remote; less of a shared pleasure and more of an opportunity for a talking to. And I could see this was where she wanted it to go now. But I had some talking of my own to do first.

"So here's the thing, Mother," I began, startling her into sitting down quickly, a surprised expression on her face. Which she masked just as quickly. I pressed on. "I can't tell you exactly why I ran out of here so fast yesterday, and I realize that I seemed quite crazy. But I'd had an epiphany, a sudden, frightening epiphany, that I couldn't marry Charles. And I knew if I stayed in this house for one more minute, I'd let everyone talk me out of it."

I paused to sip my tea, and burned my tongue. "Dammit," I swore under my breath, making her raise the stoniest eyebrow this side of Mount Rushmore. "Oh, for goodness' sake, I burned my tongue," I snapped, this cup-and-saucer game wearing so very thin.

"What a charming vocabulary you seem to have developed all of a sudden," she replied, fluttering her eyelashes.

"For God's sake, Mother, its 2014. This isn't some Edith Wharton novel. No one wears white gloves anymore, no one sends calling cards, and *women fucking swear!*" I banged my fist on the table, spilling tea and tumbling cubes.

"That's enough, Chloe. I did not raise you to speak to me in this way—"

"It's *not* enough! I was about to get married, possibly have a child by this time next year, but I'm not old enough to curse? I'm a grown-up, for pity's sake! I need to be able to say what I want and do what I want, and not worry about you frowning at me all the time." I paused to take a breath, adrenaline rushing through my veins. "Maybe this is exactly what I need—to shake things up a bit, ruffle some feathers!"

"You certainly did that. You can't imagine the phone calls I had to make yesterday; the conversations I had to have. I had to call your mother-in-law and try to explain that my daughter had run out on her own wedding and I had no idea where she might be!"

"She's not my mother-in-law!" I yelled.

Now the gloves were off. Her forehead was showing the tiniest glisten; that didn't happen even when she played badminton.

"Mother, do you realize that every single time you've mentioned yesterday, it's all been about how this affected *you*? I know how worried you've been about appearances, but haven't you been worried about *me*? Not even once have you asked me if I'm okay, or if Charles did something to make me flip so quickly."

Her head snapped up and she looked at me intently. "Did something happen? He didn't hurt you, did he?"

For the first time, I saw concern for me. Is it weird that I almost hated having to tell her no?

"No, not at all. It'd almost be easier to say yes—then my decision would be much more black and white, and not so gray. But, no. He never raised a hand, he never even raised his voice to me."

"Then why, Chloe? Just tell me why you can't marry him?"

The million-dollar question. Literally, since Charles was loaded.

"I don't love him," I said on an exhale. And there it was.

"That's it?" she asked, incredulous.

"Isn't that kind of the *point*?" I asked, joining her in the incredulous boat.

"Love isn't everything. It's not even the most important part of a marriage," she said. But she looked younger, softer, for a split second. Wistful?

"Shouldn't it be?" I asked.

Her eyes cut to mine, hardening again. "Oh, grow up, Chloe," she snapped, grabbing the teapot and heading for the sink. Teatime was over.

"Don't you see that I'm trying to do exactly that? How in the world can I grow up if I continue to do as I'm told, smiling and nodding like some pretty robot? What kind of a life is that?"

"Yes, what a terrible life, married to one of the most powerful lawyers in California, living in a beautiful house, raising beautiful children—it sounds just dreadful," she mocked, and my blood boiled.

"It *does* sound dreadful to me. It's not happening, Mother. We can go around and around about this all you want, but it's not happening." I walked to the window and gazed outside, looking over the manicured lawn, the pool, the good life. "I'm sorry for rushing out of here yesterday, and I'm sorry that you had to deal with the ramifications. I really *am* sorry to have put you through that. It wasn't fair of me to do that to you."

She stood at the kitchen sink, her back to me, rinsing out the teacups. As she finished she slowly straightened to her full height, regaining her composure with each vertebrae stacked. When she turned back to me, she wore a gracious expression.

"Thank you for the apology, Chloe. I appreciate that."

We stood there in the kitchen, no words being said, but I couldn't help but feel like something more was coming. "So . . . what needs to be done?"

"Done?" she asked.

"Yes. What phone calls still need to be made, who do I need to contact, what can I do to—"

"Heavens, Chloe, I've already handled everything. You don't think I would let all those people just wait around, do you? No no, I've already cleaned up this mess."

Again, silence.

"Okay, well, thank you again. I'll just go up to my room, then, and—"

"Your room?"

"Huh?"

She set the teacups back in the cupboard, everything where they belonged. "It seems to me, dear, that if you're so sure you want to be a grown-up, then you should start immediately. Don't you agree? Look at how strongly you felt yesterday, and poof! You made it happen."

"Okaaaaayyyy?" I said, no idea where this was going.

"So grown-up to grown-up, I think its time you leave the nest."

"You want me to move out?" I asked, confused.

"Yes, living here would only get in the way of your lofty grown-up ideals. So I think it's best that you fly this confining coop. Right now."

And with that, she slipped on her gardening gloves, set her big floppy hat on her head, and went outside to trim her rosebushes.

Point: Mother.


And the hits just kept on coming.

The good thing about being already packed for my honeymoon and subsequent move into my new husband's home is that I was pretty much ready to move out when my mother politely told me to do so. But when I walked out the front door twenty minutes later with my last suitcase, there was Charles, exactly where I'd told him not to be. In my driveway. Excuse me—my mother's driveway.

"Didn't I say I'd call you?" I said, rolling my suitcase toward my car.

"Didn't you agree to marry me?" he asked, going for my suitcase.

"Didn't I tell you I needed some time?" I grabbed my suitcase back, then opened the passenger side and tried to cram it into the crowded car.

"Chloe, baby, talk to me. And where are you going with all this stuff?"

"Don't call me that." I pushed the car door shut with my butt, the latch finally engaging. "I'm going to my dad's. My mother told me to move out. She's not so thrilled with me right now."

"She just wants what's best for you," he said, leaning against the car next to me. I could feel the warmth of his skin next to mine, his arm close to mine.

"*She's* so sure that she knows what's best for me, and *you're* so sure that you know what's best for me, but I don't have a clue. Except that I can't do this, Charles," I said, looking straight into his eyes.

"Bab—Chloe, you've just got cold feet. Don't throw everything away just because you're nervous," he coaxed, wrapping his arm around me and pulling me into his side.

I wondered if any of the neighbors were watching this. My mother believed every last one of them was always perched on their sofa with binoculars and a bowl of popcorn, settling in for another episode of *What Is Marjorie's Daughter Chloe Doing Today and How Will It Impact Life as We Know It?*

The thing is, his arm *did* feel good around me. It would be easy to let him kiss me, let him clean up the mess I'd made, and settle back in, all the loose ends tied up. Or is it tied down?

"Are you in love with me, Charles?" I asked.

"What kind of a question is that?"

"It's kind of an important question, don't you think?"

"That's just silly. Why would you ask me that?"

"Still not really an answer."

He tried to pull me closer, but I resisted.

"Of course I love you, Chloe," he finally said, not meeting my eyes.

"But are you *in* love with me?" I pushed.

"Are you in love with me?" he asked quickly, now meeting my eyes. And for the first time in my entire history with this very golden boy, he looked . . . unsure.

"No. No, I don't think I am," I answered, my eyes stinging. Endings were never good, even when they needed to happen. I slipped out from under his arm and stood before him as he leaned on my car.

He ran his hands through his hair, scrubbed at his face, and when he looked at me again, he was in problem-solving mode. "You go back to your dad's, relax a bit, get a good night's sleep, and then let's talk tomorrow, okay?"

"No, Charles, I don't think that—"

"This is all happening too fast. We need to slow down a bit, look at the practicality of this, figure out the best course of action to move forward."

"You're not listening to me, Charles. This isn't going to—" I started, and he talked over me again as he walked toward his own car.

"I'll call you in the morning, or stop by. Yeah, I'll stop by and we can go for a drive, talk some more."

"I don't *want* to talk more tomorrow. Not if you're going to continue to—"

"Okay, see you in the morning," he finished, getting into his car while I still stood there sputtering. He peeled out of the driveway, and I was left alone and frustrated.

"I can't believe that just happened," I said to myself, turning to get into my car. And as I did, I saw the curtains in the living room flutter. I waved to my mother—she knew she was caught.

I drove back to my dad's, brought in my first suitcase, set it down in the living room, and told him, "I need to get the hell out of this town."

He totally agreed with me. Which is why the next day I found myself driving up the coast, headed for Monterey.

# chapter three

Here's why my dad is the best. Without badgering or hounding, he asked only enough questions to understand why I needed some space. And he came up with a wonderful solution right away.

My father's family had a ranch in Monterey, up in the hills just outside of Carmel. Almost smack dab in the center of the California coast, it was like another world. I hadn't spent much time there in recent years, but when my grandfather died the property went to my father and his sister. And when Aunt Patty passed away a few years after that, the ranch stayed with my father. My mother hated it up there, so over the years our visits became fewer and fewer. It was a beautiful property, but it hadn't been renovated in years and was badly in need of an update. It had a very specific look to it, sort of a time capsule scenario. But for what I needed right now? It was going to be heaven.

And heaven was also currently in this car, which currently held me, my suitcases, a forty-eight-ounce Coke (*not diet*), and three fried cherry pies that I'd bought at a roadside stand.

As I sped north, away from the questions and the talking-to's in San Diego, I was both excited and nervous. I'd never lived alone before. I hadn't been to the ranch in probably five years, and Dad hadn't been there in over two.

He had someone up there who kept an eye on it, people to come in and clean every so often, and a handyman who made the necessary repairs. Since no one had stayed there in quite some time, my dad had called in a crew to get it ready for me, and now I was moving in for as long as I wanted it. When my father offered it to me, I knew how lucky I was.

*"You want to head up north to get some space, that's fine with me, kiddo. I think it'll be good for you to be alone for a while. Who knows, you might find you like it up there and want to stay."*

*"I can hardly stay there forever. How adult would it be for me to just go from living in my mother's house to living in my father's vacation home?" I asked.*

*He laughed. "It's not just my vacation home, it's yours, too."*

*"That's sweet, Dad. I appreciate your letting me head up there for a bit," I said as I went upstairs, thankful for the lifeline he was tossing me.*

*"The house is yours for however long you want it."*

*"Pardon me?" I asked from the landing.*

*"Just keep it in mind."*

*"I say again, pardon me?" I leaned down to peer through the banister at him.*

*"Pardon you nothing—take as much time as you need," he said.*

*"You're kind of amazing, you know that?"*

*"I do know that, actually," he said, his eyes twinkling.*

So while I had no real plans to stay up there very long, the idea that I could? If I wanted to? Options . . . kind of a good thing.

And options in a small, beautifully quiet town felt like exactly what I needed. I'd grown up on a stage. With dance competitions, modeling competitions, pageants almost every other weekend, I'd learned very early on that anything worth doing is worth doing in front of people.

As I drove the longer, more scenic route up the Pacific Coast Highway, I realized that for so much of my life, I'd been posing. Literally posing, mentally posing, acting a part, or some version of the best foot forward. Even my engagement was for public consumption. At a San Diego Padres game.

*"And as we pause for our seventh-inning stretch, there's a certain young man in the stands today who has a very special question for a lovely young lady."*

We were in box seats behind home plate. And there was my face on the Jumbotron, just after I'd bitten into a hot dog. A hot dog that was not on my diet, and don't think *that* didn't get mentioned later on. Ladies, if you're going to cheat on your diet, don't do it in a place where there's a Jumbotron.

Also, ladies? Don't go on a fudging diet.

Back to the flashback.

*As I hastily wiped the mustard from my chin, Charles sank to his knees in front of me—angled toward the camera, mind you—and presented me with an iconic blue ring box.*

*"Oh my God, what are you doing?" I whispered from behind the hot dog—angled away from the camera, mind you.*

*"What does it look like? Chloe, baby. Will you marry me?"*

*He opened the box, and the diamond was so large that the blimp flying overhead could have seen it.*

*"Wow," was all I could manage.*

*By that time, the entire stadium began to chant.*

*Yes.*

*Yes.*

*Yes.*

*"Yes," I repeated.*

*And as Charles swept me up into a hug, then dipped me back-
ward in a romantic fashion for a kiss seen in every romantic movie
from the beginning of time, all I could think was: Too Much. Too
Public. Too Not Private.*

*But it was a version of romance, and I let myself be swept away
by it. I was only a year out of my reign as Miss Golden State, and
now I'd been proposed to with a glob of mustard on my chin not
only for the fans in the stands to see, but to be rebroadcast on the
nightly news later on. Slow news day.*

Slow news day indeed I thought as I turned my stereo to
something hip-hoppy. I bounced a little in my seat as I sped up
the coast, looking forward to some quiet time with nary a Jumbotron in sight.

Hours later, I rounded the last bend of my journey and saw
Monterey spread out before me. Situated on a natural bay, the
city curved in on itself as it continued up the coast, the town
twinkling in the early dusk. I'd driven all day, I was exhausted,
and more than that, I was hungry. Not wanting to come all the
way back down from the hills into town after getting set up in
the house, I pulled into the parking lot of a small restaurant and
slid my car into the last spot.

I stretched as I climbed out of the car, feeling my joints
crackle and pop in the best of ways. Quickly braiding my hair
and dotting on a little lip gloss so I didn't look *so* road weary, I
grabbed my purse and headed inside. Wide front windows took
in the view of the bay, and cozy candles sat on the tables and
booths. Tables and booths that were full, so I elected to eat at
the bar rather than wait for a table. As I took a peek at the menu,
I sipped a club soda. I still had a twisty, windy drive up to the

house that would now be happening in the dark, so I stayed away from the glass of wine I was dying to have.

When the bartender came back to take my order, I looked up and locked eyes not with him, but with a set of baby blues at the other end of the bar. The mirror that stretched behind the bar reflected everyone sitting there, including the guy the baby blues belonged to. Red hair that was just two or three shades deeper than strawberry blond, gorgeous hair. Prince Harry hair. Unbelievably, this guy was better looking that his royal highness, with an incredible tan, and—oh, look, now he's smiling. Great smile.

While telling the bartender I'd take the daily special of local sablefish, my eyes kept going back to the blue eyes. I tried hard to keep my eyes on the man who was trying to decipher what kind of salad dressing I wanted from my "Hmm?" but I kept finding myself drawn back to the man in the mirror.

When I finished placing my order, those smiling blue eyes were gone. Which was a good thing; I had no business making eyes at anyone right now. I had a car full of suitcases packed with honeymoon clothes, and an engagement ring the size of a quail's egg on my hand.

Wait. Why was I still wearing my engagement ring?

I looked down at it, stunned as I always was when I looked at it. J. Lo would be impressed, is all I can say. Every time I'd teased Charles about what a big ring it was, he'd told me it was bling for his baby. Yuck. The guy actually used the word *bling*.

Was he overcompensating for something? I preferred to think no, that this was a very generous and sweet and very public display of how much he cared about me. And yet . . .

I'd take the ring off after I got to the house; it wasn't right that I still wore it. But for now, I sat in a bar 455 miles away from

it all, thinking semi-blushworthy thoughts about the cute guy
with the blue eyes.

I ate my salad, I ate my fish, I even managed to eat some cheese-
cake, and eventually packed myself back into the car. Following
the GPS directions, I twisted and turned my way into the hills,
each bend in the road affording me an even better view of the
lights of the town below. My father had hired someone to turn
on some lights and make sure I'd have no problem getting in.
And as I saw the gate for the ranch, I realized I was grinning
big. I was so excited to see the house—it always felt so cozy and
comfortable and gorgeous, all at the same time. I punched in the
code, the old gates swung open, and I headed down the gravel
drive.

It was originally a small cattle ranch, and though animals
hadn't been raised here in years, the old pastures and fence posts
remained. Every ten yards or so there was a gas lantern atop a
post, alternating sides, illuminating the driveway in flickers of
flame. In the sixties my grandfather had expanded the original
house, creating a wonderfully open space that was great for entertaining. And as I rounded the last curve and finally caught
sight of the house, my grin got even bigger.

It was straight out of the Rat Pack. Pure California ranch
style through and through, it was low, open, one story, and full of
floor-to-ceiling windows. Incredibly innovative at the time, they
slid on tracks so that you could open them all the way, creating
an indoor space that was equally outdoors.

I grabbed my overnight bag, crunched up the gravel walkway, and took out my keys. Light spilled through every window;
they *had* really left the light on for me. When I pushed open
the door, a wave of nostalgia washed over me. Pine, sage, and a

night-blooming jasmine seeped in from the back garden. I set my bag down and turned in a 360-degree circle.

I could easily envision Frank Sinatra and Dean Martin hanging out, paling around. Low modular furniture in tangerine leather in the living room off to my left, offset by an enormous glass coffee table in the shape of a kidney bean. Big glass balloon lamps floated over matching deep red oval end tables. An area rug in a black-and-white diamond pattern screamed from the floor, but was tempered by the fountain—oh, yes, a fountain—that was bubbling away on the inset bar in the corner. The most authentic tiki bar you ever did see. Stacked with highballs, lowballs, old-fashioned bowl-shaped champagne glasses, and several sizes of metallic cocktail shakers. I told them I'd be taking one of them out for a test run tomorrow.

On my left was a dining room with a table that could seat twenty. An oblong tortoiseshell, it had chairs with alternating cushions of turquoise and gold. Over the table soared a chandelier that had always reminded me of the old-fashioned game of Jacks, with silver rods jutting out at all angles and spheres of blown ruby glass at the ends.

Under my feet a terrazzo floor poured out in a wave pattern toward the kitchen, where it met polished concrete. An enormous wall of custom cabinets, light blond wood above the largest orange Formica countertop anyone had ever seen. At least in my generation.

Down the hall were several bedrooms, including the master, where I'd be sleeping. But off the kitchen? That's where I was headed. Through one of those enormous floor-to-ceiling glass doors was the most gorgeous terraced patio, inlaid Spanish tile set against adobe brick. There were tables and chairs and umbrellas everywhere, all in shades of sunny yellow and gold, like you might see outside a Tastee-Freez in the summertime. Three levels of terraces with potted olive and lemon trees, and then the pool. Free form and lush, it was painted dark green, giving it a tropical lagoon feel. I gazed at it a moment, considering a swim, but my sore muscles were singing a different story.

Collecting my overnight bag, I headed for the master bedroom (shades of green and pink with palm tree wallpaper, very Beverly Hills Hotel) and took a quick shower in the bathroom (shades of aqua and mint with golden mirrors, very Liberace in the Desert), and fell into the low platform bed (shades of I'm exhausted, so I have no idea what color it actually is).

I lay there feeling my muscles begin to relax, and listened to the house settling around me. There was a strong wind blowing tonight, whistling through the trees outside the window and scuttling leaves across the patio. It was a lonely sound, but I didn't *feel* lonely. I was alone in a strange bed in a semistrange house in a semistrange town, but there was still that hum of electricity running under my skin that I'd felt ever since my dad suggested coming up here.

As I rolled over on my pillow, my thoughts were suddenly filled with images of blue eyes. I smiled to myself in the dark and imagined what it might be like to date again. It was way too soon right now, but one day it'd be an option.

And there's that word again: option. The world was full of possibilities, and meeting handsome men in restaurants was just one.

I allowed one more moment of dreamy over the blue-eyes guy in the mirror, and then hummed myself to sleep. Sinatra, of course.

# chapter four

The next morning I woke up to not one, not two, not even three, but four texts from my mother. Which proves how much she didn't want to actually speak to me, since texting was something she hated to do. And was terrible at—she never really grasped the concept as a medium of communication. Case in point . . .

Text #1:

Dear ChLOE!

Text #2:

Your father tells ME
YOU HAVE GONE TO
MONTEREY. HOW VERY
grownup of youDON'T
YOU THINK PART OF
BEING A GROWNUP
MIGHT BE NOT LETTING

YOUR PARENTS GIVE YOU
ROOMand bonobo??????%

Text #3:

Pleasefilloutachangeof
addressformatthePOST
OFFICESOTHATYOUR
MAILWILLSTARTGOING
STRAIGHTTOYOUAND
youcanstartdoingthe
verygrownupexerciseof
answeringyourownsorryyou
didn'tgetmarriedCARDS)

Text #4:

FROM: YOUR MOTHER

She had large thumbs. Pretty sure *ROOMand bonobo??????%*
meant room and board, but I can't swear to that. But she did
have a point, and as soon as I had some breakfast, I intended to
begin addressing her concerns. The *room* I wasn't even going to
dignify. This house was way too cool to not enjoy. So stick that
in your tea cozy. But the *bonobo?* That I should, and would take
care of on my own.

I had some money squirreled away from my days on the pageant circuit, although it wasn't much. Even when you're winning,
which I did the last few years, it was mostly scholarship money,
not a ton of cash payouts. But I'd saved what I could, and would
be able to get by for a while. I knew what my mother was saying:

don't take your father's money. Funny, she had zero problem with that when it came to her alimony checks . . .

And my father would happily fork it over to keep me happy, but that wasn't the point. I'd felt funny about jumping from my parents' payroll over to my husband's. And it wasn't as if I hadn't tried to get a job over the years; I had. But my mother wanted me to focus on school, and then pageants, and then I was engaged. My year as Miss Golden State had taken place my senior year of college, and then once I graduated I was still volunteering extensively for the therapy dog charity. And once the wedding planning began, that became all consuming. I'd attempted to broach the subject several times to Charles about working once I was married, but it wasn't something he was too keen on. So my résumé, other than countless titles and work for my charitable organizations, was thin at best.

I'd been thinking more and more about the conversation I'd had with Lou Fiorello the other day.

*"We're finally ready to open a second Our Gang location, and we're starting to scout possible sites. We know we want to go north, somewhere like Santa Cruz, Salinas, maybe even as far north as San Jose."*

*"That's so great!"* I said. *"I'm sure they'll be thrilled to have a location up there. Same business model as the one you have now?"*

*"Yeah yeah, pretty much the same,"* Lou said. *"Part rescue, part shelter, part rehab, and of course, the adoption center. That's the whole point: getting these guys a good home."*

*"Sounds amazing. If there's anything I can do to help, just let me know."*

*"Well, why do you think I emailed you, princess?"*

*"To be honest, I wasn't exactly sure,"* I said.

"I thought maybe we could persuade you to come join us, get your hands dirty a bit."

"You want me? To work with you?"

"Hell, yes. You love dogs, you're great with the pits, and they need all the good PR they can get. Having a Miss America running a shelter for rescued and abandoned pit bulls? How great will that look on the six o'clock news?"

"Miss Golden State," I corrected as I doodled on the legal pad. "So what are you asking me, exactly?"

"We've already got the startup money for the new location. We just need to find it, staff it, and train the team that'll be working there. Interested?"

Goodness yes, but there was something that was a bit off here . . . "Lou, you knew I was supposed to be getting married this weekend, right?"

"I did."

"Yet you're offering me a job that would move me out of San Diego, right?"

"I am."

"Well, now, how's that gonna work out?"

"I got that pretty invitation you sent me stuck up on my bulletin board. The wedding date was yesterday, right?"

"Yeah."

"How'd it go?" he asked.

"Well, I'm not calling you from my honeymoon, if that gives you any clue." I grimaced.

"I had a feeling," he said, and I rolled my eyes.

"Would have been nice if you'd told me," I replied, and he chuckled.

"Well now, that was something you had to figure out for yourself. Sounds like you did."

"Humpf," was my reply.

"*Listen, I gotta get going, making a run to Torrance to check out a fighting ring we heard about. You think about what I said. If you're interested, let's talk soon, okay?*"

"*Okay, Lou. Thanks for thinking of me.*"

"*You kidding? I've already got fliers designed in my mind: you in your tiara and sash, surrounded by forty pit bulls. It'll be a hoot,*" he cackled, and I grinned into the phone.

"*I don't like the idea of you daydreaming about me in my tiara, Lou,*" I teased, and he gave a whoop of laughter as he hung up the phone.

I'd thought about that conversation a lot over the last few days. And while driving up to Monterey, I couldn't help but think that it was situated right between two of the towns he was considering.

I fired off a quick email to him now, while I was thinking about it, then got ready to head out and grab some breakfast and hit up a grocery store. And then maybe take a dip in that gorgeous pool. By the time I got my hair brushed and tucked into a neat bun, dressed in a simple sundress with a jeans jacket, and added the barest hint of makeup, there was already a reply waiting for me from Lou.

Hiya princess,

So you're spending some time in Monterey, huh? Beautiful town, probably a great place to get some space, am I right?

I'd love to have Our Gang in a town like that. Land can be pretty pricey there but it's worth looking into. Sounds like you're warming up to the idea? There's a vet there that I've worked with for years, Dr. Campbell. He's got his own clinic set up in town there, Campbell Veterinary Hospital. He volunteers his time down here when he can and does a lot of work with cities all over California, fighting those breed specific laws that get put

on the books without merit. I'll tell him you're in town, so stop
by and see him anytime. He'd be a great person to talk to, get
another perspective on what we want to set up. Also a great
person to partner up with, especially since he might have some
ideas about space around town we can look into.

Our Gang in Monterey? I like where your head's at . . .

Lou

Options, options everywhere. I grabbed my keys and headed
out to my car. With a clean breeze blowing in off the sea that
I could taste even up here in the hills, today was looking like a
great day. Especially if I could find some killer donuts.

Turns out the killer donuts are located at Red's Donuts, and as
my mouth can tell you, they are delightful. Especially the kind
with the maple frosting. I may have had three. Which may be
closer to four. Okay, truth time. Four and a half—but that's all.

Stopping after I could practically see the food baby I was creating, I headed for the grocery store I'd passed the night before.
I thought I'd leave the GPS off and try to navigate on my own,
which wound up getting me lost within three turns. Twenty minutes later, I pulled over into a parking lot to turn my GPS back
on to lead me to the grocery store. As I tried to remember the
name of the store, I looked around, hoping to get my bearings.

And there, right in front of me, was a building with a sign
that said Campbell Veterinary Hospital.

*Options.*

Lou had said he'd email this Dr. Campbell, but who knows
when that would actually happen? I'd probably have to make an
appointment, though; it'd be rude to just pop in . . .

*Options.*

Fudge it, I was going in. I checked my face, reapplied my lip gloss, and headed inside. The parking lot I was in must have been on the side, because as I rounded the corner I realized the building was enormous. Giant windows, big friendly pictures of dogs and cats, and special parking slots for "Pet Emergencies."

As I went through the automatic door, my nose was immediately met by the smell of disinfectant, butterscotch candies, and good old-fashioned doggie breath. The warm and inviting waiting room was packed with all manner of adults, kids, and dogs and cats. A German shepherd played with a dachshund in the corner, while three cats in a carrier explained to everyone why it was a crime against nature that they'd been brought here.

It was pretty crowded; maybe this wasn't such a good idea today. I'd call when I got back—

"May I help you?" A voice coated in southern charm pierced through my waffling, and I approached the desk. And saw quite possibly the brightest polyester pantsuit ever created. An almost electrically charged aquamarine blue, it was something Sally O'Malley would kick—and streeetch—and kick to get her hands on. An actual beehive, at least four inches of teased and twirled brunette fluff, was stacked on top of her head, a head that had eyelids full of an iridescent blue eye shadow almost exactly the same shade as the pantsuit. Stripes of what can only be called rouge (I'd blush to call it blush) accented plump cheeks, pointing down to a cherry-red glossy mouth curved in a welcoming smile. And on her ample bosom? A rhinestone-bedazzled name tag proclaiming her to be Marge.

"Hi there, sugar, step right up. I don't bite," she cooed.

A disembodied voice from behind a row of filing cabinets shouted, "That's not true!"

"Shush!" she ordered, then waved me forward. "You pay him no attention, sweetheart. Now, what can I do for you?"

"Well, I don't have an appointment, but—"

"Or an animal," she said, looking over the counter to peer down and make sure that I did in fact not have a pet. She couldn't be more than five feet tall, so it was quite a lot for her to lean, and as she did, I marveled at the beehive. It didn't move, not even when she was half upside down. She righted herself, then looked at me expectantly, still with the friendliest smile I'd ever seen.

"No, ma'am, no pet. I wanted to see if Dr. Campbell might be available?"

"Which one did you want? What is this about?" she asked.

"My friend Lou mentioned that Dr. Campbell would be a good person to talk to about pit bulls. Or rather, rescuing them. I probably should have called—"

"Wait, Lou. You mean Lou Fiorello?" she asked.

"Yes, Lou Fiorello mentioned that Dr. Campbell would be a good person to speak to about a shelter for rescued pit bulls in the area," I finished, my pageant training taking over and slowing down my speech so I enunciated each word. My tummy had automatically pulled in as well.

She giggled. "Oh yes. Lou called this morning." She sighed dreamily and an actual blush began to bloom around the rouge stripes. Interesting. "So you're Chloe, right?" she asked, and I nodded. "Lou told me he was sending some pretty young thing in here to talk to the doc—something about picking his brains about opening up a gang here in town?"

"Well, kind of, yes. Is he in? It looks really busy; I can come back."

Marge got a different look in her eye—one that appeared much more like problem solving than dream weaving.

"It's busy, but I know he'll be glad to meet you. Why don't

you come with me, sugar, and we'll get you all fixed up. Amy, take over the desk for a moment, won't you?" Marge called.

As a young woman in scrubs took her place, Marge led me through the waiting room and down a corridor filled with exam rooms.

"You just go right on in here to exam room six and I'll send the doctor in to see you, okay? Here's some pamphlets about heart-worms while you wait; make yourself comfortable," she cooed, her voice literally dripping Spanish moss and tall lemonade.

Spying a stool in the corner, I took a perch, waiting for Dr. Campbell. And I did in fact do my assigned reading. I was so engrossed that when the door opened, it took me a second to register who had just come in the room.

Blue-eyed guy with the Prince Harry hair.

Well, hello.

His gaze was down on his clipboard and medical charts, and he came through the door saying, "Okay Mrs. Winkle, it says here that our pal Stanley swallowed an entire roll of quarters. Has he passed them yet?"

When he looked up at me and I caught the full force of those ice-blue eyes, the impact was a thousand times more lethal than the reflection in the bar mirror.

Gingers are my kryptonite. Always have been, always will be. Show me a hot redheaded guy and my pulse will start a'racing. And *this* guy? At least six feet three, sun-kissed skin, freckles scattered across his nose, his hair swept back from his chiseled features. Cheekbones that could cut glass. And those eyes, currently giving me the three-second inventory. I drew my-self up to my full seated height and took another two seconds to catalog the strong forearms, also splashed with a few freckles, the long and tapered fingers holding the charts. Oh yes, a very good-looking man. And did I mention the scrubs? Oh my yes, he was all wrapped up in dark navy blue surgical scrubs, which accented the eyes magnificently. I finished my perusal, and met those eyes on the return trip.

"You're not Mrs. Winkle," he said, one corner of his mouth turning up, then looking behind him to make sure he came into the right room. That's when I noticed the name tag. Dr. Lucas Campbell.

"I'm definitely not Mrs. Winkle," I said, jumping off my stool and crossing to him.

"Obviously," he answered with a twinkle in his eyes. Fudge, the kryptonite had a twinkle.

"Dr. Campbell, right?" I asked, and he nodded his head. "I'm Chloe, Chloe Patterson?"

"Nice to meet you Chloe, Chloe Patterson," he replied, tilting his head at me, looking a little confused as he took the hand I offered.

"From the email? Lou told me I should stop by and introduce myself."

"Thanks, Lou," he murmured, shaking my hand.

"He thought you might have some advice for me about setting up here in town."

"Setting up here in town?" he repeated, still shaking my hand.

"Our Gang. He wants to set up an operation somewhere up north, and he was considering Santa Cruz or Salinas until I suggested Monterey. I just got into town last night and—"

"—had dinner at Spencer's Grill," he interrupted. Still shaking the hand.

"Yes, yes that's right," I replied, going a little starry-eyed. But

I quickly rallied. "Were you there?" I asked, not so much flutter-ing my eyelashes as just blinking once or twice. Rapidly.

Still shaking hands—just a reminder.

"I *was* there. In fact, I could have sworn you saw me too. In the mirror?" he pressed, a knowing grin on his face.

I blinked my wide eyes, but my blush gave me away.

"I may have seen you," I allowed, and his eyes danced. Danc-ing and twinkling. I was in trouble here. "I was exhausted; I'd just driven all the way from San Diego."

"To set up your operation. Not in Salinas or Santa Cruz."

"Exactly. So, think I could pick your brain a bit sometime?"

"Absolutely," he answered, squeezing my hand firmly. Be-cause we were *still shaking the hands*.

"Chloe?" I heard from the door. Another tall man, with silver hair and welcoming smile, dressed in a suit and tie, white lab coat, and a name tag that said Dr. Campbell.

I nodded my confused head.

"Hi, Chloe, I'm Dr. Campbell. Lou said you might be stop-ping by, but I didn't expect you so soon. I see you've already met my son, Lucas."

"Nice to meet you, Chloe," Lucas said, finally letting go of my hand. "Well, I've got to see a poodle about some quarters," he said, meeting my eyes one more time.

"I think the Winkles are in exam seven," the elder Dr. Camp-bell said.

"Could have sworn Marge told me I needed to go to six," Lucas said, which was confirmed a second later by Marge her-self as she breezed down the hallway in a cloud of Jean Naté.

"I did tell you exam six. I needed someone to keep Chloe company until your dad was ready for her," she called over her shoulder.

"Could've clued me in, Marge," Lucas shot back.

To which Marge responded, "Now where's the fun in that?"

"She's got me there." Lucas looked back at me and I shot him a knowing glance, which made him unleash that killer grin once more.

"Um, son? The Winkles in seven?" Dr. Campbell nudged.

"On it. Nice to meet you, Chloe. You'll have to tell me all about this operation you're setting up; sounds fascinating."

Then he was gone and I was ushered into Dr. Richard Campbell's office, where we did indeed discuss the possibilities of opening up another Our Gang in Monterey. And while we talked, I didn't think about how great Lucas' butt looked in his scrubs. And by didn't, I mean only for a little while.

Dr. Campbell had a wealth of knowledge. He worked with pit bull rescue all over California, and was instrumental in helping towns get rid of the laws that made it illegal to own dogs like pit bulls. He also donated his services to provide free medical care to some of the dogs pulled out of the fighting rings that were a popular pastime for very sick and cruel people.

He thought it was a great idea to open up an Our Gang here, and with some of his close friends being county supervisors, he was confident that the approval wouldn't be a problem.

I left his office feeling like a plan was literally taking shape before my eyes. On my way out, I stopped at the front desk to say good-bye to Marge.

"Thanks for making the meeting with Dr. Campbell happen this morning," I told her as she sorted folders at a dizzying pace.

"Which Dr. Campbell are you referring to?" she asked with a coy smile.

I raised an eyebrow. "The father, of course."

"And the son?" she asked, raising her own eyebrow. Oh boy.

"You're a little bit wicked, aren't you, Marge?"

"Only a little bit?" she asked, and I laughed out loud. This woman was a trip. "So Lou mentioned that you just moved into town from San Diego, is that right?"

Whoa. Subject change. "Well, I wouldn't say I've *moved* into town. Visiting would be the right word."

"Visiting . . . all by yourself?" she asked, nonchalantly. I noticed that she slowed down the pace of her filing, however . . .

"Yep. All by myself." I widened my smile. I knew where this was going, and I knew I had no business going along with it. But I was glad I'd removed the engagement ring last night. What a strange thought for someone who should be sunning on a beach on Tahiti with her new husband at this very moment.

"What perfect timing. Lucas just got back after being away for a while. If you need someone to show you around town, I'm sure he'd be more than happy to—"

"No no no, Marge, I'm going to stop you right there." I leaned over the counter toward her excited face. "I'm not interested in dating anyone right now. I just got here, and I'm dealing with some stuff—"

"*Everyone's* dealing with some stuff, darlin'. Sometimes it's just nice to deal with it while looking at a gorgeous hunk of a man." She reached below her chair and plopped a giant yellow purse in the shape of a sunflower on the desktop, then pulled out her phone. "Now, take a look here. Here's Lucas at the clinic picnic last spring—isn't he so handsome? And here he is in his kayak—did you know he loves to kayak?"

"How would I know that? I just met him." I shook my head, letting this play out since she seemed to be having such a good time showing me pictures of Lucas. And I'll admit, the shirt-less picture of him on the beach was worth listening to this kooky old bird for a few more minutes. I also learned some interesting things. He'd gone into practice at his family's animal hospital right after finishing up veterinarian school, third generation, don't you know. And he indeed loved to kayak, he loved the ocean in general, don't you know. He'd spent the last twelve weeks in Guatemala working for Vets Without Borders. That explained the tan.

Finally, with a cheery good-bye and a promise to stop by any ole time, I scooted away. And on my way out, I saw Lucas come walking down the hallway with a very relieved looking poodle. I waved, he waved, and I found myself strutting a bit as I headed out the front door.

Back in my car, I found the address to the grocery store I'd started out for an entire morning ago, stocked up on food, and headed for home. And as I went up my driveway and parked around back, I looked out at the old pastures, the trees, the open space almost as far as I could see . . . and I suddenly had a very good idea of where Our Gang Monterey could set up shop.

I just had to convince my father.

# chapter five

I spent three days lying by the pool, listening to sad songs, taking long, hot baths, drinking wine, and eating chocolate. I tried to will myself into mourning the relationship that I'd walked away from, thinking that I should be suffering for the emotional turmoil I'd caused Charles. That I should be crying and sobbing for the love that was no longer, for the good times and the bad, for the laughs and for the tears . . . But it wasn't happening.

I knew what I truly wanted to do; the idea had been percolating from the moment my dad offered me the house in Monterey. So after three days of self-imposed sad sack I called my father and broached the idea of using some of the land to set up Our Gang. He was familiar with Lou's name, since I'd told him about the organization when I first found out about it. And about how angry I was at Mother for not letting me participate. So when I mentioned Our Gang, he knew instantly what was involved. He supported the idea of me going to work with Lou, and I was pretty sure that's what I wanted to do. But when it came to using the land, he wasn't 100 percent sold.

"Okay, tell me again what this would entail," he said on the phone the night I brought it up. I didn't have a ton of information, as I didn't want to suggest the idea to Lou until I knew whether my father would even entertain the idea. He was cautious. "You're going to be living with forty pit bulls?"

I grinned, knowing he was intrigued now. I tossed a handful of mushrooms into the wok I was cooking my dinner in. "I thought we'd use the field behind the barn, the one where Grandpa used to have his vegetable garden. We could house the dogs in the barn—there's plenty of room for individual pens, an exercise yard—we could make it really comfortable."

"And *you're* comfortable with all those dogs?"

"Well, sure. You know I love working with animals."

"And you're great with them, there's no question about that. But, honey, working with golden retrievers in a nursing home is totally different than rehabilitating dogs that have come from some very violent places. Are you ready for that? Do you even have the training to deal with that?"

"I don't yet. I'd work with Lou; learn more about obedience training and how to handle more powerful breeds. And someone he's worked with at his place in Long Beach will be coming on board in the new location, so I'll literally be surrounded by people who know more than I do. Didn't you always tell me to make sure you always work with people who are smarter than you, because then you become a smarter person as well?"

"Well played, kiddo," he said with a chuckle. "Sounds like you're staying in Monterey, huh?"

The million-dollar question. I took a deep breath, turned off the burner under the wok, and walked out onto the patio, sitting down in one of the giant lawn chairs upholstered in daisy-covered plastic. "I realize I'm probably having a knee-jerk reaction to what I just did to everyone down there, including you, who spent so much money on that perfect wedding." I winced, remembering seeing one of the bills Charles let my father pick up. Zeroes upon zeroes.

"But I also realize I need to do something totally different from what I'm used to, to try living a life that's a one-eighty from what I've been doing. And boy, this would be different." And hard. I wasn't fooling myself thinking this was going to be, "Hey, let's open up a pet store!" This was going to be very hard work, physically and emotionally. Seeing how damaged some of these animals were would be tough to take. But I also knew I needed this. I needed a challenge. I needed to get my hands dirty.

"Tell you what, Dad. If you can get some time off, why don't you come up here? I'll have Lou come too, and we can all talk, see if this is something you'd be interested in doing. Because this is your place, and you'd need to be totally on board with it. And if this is going to work, I'd insist on paying rent. It might not be a lot at first, but I'd pay you something."

"Hell, Chloe, you said it yourself—I'm never up there; the place just sits empty fifty-one weeks of the year. It *would* be nice to have some activity around there again. I hate to think of all that land going to waste," he mused. In my mind's eye he was sitting at his desk in his office, rubbing his jaw and looking off into space.

"So you'll think about it?" I asked, and I could see him nodding.

"Call your friend Lou. If he can come up some weekend, I can make that happen too. And then we'll just see," he said.

I kicked my legs into the air. *Yes!*

And I went back to my stir-fry and to my glass of perfectly chilled rosé, and enjoyed them with a side of wonderful options.

• • •

Those options turned into reality a week later, when my father and Lou shook hands and agreed that this would be the place that Our Gang North would be putting down roots. I'd thought it would take several meetings and several rounds of convincing, but when my dad saw the photos and videos Lou brought, not only of the dogs when they came in, but when they were adopted into loving forever-homes, there wasn't a dry eye in the house.

And that was it. Lou offered me the position of director of operations, I accepted, and I was suddenly in business. I had a salary, I had a title, I'd even have business cards! And the money that was allocated for leasing land would be paid to my father as a monthly stipend for using his property. I had brought some income in for my dad; I wasn't a freeloader. And I had business cards!

Not exactly how I was going to sell it to my mother, but that was a conversation that could be put off for a few days. Since I'd been in Monterey, my communication with my mother had been limited to a few very short, curt phone calls, and one more round of exhausting texts.

Text #1:

Dear Chloe,

Text #2:

I've taken the liberty of
sending BACK ALL OF
YOUR WEDDING GIFTS,
MOST OF THEM WERE
OFF THE REGISTRY AT

Sakssolwasabletogetthat
takencareofquite
efficiently!!!!

Text #3:

Your father tells me that
you're staying in Monterey
indefinitely, although I'm
not sure whyyouDIDN'T
TELL ME YOURSELF

Text #4:

Don't forget that in the
midst of all this soul
searching you're currently
doing that you made a
commitment to speak
at the Miss Golden
STATUATORY conference
on the 30th. I'd hate to
have to tell them you're
canceling because
you haven't been able
to FINDYOURSELF or
whatever it is you're DOING
up THERE*%

Chuckle. Eye roll.

• • •

What I was doing was moving along at a pretty fast clip. Lou's contractors started leveling the ground in the pasture beyond the garage, which would be the main area where the dogs would be concentrated. As I'd hoped, we were able to repurpose the old milk barn into housing for the dogs. Rows of indoor/outdoor pens would be grouped together, with a row for cases that needed more isolation. Dogs just coming out of fighting rings could be unstable at best, and keeping them away from other dogs was vital to their rehabilitation, introducing them to the rest slowly, over time.

An exercise area was quickly constructed with an obstacle course and a kiddie pool for playtime, and the contractors fenced in an extensive pasture for the dogs to run free.

An old shed was insulated and converted into an adoption area, with plenty of room for potential adoptive families to meet their new pup. Another shed was perfectly situated for storage of all the Puppy Chow, chew toys, and doggie beds we'd need, mostly donated, sometimes from stores and sometimes from peoples' homes. When you looked around a house, there were so many unused things that could be useful to someone else. That twenty-year-old bedspread that's taking up valuable real estate in your linen closet would feel like heaven to paws that have never known anything but concrete. That bucket of balls in the garage from when you tried to take up tennis is exactly the kind of thing dog shelters needed, and would be put to immediate use.

Dr. Campbell senior was an enormous help. He was able to get us approval from the county faster than we could have on our own, to make sure we'd be open for business as soon as we could get things ready. And with his good standing in the community, anyone who had something negative to say about pit bulls being sheltered in their town was immediately converted after they heard him eloquently speak about these misunderstood animals.

As things began to take shape, I found that I was thinking less and less about the life I left behind in San Diego, and more and more about the life I was creating here in Monterey.

One afternoon I was whitewashing the old milking stalls when I saw a truck with Campbell Veterinary Hospital emblazoned on the side pull up in front of the house. Dr. Campbell had said he might stop by after work to drop off some donations. Wiping my painty hands on my jeans, I headed out into the driveway and saw that it was the son, not the father. I quickly ran my hands through my hair, realizing too late that I'd just striped myself like Pepé Le Pew. Ah, well.

Lucas climbed out of the truck, clad in jeans and a tucked in black button down. (Mercy.)

"Hello! I thought your dad was stopping by," I said as he walked toward me.

"Disappointed it's not him?" he joked.

Standing in front of me, he blocked out the sun, making a halo of his hair. I bit down on my lip to stop myself from telling him this very thing.

"Just surprised, is all," I said, tilting my head back for another halo peek. "How've you been?"

"Good, good. You?"

"Busy. Which is good for me."

"Sounds like things are really coming along up here. When my dad told me he was running some stuff up here, I offered to come so I could see . . . the place." He grinned.

"Oh, I bet Marge loved that." I laughed.

"She sure did," he admitted. "So, give me the tour."

"The tour?"

"Yeah, I hauled eighteen bags of Dog Chow up here for you. The least you can do is show me around the place."

"You hauled them in a truck—don't make it sound like you lugged them up by hand," I teased.

"I *loaded* them by hand. Does that count?" he asked, showing me his hands. They were calloused. And looked strong.

"Those callouses from kayaking?"

"Mostly paddleboarding. How'd you know I kayak?"

"Your agent told me." I rolled my eyes. "She even showed me pictures."

"Crazy old woman." He laughed with affection.

I'd stopped by the clinic twice in the last two weeks and never saw Lucas, but Marge made a point to show me more pictures of him.

I hadn't exactly protested.

"Tour, huh?" I asked.

"As long as you don't put a paintbrush in my hand," he teased, reaching out to tug on a piece of my hair that was striped. My skin tingled pleasantly. "So where do we start?" he asked, looking toward the hill. "Up there?"

"Hey, buddy, this is my tour. We'll start where *I* say." I turned and headed up the hill. "We're gonna start up the hill."

I could hear him chuckling behind me. I put my hips into it. The chuckle turned into something a little more desperate, and I chuckled right along with him.

Showing him around the property, I pointed out what was completed and what we were still working on. Some of Lou's volunteers were coming up in a week to help fine-tune everything, setting up the office and things like that. Since we were a satellite operation, we were essentially copying what was working in Long Beach, on a smaller scale. I'd visited Lou several times over the last few years, and always marveled at what a tight ship he ran. I was hoping to copy that as well.

As we walked down the center of the barn, I explained how the dogs would be kept. "They'll have a lot of time out in the yard every day, but they'll each have their own pen to come back to, with beds and their own food and water. Shared spaces sometimes, but at the beginning, at least, they'll each have their own space."

"Dad's told me all about it, but seeing it is a very different thing. What you guys have done up here already is impressive."

"Not just us. You'll be here too," I said innocently.

"I will?"

"Sure, your dad volunteered your services evenings and weekends, free of charge. He didn't tell you?"

"He seems to have neglected to mention that." He leaned against one of the stalls. "But it sounds good to me."

"Nights and weekends? Free of charge? Fantastic!" I clapped my hands. He pushed himself off the stall and moved a bit closer.

"Might as well. My nights and weekends aren't too exciting these days."

"Oh, I can't believe that. A good-looking guy like you?"

"Good looking, huh?"

"Well, you kind of set me up for that one, didn't you?" I laughed, noticing how close he'd gotten. "Besides, all the good-looking guys are going around with white stripes on their black shirts these days—it's all the rage. I'm sure you won't have any trouble picking up the ladies."

"White stripes?" he asked, puzzled.

I stepped to his side and ran my hand across his back, then showed it to him.

"You could've warned me!" he exclaimed, spinning around quickly as if to see the back of his own shirt.

"What part of 'I'm painting the stalls in the barn' did you not get?" I laughed, and it felt good, easy. "Don't worry, it's milk paint. It'll come right out in the wash."

"Good. I should get those bags out of my truck and let you get back to your afternoon. Or night, I suppose now. Dusk. Whatever."

"Yes, let me get back to my dusk, please," I teased, and we headed back toward the truck. We walked in silence, and within a few seconds I felt the need to fill it. "My nights and weekends are pretty thin on excitement too, you know."

*Overshare. Overshare. Overshare.*

"Oh, yeah?" he asked, and I could feel my cheeks begin to burn.

Why in the world had I said that? I quickly said, "Yes, I'm actually enjoying the peace and quiet. It's a good change of pace. So, Marge said you were involved with Vets Without Borders? Tell me about that."

We'd reached the truck, and he went around to the back and started unloading the big bags of Dog Chow as I directed him toward the shed. As he unloaded, he told me all about this wonderful program. It's exactly like what it sounds like: they go where the vets aren't. They identify areas that need quality veterinary care, and doctors donate their time and service to that community. Pets, strays, you name it, they care for it. And as eighteen bags of Dow Chow were unloaded, he painted a picture of a coastal village in Guatemala, and the sweet people he met there. Sleeping in barracks with other volunteers, spending evenings around beach bonfires, working long hours in the hot sun. He was heading out again for another tour in a couple of months, to Belize, and he'd be gone twelve weeks again.

"How'd you get involved with them?" I asked as he stacked the last bag. For every one bag I lugged across the yard, he fireman-carried three. He wasn't even out of breath, and I wondered what it took to make him pant a little. I further wondered why I was already a bit sad he was leaving for twelve weeks, when I barely knew him.

"Let's just say I needed to get out of town for a while," he said, his eyes darkening a bit.

"I totally understand. That's why I'm up here. I couldn't stand being in San Diego any longer," I said, playing with a leaf that had fallen into his truck bed as he sat on the truck gate.

Looking intrigued, he said, "Oh, you have a story too? I bet it isn't as bad as mine."

Well, fudge. Now *I* was intrigued.

"Oh, mine's pretty bad," I warned, twirling the leaf.

"I'll show you mine, if you show me yours?" he asked.

"You think I'm just going to whip out my sad tale to see if it's as big as yours?" I teased.

"Yes, that's the general idea." A last ray of sunshine beamed through the gathering clouds, gilding his face.

"You go first," I said with a sigh.

As he began, his shoulders fell a bit. "Well, it's very simple. Boy meets girl, boy and girl fall in love. Boy and girl date all through the end of high school and through college. Boy asks girl to marry him. Girl agrees. Boy and girl plan wedding, boy and girl move in together, boy and girl are very very happy—boy *thinks*. Then minutes before they're to be married, boy gets left at the altar when girl decides she doesn't want to be stuck in a small town the rest of her life. Girl leaves church, packs a bag, and moves to Los Angeles, leaving boy to explain to everyone in the church where the hell the bride has gone. Boy knows where, because girl was thoughtful enough to send a bitchy note with an even bitchier bridesmaid. Boy hears about a spot that just opened up in Guatemala, and takes the chance to get the hell out of town and away from everyone with their sad faces. Not unlike the one you're making right now, although the gaping mouth is a nice touch I haven't seen before."

I closed my mouth immediately. "Let me get this straight," I began, shaking my head in disbelief. "Your fiancée walked out on your wedding?"

"She did."

"Oh, fudge."

"Sorry?"

"Nothing," I said, eyes wide. "Continue."

"That's about it. We'd been together for a really long time; we'd practically grown up together. I knew her better than anyone—at least I thought I did. I just . . . I still can't believe it happened. When someone you trust can do something like that to you . . ." He trailed off, his voice dark.

"I know," I echoed, my brain whirling.

"Anyway," he said, life sparking back into his eyes. "I showed you my sad story. Now . . ."

"You want to see mine?"

"Like you wouldn't believe." He grinned.

I felt my heart pitter-patter. And also an icy stab—how could I tell him my story? His fiancée had ripped his heart out in front of everyone, and now he wanted me to tell him I essentially did the same to Charles?

Technically, Charles never made it to the altar. And technically, mercifully, we never had the kind of love it sounded like Lucas had with his ex. So technically, I could tell him and make him understand.

Yet this wonderfully sweet and ridiculously handsome guy was looking at me with those piercing eyes and that sexy half grin, and dammit, I wanted to keep those eyes and that grin on me a little bit longer. So . . .

"Oh, well, it's not that interesting a story. Just recently got out of a long-term relationship, is all. I was engaged too, until very recently, as a matter of fact." I plowed ahead, punctuating my words with a little toss of my hair and shoulder shrug. Minimize. Minimize. Minimize! "But I'm not anymore; that's all over. So yeah, no stranger to heartbreak here." I sounded like a country-western song. And not even a good contemporary one, more like an old twangy one.

"You were engaged?" he asked, sympathy apparent.

"Yeah, but you know . . ." I started to shrug, when I saw his eyebrow go up at my nonchalance. "I mean, yeah," I said, maudlin, "you know." Sigh. Blink. Blink.

Oh, what tangled webs we weave, when first we practice to pretend to be more broken up about leaving your fiancé than you really are. Hey, it was poetic inside my head.

"So your engagement fell apart, and I got left at the altar," he said, that slow grin beginning to reappear.

"So it would seem," I agreed.

"So we're both pitiful," he said, holding my gaze. For exactly three seconds.

Then we both broke into crazy laughter, mine because I'd successfully sidestepped this land mine for the moment.

We began to quiet down, the twilight settling in around us, the air fresh and beginning to fill with the sounds of the hillside. Crickets, birds heading home, a few bumblebees making one last honey run.

"Want to hear something weird?" Lucas asked, bumping my shoulder with his own.

"Always."

"You look like her."

"Her who?"

"My fiancée. Ex-fiancée."

"Oh, fudge, really?" I said, covering my face.

He laughed, grabbing my hands and placing them back in my lap. "What's with the fudge?"

"Hmm?" I asked, not paying attention to his words since his hands had just been on my skin. Something my skin apparently enjoyed immensely, as it was all zingy now.

"You just said 'oh, fudge, really,' and when you dropped a bag of dog food earlier I'm pretty sure you said 'fudge it.' So . . . fudge?"

"Oh, yeah, well. That's a holdover from my mother. A lady never swears, you know. It's simply not done," I answered, making my voice go higher and poshier.

"Ah, so fudge means . . ." He trailed off.

"Yeah, fudge means . . ." I echoed.

"What does it take for you to say the real word?" he asked, his blue eyes teasing.

"I have to be pretty worked up," I admitted, becoming aware of every single point of contact between us, everywhere the right side of my body was connected with his left side. Thigh, yes. Hip? Uh-huh. Elbow? Hell, yes. "So, I look like your ex, huh?"

I'd just thrown a virtual bucket of water on us both. Whew.

"Oh—yeah, a bit. Same long blond hair, same green eyes, but you're a bit taller and slimmer than her."

"Hmm. I'm surprised that Marge has been playing matchmaker, then."

"I know, could she be more obvious? Every morning when I get to work, she greets me with an update on how things are going up here, how pretty you are, and how she wonders why no one has taken you out and shown you the town. I usually get another update at lunchtime."

"Oh my God, I'm so embarrassed," I moaned, lying back into the truck bed. His face appeared over mine.

"Don't be embarrassed; she does it with everyone. I've just never been in her sights before."

"If she knew that I'd just bro—that my fiancé and I had just broken up, she wouldn't be so quick to play matchmaker," I said, digging my hands into my hair. "Setting up two people who'd be sooooo on the rebound is not good."

"Yes, rebounding off each other sounds like a terrible idea." He chuckled quietly, and I peered up into his face through my fingers.

"It *is* a terrible idea. Which is why you and I, Mr. Blue Eyes, are not going to let Marge be in charge." I scrambled to sit up, pushing my paint-encrusted hair out of my face. "This would be a mistake of epic proportions. Especially if you started dating some new chick who looks just like the girl who just . . ."

"Fudged me over?"

"Yes. Can you imagine? Everyone would be talking."

"But I bet you're nothing like her. Unless you're a pageant girl too. That *would* be just too weird." He laughed.

Instant quiet. I looked up at him with wide eyes and a guilty expression.

He wrinkled his forehead.

I lifted my arm in answer. Elbow elbow wrist wrist.

"What? No . . ." he breathed, looking horrified.

I patted him on the cheek. "You sweet, sweet boy."

After a moment he fell back into the truck bed, groaning. Which quickly became laughter. Which I joined in, two new, not-rebounding friends laughing like fools under the new moon.

# chapter six

"Chloe! Great to hear from you—I've been wondering how you've been doing!" Clark said.

"So far, so good. Sorry I didn't get to see you longer when you were down here for the wedding."

"No problem, you had a lot on your mind. How are things down in San Diego?"

"I assume okay, but I'm in Monterey now. I'm moving here, actually."

"Holy mackerel." I could hear him processing. After a few seconds, "Okay, tell me how *that* happened."

My cousin and I were only a few months apart, and were thick as thieves when we were kids. I used to spend summers up in Mendocino with his family when I was little, before the call of the pageant got to my mother and we started spending our summers driving around California, entering me into Little Miss Anything & Everything with a Crown. As we grew older we grew apart a bit, but a family reunion our senior year in high school brought us back together, and we'd become close again.

Both being an only child, we'd missed out on that sibling bond, and over the years we'd become honorary sibs to each other.

When I'd visited Clark a few weeks before the wedding, I'd given voice to some of the cold feet I was having, which I'd written off as just a case of the jitters. He listened; he'd always been a good listener. And while at the time I felt that getting married was still the right thing to do, he was one of the few who would understand why I couldn't go through with it.

I'd also met his Vivian on that trip, or Viv as she preferred to be called. She was a piece of work—a little rough around the edges, but she seemed a perfect match for the steadfast and somewhat buttoned-up Clark. The night after I'd left Mendocino was apparently the night things changed for them; ever since then, it'd been a whirlwind romance. According to Clark, she was the cat's meow. And they were already living together. I remember when he called to tell me.

*"Wait, hold up. You're moving in?" I asked, incredulous. "It's only been . . ." Fudge, I sucked at math. "It hasn't been very long."*

*"True, but it's kind of perfect, actually."*

*"If you're sure you know what you're doing," I cautioned, not wanting him to get his heart broken. My cousin was sweet, kind, and hopelessly old-fashioned when it came to love. Apart from the "living in sin" bit.*

*"Chlo, have you ever known me to do anything impulsive?"*

*"No, actually."*

*"And that's exactly why I'm doing this—so just be happy for me." He laughed, and I was taken with the excitement in his voice. He did seem really happy.*

Now he told me, "And we're learning to can vegetables! Vivian's been trying to figure out how to replicate her Aunt Maude's recipes, especially her famous homemade pickles. Our kitchen is full of cucumbers and glass jars, and I'm pretty sure we both smell like vinegar."

"Whatever makes her happy, right?" I laughed, knowing my cousin. He was the type of guy who'd do anything for the woman he loved. Including smelling like salad dressing.

"But enough about us; tell me what's going on with Monterey. I'm happy to have you in my half of the state."

"I know! You guys will have to come down for a visit and see me. Remember that place in Long Beach I told you about, Our Gang?"

I filled him in on everything I'd been up to, and as I told my story, I realized that I'd really done a lot in such a short time. He was interested in the shelter, and was impressed with how much work we'd completed already. He shared my father's concern about aggressive dogs, but overall he was happy for what I had going on.

"You know, Viv has been talking about wanting to get a dog . . ." he mused.

"As soon as we've got some ready to be adopted, I'll let you know." I was excited to think of this becoming something real. Something that was mine, that I'd worked hard for.

I'd never really given much thought to what I wanted to be when I grew up. Strange, yes, but everything seemed so predetermined. There's nothing wrong with being a wife and a mother, when you choose it. Only a few girls I went to school with truly *yearned* for that. They couldn't wait to have babies and build homes and start a life with their own family unit. Their paths were clear, and they were honest with themselves.

But most of the girls I went to school with? I always got the sense that they were rushing toward that life because they thought the good life was something that was just handed to them. And believe me, if you were young and beautiful, there were scores of men who were interested in arm candy. And sometimes arm candy turned into wife candy. That was the endgame—that was the pinnacle. Marriage was just a means to an end.

I'd hoped to marry a man I loved. And now, listening to Clark talk about Viv, I thanked my lucky stars once again that I'd panicked and fled the morning of my wedding. One day I might crave pickles, and I'd love to think I'd be craving pickles with a man who also wanted to learn how to make pickles. Charles would have just bought pickles. Nothing wrong with that. But I wanted something a little more homegrown.

As Clark the Pickler and I ended the call, I agreed to keep in touch about a dog that might be right for them, and he agreed to keep me up to date on their ongoing adventures. I sat back in my chair in the breakfast nook, coffee cup in hand, and thought about what I wanted to eat for breakfast. I'd been buying donuts too often lately, and it hadn't gone unnoticed that my pants were feeling a little more snug than they used to.

I headed over to the fridge and began poking around, deciding to make an omelet. I was just starting to chop up some onions when I heard a car in the driveway. I'd gotten used to workmen coming at all hours of the morning, but on a Sunday? I looked down at my nightgown, and hastily tied my robe around me. Which I was glad to be wearing, when I saw the truck coming around the corner with the Campbell Veterinary Hospital decal. And before I knew it, I saw Lucas climbing out of the front seat dressed in old jeans and a paint-splattered T-shirt, carrying a bucket of painting supplies.

I waved at him through the kitchen window, and he approached.

"What's going on?" I called through the window screen.

He held up his bucket. "You told me you needed help painting, so here I am."

"But I haven't even had breakfast yet!"

"Great!" He set the bucket down in the yard and grinned. "I'm starving!"

"Oh, for pity's sake," I mumbled under my breath, and pointed him toward the front door. As I walked, I saw him following me around the side of the house, each huge window providing me with another glimpse of this dangerously charming guy. I tightened the ties on my robe, and opened the door.

"Good morning, Rebound," he grinned, stepping up onto the porch. "Nice," he complimented, his eyes raking over my nightgown and robe.

My hand gripped the knob. *Door*knob. "Well, I was hardly expecting company this morning," I answered. "And don't call me that. No one is rebounding anything."

"Hmm," was his reply, then he looked past me into the house. "Aren't you going to invite me in?"

"You're used to getting your way, aren't you?"

"Pretty much," he replied, letting loose the grin.

I smiled back in spite of myself and waved him in. "Come on, then; hope you like omelets."

"I love them." He followed me into the house. "Whoa, time warp," he exclaimed, taking in the retro styling.

"Oh, yeah, wait till you see the kitchen. It's where orange Formica went to die." I laughed, pointing out some of the more kitschy features. "I still can't believe you came to paint."

"We made a deal last night, and I intend to honor my commitments," he replied, leaning in a bit closer. "Unlike my ex."

"Ouch. I winced, a tiny ball of awful bubbling up unexpectedly.

"I shouldn't say that. It makes me seem pathetic, doesn't it?"

"Pathetic, no, not at all," I said, tightening my ties a little more. "But maybe it was the best thing? I mean, obviously it was hell, but wasn't it better to find out before rather than after?" I asked, and not just to Lucas. Justifying to the universe a little?

"Pretty and practical," he mused, smiling down at me. "You're lethal, you know that?"

My breath caught as I looked up at him through my lashes, peeking at the cute in front of me.

"You're blushing," he murmured, and I turned toward the kitchen, knowing he'd follow.

"Let me blush while I make breakfast," I said, keeping my tone light.

"Challenge accepted," he said, stepping into the kitchen behind me.

"No challenge was offered. You can't accept something that wasn't offered," I said, taking a position on one side of the enormous kitchen island. I leaned forward a little, my robe falling open just slightly.

"Lethal," he whispered, leaning against the island on the other side, eyes a bit dazed.

"I'm going back to my onions now, okay?"

"Do it," he breathed, and a maniacal giggle escaped my lips.

Shaking my head, I turned to the stove. "Can you grab the butter from the fridge? Top shelf, on the right."

"Got it. Need anything else in here?"

"The cheddar cheese, actually, bottom drawer."

"Cheese doesn't go in the bottom drawer."

"Sure it does."

"No, it doesn't. Vegetables go in the bottom drawer. Cheese goes in this small drawer here, marked Dairy," he insisted, pointing it out to me. "But you've got—good lord, are you hoarding pudding?"

"You. Get. Outta there." I laughed, tugging at his arm and moving him away from my stash.

"Seriously, I'm pretty sure that's all the chocolate pudding in town. You some kind of doomsdayer?"

"What?" I asked, grabbing the cheddar cheese and shooing him away from the fridge.

"You know, like those guys who hide out in bunkers and squirrel away canned food and guns in case of a zombie apocalypse. Except you're going to fight the zombies with pudding," he explained as I marched him to the table in the breakfast nook and sat him firmly in a chair.

"Yes, that's exactly my plan. However did you guess?" I replied deadpan, batting my eyelashes at him. "You want bacon in your omelet?"

"Of course," he answered, and I started whisking eggs and crumbling up bacon I had left over from yesterday. I began sautéing the onions in a bit of butter, then turned to ask him why he had nothing better to do on a beautiful Sunday morning than paint my barn, when I noticed he'd disappeared.

"Lucas?" I asked, and he popped his head out from the pantry.

"Holy hell, there's another case of pudding in here! And seven, no, eight boxes of chocolate Pop-Tarts!"

"Okay, that's it. Get out of my pantry; you're a pest!" I shouted, marching him once more to the table. "Don't make fun of my consolation chocolate."

"Your what?" he asked, confusion all over his gorgeous face. Oh, man, I was in trouble.

"My consolation chocolate. I went through a breakup. I'm entitled. Besides, you should have seen the diet my mother had me on to fit into my wedding dress. Ugh." I cracked eggs angrily into a bowl and whisked with a vengeance. "I am *owed* that chocolate."

"I believe you," he replied, watching me pour the eggs into the onion mixture.

"I'd ask you to pour the orange juice, but I'm afraid I'd have to hear about the chocolate milk," I said, looking at him over the burners.

"Can I have some of it?"

"My chocolate milk?"

"Yeah."

"Sure."

"Then you won't hear a word about it," he answered promptly, heading back to the fridge. He got out both, and I nodded him toward the cupboard where the glasses were kept. A few minutes later we were sitting at the table with full plates and glasses in front of us. We grinned at each other across the tops of our glasses and dug in.

"This is really good," he told me as demolished half the omelet in two forkfuls.

"Thanks."

I sat contentedly for a moment, listing to the scrape and clink of his fork as he polished off the other half. In just a few short weeks I'd gotten used to the quiet, but the silence of one is very different than the silence of two. It was nice to have another scrape and clink in the kitchen.

"So what's with the house?" he asked suddenly and, surprised, I choked on my orange juice. "You okay?" He thumped me on the back.

"Sorry, wrong pipe. What did you mean?"

"This crazy pad, man—these ring-a-ding-ding digs. I feel like I should be saying things like chickie baby."

"Ah, yes. Well, it's not my taste, if that's what you're asking."

"Are you kidding? This place is great!" he said with such

enthusiasm that I found myself smiling again. I sure did smile a lot around this guy.

"Thanks, it's my dad's. It's been in the family for years, but we hardly ever use it. Hence, the very out-of-date decor."

"And now it's the home of a pit bull rescue. Very cool."

"Yeah. Not at all what I was expecting when I came up here; I just needed some space. And how lucky for me that I've got the land to do this here."

"Is this what you did in San Diego? Like, for a living?" he asked.

I took the opportunity to examine my plate. "Not exactly."

"What kind of work did you do?"

"I've never had a paying job before. I was good at one thing, and that was winning crowns. Then I volunteered. Then I was engaged. And I wasn't going to work once I was married. So this is kind of a big step for me," I snapped, throwing my fork down. Where had that come from, and why was my chin wobbling?

Ah, fudge.

"Sorry, it's a bit of a touchy subject for me, I guess." I sniffed, dabbing at the corners of my eyes with a napkin.

"It just happened; I think it's normal to be a little touchy. You should have seen me after Julie and I broke up. When I first got to Guatemala, I was . . . not myself," he admitted, pushing his plate away.

"Oh, yeah? Did you cry over omelets like a big baby?" I asked, my voice going all warbly now. Warbly voice and wobbly chin, what a combo.

"Over omelets? No. But I drank more than I usually do, and made a few late-night phone calls that I'm not proud of." He leaned closer and motioned for me to do the same. "Okay, there was one night when there might have been a tear or two. But that was over some weird goat stew—not an omelet in sight."

I laughed into my napkin, an ugly, weepy laugh. "What a mess I am."

"Yeah, you barefoot and in your nightgown," he said quietly, reaching out to swipe my cheek with his thumb. "What a mess."

He stood to clear the table, reaching for my plate first. "Okay, we wash dishes, and then we paint. How's that sound, weepy girl?"

"Good," I whispered. I whispered because I didn't trust my voice in that moment. Because there were suddenly other things I wanted to do instead of washing dishes and painting . . .

I'd done most the work the day before, but there were some high spots that were hard for me to reach that I'd saved for last. Being so tall, Lucas was the perfect guy. To hit the high spots, of course.

We talked as we worked. And laughed as we worked. And over the course of the morning, I decided that Lucas Campbell was not just great looking and funny, he was also . . . a nice guy. With Prince Harry hair.

Kryp-to-nite. *So* much trouble.

I learned that he was an only child but had a lot of extended family, mostly in Northern California. He'd been on the water since he was a kid, originally surfing and now kayaking and paddleboarding—a real beach rat. I learned that he'd never wanted to be anything other than a veterinarian, and to go into the family business that his grandfather started back in the sixties. And I learned more about his ex, Julie.

She hadn't been on the pageant circuit as long or as extensively as I'd been, and had held mainly local titles, which could

be why I'd never met her. She was always more interested in acting, which is what she decided to do when she left Lucas to run
off to Los Angeles. Who would ever leave this guy?

*Someone is saying the exact same thing about you every time
they look at Charles.*

Touché.

"So who ended it?"

"Hmm?" I asked from the corner of one of the stalls. I was
almost finished, sitting down to paint the baseboards. The old
floors had been power washed, then sealed to keep down the
dust that was always floating around in old structures like this.
With the whitewashing, the entire place looked bright and inviting, the old beams sailing overhead. Things this old were built to
last, by God, and the roof only needed minimal patching to keep
the dogs dry in even the nastiest of storms.

It was cozy.

And speaking of cozy, Lucas was standing on a stepladder
in the stall next to mine, looking down on me from above as he
tackled his own last corner. Lucky corner, I mused.

But wait, he asked me something? Oh, yeah. "Ended what?"

"You and your guy. How close did you get to the big day?"

I almost dropped my brush into the pail. "Oh, please, like
I'm going to tell you that," I scoffed, staring up at him. As he
reached for the highest rafter his T-shirt slipped up, revealing an
inch or so of tanned skin. I licked my lips without thinking, then
grimaced at the taste of paint. Gross.

"Come on, I thought we agreed last night that we could talk
to each other about this stuff. Swapping our sad stories?"

"Oh, story this, you nosy veterinarian," I replied, slapping the
last bit of paint on and throwing my brush into the pan. "Done!"
I laid down on the floor, feeling the muscles in my back stretching out gratefully.

"Great! You can entertain with me while I finish this last part. Talk, woman." he instructed, and I shamelessly watched him work.

Could I tell him? Could I talk around the part where I ran out on my wedding hours before it happened? I could give it a shot.

"So you want to know why my fiancé and I broke up?"

"Yup."

"It's complicated."

"I assumed."

"Hmm, okay. Well, I guess for me, it all boiled down to a feeling I—er, we had. I'd been feeling like something was off for a month or so before the wedding; I think we both felt it. But it didn't all bubble up and become clear until that last . . . week or so." So far, so good. *We. Stress the* we. "And we just knew it wasn't the right thing to do." Whew.

But like an idiot, I pressed on. "The funny thing is, I think he'd still have gone through with it. I mean, if we didn't talk about it ahead of time. He wasn't in love with me, and I wasn't in love with him, but somehow I don't think he felt that was necessary for a good marriage."

"And you?"

"I want it all. I want all-encompassing, knock-your-socks-off, can't-live-without-you, can't-be-in-a-room-without-wanting-you-naked love," I said, closing my eyes and smiling as I said the words. When I opened them, there he was. "I can't believe I just told you that," I said, wanting to disappear. But he wouldn't let me. He stared me down, his eyes searching and strong. I could barely breathe. His body now full of tension, his knuckles whitening on the brush he was holding, he licked his lips.

"Well, that's what everyone wants, right?" he asked, finally returning to his whitewashing.

I returned to my regularly scheduled breathing. "Is that what you had with Julie?" I asked, my voice unsteady.

He stopped for a second, then continued painting. "We did at one point. And if you'd asked me that question the day before we were supposed to get married, I'd probably have said we still did. But in reality?" He finished up his corner with a resounding smack, then tossed his brush into the bucket. "We didn't have that. Not anymore."

He came down the ladder, disappearing from sight while he was on the other side of the stall, but then coming over to sit next to me. We both looked at our handiwork in silence. Then he asked, "What was his name?"

"Charles. Charles Preston Sappington."

"Yuck."

"Yuck? You don't even know anything about him!" I protested, sitting up in a huff.

"Rich guy, right?" he asked, a knowing look on his face.

"Yes."

"Country club? Well connected? Shirt never untucked?"

"Yes. Yes," I said, then thought for a moment. "Yes," I admitted to the last with a sheepish grin.

"I stand by my yuck. Yuck to Chuck."

"Who was *never* untucked," I added and he nodded seriously, as though that explained it all. We sat there another moment or so, looking at the work we'd done. "Thanks for helping me finish this up, by the way. Especially on a Sunday. "

"It's in my contract, right?" he replied. "Nights and weekends."

"Oh, yeah. Nights and weekends."

A patch of sunlight had been working its way across the barn floor through a window high up in the rafters. It had finally reached us, and the day immediately felt lazy and unhurried. Like a sunflower, my head turned to follow the warmth, and I felt content for the first time in a long while. Warm, safe, and altogether gooey. When I turned to share this little bit of nonsense with Lucas, it felt perfectly natural to instead lean in and press my lips to his.

And I very nearly did. I looked at his mouth, those soft lips smiling back at me curiously. I tilted my head just enough to the left, and actually began the leaning in . . . but then stopped myself. He raised an eyebrow—he knew what I'd been thinking. Horrified, I leaned back, shaking my head.

"Did you just—"

"No!" I replied, hiding my face.

"Pretty sure you just tried to—"

"No!" I yelled at my knees.

"I think you almost—"

"No!" I repeated once more, thoroughly embarrassed. And then he was tugging at my arms and unfolding me and pulling me across the floor toward him. "Oh, God, I could just die."

"Oh, would you quit." He chuckled, and suddenly I was tucked against his side, his arm around me. "I've been thinking about this nights and weekends thing."

"Uh-huh," I said, holding my hands over my face so he couldn't see my flaming cheeks.

"My friends are all married, and most already have kids, so they're usually pretty busy."

"That's great," I said, monotone.

"So, since I've been back from Guatemala, I've spent most of my nights and weekends alone. I take extra shifts when I can, but mostly I've been . . . well . . ."

"Been what?" I asked, peeking through my fingers at him. He was chewing his lip. His thumb was also absently stroking my hip where he held me close. I let him stroke. It was soothing.

"Moping, I guess. Julie and I were together so long, almost

everything I did was as part of a couple. And alone, it's just . . .
I don't know."

"I know what you mean," I offered. "I miss certain things—
not just with Charles, but just . . ."

"Having someone else there?"

"Yeah." I sighed, leaning against him. He smelled so very
good. Equal parts pine and salt air and a hint of sunscreen.
Beach rat.

"So I was thinking, let's just hang out a bit. Run around
town, drive up the coast, go do some stuff. How much time have
you spent exploring Monterey?"

"Zero," I admitted. "I've been so busy, which is a good thing."

"It is a good thing, but this is a fantastic town and you should
see it."

"Nights and weekends, huh?"

"Nights and weekends. I've been bored out of my mind, and
it'll be nice to hang out with someone again."

"Just hanging out, right? That's it?" I asked.

His eyes darkened slightly. "That's it."

But there was an undercurrent now, something intangible in
the air. He knew it, I knew it, but we were both going to ignore
it. Because . . .

"Because it's just . . . it's too soon . . . you know?" I said, and
he nodded.

"I get it," he replied, and planted a kiss on my forehead. "I
actually do."

And so we sat, in the sunshine on the floor of the barn, until
it moved on. Just me and my kryptonite. Who'd be filling my
nights and weekends.

Mm-hmm.

# chapter seven

Turns out that nights and weekends had to wait a bit, as I had work to do out of town. I spent a few days at Our Gang in Long Beach, working with Lou and his team on the day-to-day operations of running an organization like this. The amount of fund-raising required was astonishing; just the phone calls to sympathetic ears was staggering. As a satellite operation we received funding mostly through the mother ship, but I'd be responsible for doing some of my own outreach in Monterey. I was already thinking of ways I could not only generate donations, but get the community involved with the placement of the animals by partnering with the local scout troops.

And I got to spend time with the dogs at Our Gang Long Beach. I learned how to socialize the newer dogs, how to work one-on-one with those that came out of more aggressive households, and how to approach a dog that wasn't used to humans who were actually *kind*. So many of these animals had been mistreated, tied up, left alone on chains in empty lots and backyards, *they'd never known that anyone cared about them.*

But when they realized that someone did care, and someone

would let them just be dogs again, to run and jump and play, they could have the same personality that anyone would want in a family pet. Friendly, eager to please, and loving, they'd run with you all day and sleep by your side all night. And that was the image I was taking back with me to Monterey; that was the image I was determined to show anyone who questioned why we were running a rescue for these amazing creatures.

When I got back from my training, I was floating high above the clouds and eager to get our operation open for business. And I came back to a place nearly ready to do just that. I was amazed at how much work had been done; we were in the homestretch. I walked the grounds with the head contractor, checking out the final punch list of things to be completed, but it was pretty close.

After everyone left for the day, I was out on the patio, working on my to-do list, when my cousin Clark called. Smiling, I answered the phone.

"What's up, mister?"

"Hey, how's my favorite cousin?"

"Good! Just got back in town, trying to get things finished up around here so we can start taking in some dogs. What's up with you?" I asked, still working on my list. Get a hose for watering bowls: check. Tennis racket for exercising with balls: check.

"Not much, I just have some news." His voice sounded different, a little high pitched and breathless, and I looked up from my list.

"Oh?" I asked, setting my pencil down. Something was up.

"Remember the pickles? How Vivian was craving them?"

"*No*," I breathed, putting two and two together and coming up with pickles. "No *way*," I squealed.

"Vivian's pregnant," he said, his laughter ringing out across the line. "She's pregnant! I'm having a baby! Well, *she's* having a baby, *we're* having a baby! Can you believe it? Ha!"

I *couldn't* believe it. They'd been dating, like, two minutes. But listening to him go on and on, babbling like a brook, his excitement was so contagious that I found myself laughing right along with him.

"And we're getting married! I mean, I already had the ring, so it was just a matter of time, really, and when she told me, I passed out—can you believe that?"

I could, actually. Once when we were kids, he passed out from excitement when he got to go on the Jurassic Park ride at Universal. All those dinosaurs, it was just too much for him. I smiled just thinking about it.

I came back from my memories to hear him say, "So when I came to, I just asked her to marry me and she said yes!"

"Clark, breathe, honey, breathe," I said. "That's fantastic news, all of it. I'm so happy for you! Congratulations! So give me all the details."

And as he told me all about how far along she was (not far) and what their plans were (they'd get married after the baby came; she wanted a big 'wedding back home in Philadelphia) and how at first her brothers were planning to come out to kick his ass (all five of them) until she convinced them what a terrible idea that was, I listened and laughed along with him. After we got off the phone, I looked down at my to-do list and realized I'd doodled right over everything I'd been working on. And I'd doodled several versions of cribs, rattles, and a stick figure family.

Christ, if I'd gotten married, I could have been pregnant already. Charles wanted a family right away. And I did too . . . I'm pretty sure I did. That was the plan, anyway, and I was all for the plan, right? Wait, I *wanted* kids, right? What the hell kind of a woman wasn't sure she wanted kids but would *probably* have had them anyway?

As I was contemplating my doodles, my phone rang again. It was the ginger vet this time.

"Hey," I said in greeting.

"Hey to you too; how was your trip?"

"Good, just got back this afternoon. They got so much done while I was gone; you should see the place."

"Great, when I pick you up in the morning you can show me what's new."

"In the morning?" I asked, confused.

"Yeah, nights and weekends, remember? Tomorrow I get to start showing you the best Monterey has to offer."

"The best Monterey has to offer? What are you, working for the tourism board?"

"Yes, exactly that. So throw all your cares away and enjoy Monterey," he said, game show voice style.

"Well now, that's just creepy," I said with a laugh. "What are we doing?"

"It's a surprise, but you'll get wet, so wear a bathing suit, please."

"A bathing suit?"

"Notice I said please. Something really skimpy and preferably see through."

"Lucas!"

"Kidding. Not kidding," he deadpanned.

"Lucas," I warned once more.

"Okay, suit is a definite, skimpy is optional."

"Uh-huh, thanks," I said, wondering what he was up to.

"Pick you up at eight. Bring a change of clothes too."

"Okay, bossy. And mysterious. You're being bossy and mysterious," I said.

"And cute. You forgot cute," he prompted.

"I can't see you. How do I know you're cute?" I teased.

"Oh, you know I am," he insisted

I blew him a raspberry, and hung up listening to him laugh.

Smiling, I laid back in my lawn chair and looked up at the night sky. This high up in the hills, it was so clear that you could see thousands of stars. After mentally going through my bathing suits—which were mostly skimpy, let's face it—I got up to head inside for a good night's sleep. Eight o'clock would come early. As I picked up my doodled to-do list, I noticed that on the bottom I'd written *Lucas*. On my to-do list.

"Yeah yeah yeah," I muttered to myself. Still smiling.

"Paddleboarding? This is why you wanted me to wear my bathing suit?" I exclaimed as he pulled up the next morning and I saw what was stowed in the back of his truck.

"Hello to you too," he said in response, jumping out of his side.

"Sorry. Hello," I allowed, then went back to my earlier greeting. "Paddleboarding?"

"What's wrong with paddleboarding?" he asking, walking around the front of the truck. Long black swim trunks, old surfing T-shirt, unzipped fleece—he was ready for a day on the water. With those legs of his that were tanned and oh so long. He really was a tall drink of water.

"Nothing," I said to his legs, then forced my eyes toward his face. What a hardship that was. "I've just never tried it. I thought we were going to spend the day lazing around a pool somewhere. Like the one I happen to have here . . . the water's warm, drinks nearby . . ." I gulped nervously. "No sharks."

"Sharks! Is that what you're worried about?" he laughed, taking my bag and throwing it into the bed of the truck. "You grew up in California. Don't tell me you're afraid of sharks."

"I have a healthy fear, yes. Not to mention the bottom of those paddleboards look just like a tasty seal."

"These boards are over ten feet long," he said, pulling me toward the passenger side.

"So?"

"So how many seals are over ten feet long?"

"The sharks will think they've hit the mother lode," I muttered as he packed me in and shut the door. Peering through the side mirror, I looked at the boards and paddles behind me. I caught sight of him running around to his side, shaking his head and grinning.

"Besides, won't the water be freezing?" I asked as he jumped in next to me.

"I've got that covered, chickie baby," he said, giving me two thumbs-ups. "Wet suits."

"Oh. Great," I replied weakly, and settled against the passenger-side window. He just laughed, and we were off. It wasn't that I was deathly afraid of sharks. Most of the guys I grew up with surfed. They all seen a fin or two, maybe even had a bump once in a while. And I loved going to the beach, loved going in the ocean. But I tended to stay pretty close to shore, and by tended, I mean I rarely went in past my waist. Paddleboarding? Definitely past my waist. Where sharks might be. Shudder.

But as we drove toward his favorite beach, I watched him tapping out a rhythm on the steering wheel, glancing over and smiling every so often, relaxed and happy as a clam.

I decided nothing ventured, nothing gained, and when we pulled into Lovers Point Park in neighboring Pacific Grove, and saw that gorgeous beach, punctuated by wind-shaped cypress trees and rippling with craggy rocks and peaks, I realized that trying something new could be a very good thing. I took a moment to breathe in all that good salty air. Lucas climbed out of the truck and came around to my side while I hung out the open window like a Great Dane, just sniffing and smelling.

Leaning on my window, he looked at me carefully. "If you don't want to do this, that's totally okay with me. We'll hang on the beach, maybe take a drive—we can do whatever you want to do."

I looked past him at the beautiful water and the beautiful day, and said, "I want to do this."

"Great! Let's get suited up," he said, helping me out.

"But if we see one mother-fudging fin, you're the sacrificial seal." I pointed at him, then grabbed the wet suit. "Now, how do I get into this thing?"

Turns out wet suits are not easy to get into. There's a fair amount of jiggling and jumping, especially if you're not used to putting one on. And while I didn't wear my skimpiest bikini, I did spend more than a few minutes picking it out. Black and white polka dots, tied tight in the back. Semiskimpy. Did I notice how his eyes bugged when I took off my shirt? Yes. Did I notice how he bit his lip when I took off my shorts? Yes. Did I notice how he tried so very hard, but failed so very miserably, to not look directly at my breasts when I jumped and jiggled my way into a second skin of rubber? Oh, yes.

The real question is, did *he* notice how I whimpered the tiniest bit when he took off his shirt? No idea—because when he did, I couldn't look anywhere but his torso. Lean, tan, lightly freckled, especially on the tops of his shoulders from a lifetime spent on the beach. He was in his wet suit in a flash, zipping up the back with practiced ease. And when I struggled to zip my own suit, he offered to help, taking his time.

He held me steady with one hand on my shoulder, while I looked over at him with a hairy eyeball. "You okay back there?"

"Oh, yeah," he teased, his eyes nowhere near my own hairy eyeball, which earned him a slap on the butt from me as he went to grab the first paddleboard.

He went easy and slow, giving me a mini lesson on the beach first. To distribute your weight on a paddleboard, you want to make sure you keep your feet about shoulder width apart and in line with your body, rather than in a surfing stance, where one leg is in front of the other. Because I grew up with surfers, it didn't seem natural to me, but I was going to give it a go.

The water was bracing but the day was warm and sunny, so it was a good mix. It was calm, hardly any waves, which was great for paddling. Once we were up to midthigh, he showed me how to sit comfortably on my knees and how to hold the paddle.

"Hold it about midshaft now. Once you're standing up, you'll want to grip the end."

"Midshaft. Grip the end. I see what you're doing there," I muttered, struggling to keep my balance when what looked like a tiny wave actually made the board move quite a lot.

"You're the one with the dirty mind, Chloe—I'm just trying to show you how to stay on top," he said with a wink. "Relax a little. If you fall off, no big deal, you get back on. And if you do fall off, fall away from the board. You don't want to smack yourself in the face."

"This is supposed to be relaxing?" I sputtered thirty seconds later, when I did in fact fall right off.

"Once you get into it, you'll love it, I promise," he said, holding the board steady as I climbed back on. "Straddle it."

"Oh, shut up," I yelled, falling in again. When I finally made it back on and felt reasonably stable, we paddled out a bit farther. Once I felt comfortable enough to look up from my board, I took in the scenery.

He sliced his board through the water, his strong shoulders moving effortlessly as he paddled just ahead of me. His back muscular even through the wet suit. That hair, messy and tousled by the wind and the water, a dark mahogany now that it was wet.

That coastline was real purdy too.

And before long, it was time to try standing up. "Now remember: go up on your hands and knees, get steady, then slowly raise up, bringing your feet to the center of the board. Not too far back, or you'll tip. Just find that sweet spot," he cautioned, demonstrating the standing-up part, not the tipping. He made it look really easy.

"Hands and knees . . . sweet spot . . . Do you have a job taking late-night phone calls that I don't know about?"

"You're stalling," he said, and I nodded. I took a deep breath, scanning the water for fins. Nothing.

"You can do this, Chloe," he said, only a few feet away.

And you know what? I did. I stood up on my first try, legs trembling a bit as I wee-wawwed trying to find the sweet spot, something that really did exist. Holding tight to the paddle, I stood up strong.

"Way to go!" he yelled, and I turned to smile . . . and promptly fell into the water.

But it was okay, that was just part of it. I stood up once more, and under his careful instruction, started paddling. And before I knew it, I was totally doing it! We went out farther and he showed me how to turn slowly, and then how to make a quick turn. He fell in, I fell in—okay, I fell in many more times—but each time it got easier, and before long I was skimming the surface, making great long pulls with the paddle, flying across the water.

At one point I looked back toward the coast and realized how far out we were. It was so quiet. No cars, no buses, no radios; just lapping water and a few gulls crying overhead. It was a bit unnerving at first, feeling so far out, but then I looked to my left and there was Lucas, gently paddling next to me, grinning.

Then I *really* looked around. When I saw the coast, this time I didn't see how far away it was—I saw how from this distance you could really take in the cypress groves, the twisted rock sawing at blue sky, the mossy green grass. It was the same coastline I'd been sitting on not thirty minutes before, but from this angle, it was a totally different thing. From a totally different perspective. "Thank you," I whispered.

It was quiet enough that my words were carried to Lucas, who simply said, "You're welcome." And then asked, "You want to go see some otters?"

Always answer yes if anyone ever asks you that question. Because they are the *cutest* fudging animals on the planet. Not far from where we started was a tiny, protected cove filled with kelp beds. And that's where we saw the sea otters, in groups, rolled up in the sea grass to keep them tethered while they ate their breakfast on their backs. Breaking open tiny abalone and mollusks on their chests, they ate while floating in the kelp bed, aware of us nearby but not bothering to hide their buffet. I could have watched them for hours, their sweet little mouths busily prying off the outer shells to get to the tasty treats inside, all the while floating on their backs.

Eventually the cold water became too much, and we reluctantly paddled back to shore. Chilled to the bone but feeling exhilarated, we plodded up the beach to the truck.

"That. Was. Amazing!" I cheered, pounding on his back in excitement as we dragged our boards up through the sand. "Seriously, anytime you want to go, let me know and I'll be there!"

"I'm glad you liked it so much. I was a little worried you were going to freak out when we saw that fin."

"You're hilarious." I stretched my arm behind me, feeling for the string connected to my zipper. "Very funny."

"Okay," he said, pulling his zipper down and peeling the wet suit down his torso, stopping around his bathing suit.

"No, really. You're joking, right?" I asked. "You're just teasing me."

"Okay," he repeated, a devilish look in his eye.

"Don't tell me. I don't want to know." I shuddered, determined not to let anything bring me down from this paddleboard high. Except this damn zipper.

"Want some help?"

"Please." I held up my damp hair so he could get to the zipper. He unzipped me most of the way, and I could feel the edge of his warm, pruney thumb graze the middle of my back, just below the line of my bathing suit top. I scooted away from the warm and pruney thumb to slip all the way out of my wet suit, wrapping up in a towel that was warm and soft from sitting in the sunshine. He grinned, peeled his suit off the rest of the way, and dropped the gate on his truck, creating a place to sit.

Sitting next to each other on the edge, watching the now stronger waves beginning to roll in, he unwrapped the sandwiches he'd made while I pulled a bag of chips open with my own pruney fingers. Licking the saltwater off my lips, I looked around for something to drink.

"I've got soda in the cooler," he said, gesturing over his shoulder.

Seeing it, I scrambled over the truck bed, losing my towel in the process. And as I leaned in to grab the soda, I realized I had very nearly hit him in the head with my bum.

"You want something to drink?" I asked, looking over my shoulder to see him grinning.

"Sure. Whatever. And feel free to take your time. Take a look at every soda in there. Twice, if you want."

I swung wide and made sure to knock him in the head with the object of his affection on my way back to my seat.

"Here you go," I said sweetly, handing him his soda while I popped the top on mine. We clinked, then sipped. The morning on the water made us famished, and as we demolished our peanut butter and jelly sandwiches, he told me about another beach not far from here that we could try next time.

"You're making an awful lot of plans for someone who's leaving again in eight weeks," I teased, my words casting a bit of a shadow on the day. Part of me didn't want to get excited about all these new plans, since he'd be leaving. But hey, this was just for fun, right? We weren't dating; just friends spending some time together.

"I'll make sure those nights and weekends are worth it between now and then, okay?" he said, nudging me with his shoulder.

I crunched down on a chip and showed him my chewed food. Even the otters heard him laughing.

We spent the rest of the day lazing around at the beach. He dug a Frisbee out of the back of the truck and we ran up and down the beach, laughing and shouting and calling foul play whenever it went into the water. When we finally packed our sunshined bodies into the truck and started for home, it was nearly five o'clock.

When we pulled up, I asked if he wanted to come in for a bit.

"Nah, I need to get home. Get some laundry done before the work week starts up again," he said, leaning his head back against the seat. "This is one of the times I really miss my ex."

"She did good laundry, huh?"

"She did!" he exclaimed with a sheepish look. "It's just not the same when I do it, you know? I used to just open a drawer and bam. Clean shirts, all folded and lined up."

"I did my own laundry, living at home with my mother. But Charles sent everything out; he liked his dress shirts pressed in a very specific way."

"I mostly wear scrubs."

"You sure do," I said on a sigh, remembering how good he looked in that navy blue heaven. I cleared my throat hastily. "Anyway, enjoy your laundry. I'll talk to you soon?"

"You bet," he answered, and I slid out of the truck. Looking through the window, I said, "This was an amazing day; thank you so much. Like, it was one of my favorite days . . . ever." I meant it. It'd been perfect. I shrugged, trying to lessen what I was saying for some reason. "So, thanks."

"It *was* an amazing day, Chloe," he nodded, his gaze burning into mine. "Thank *you*."

"Okay. So . . . bye." I whirled around and headed inside before I could say anything else. Though what else could I say? How could the day possibly get more amazing?

Oh, I had an idea—boy, did I have an idea.

# chapter eight

The next morning, I was in town filling out the last of the paper-work I needed to file with the Monterey county and I stopped by the animal clinic on the way home to pick up some blankets they'd collected for me.

Marge came pranced around the edge of the desk to catch me into a Jean Naté–scented hug. "Oh, sugar, I feel like I haven't seen you in forever! How have you been? How was your trip down to see Lou? You saw him when you were there, right? How was he—I mean, how was your trip? Is he coming to town for the grand opening? Lou, I mean?"

"Well, you are just all about my recent travels. How sweet of you to ask," I teased, giving her a knowing glance. "And, yes, he's coming for the grand opening."

"Well, now, that's just fine, just fine, indeed. I'll make sure to bring extra of my famous baked beans. Have you heard about my baked beans? Everyone back home in Savannah just raves about them, and everyone out here always asks me to bring them to picnics and potlucks and such. I'll bring some and you just watch . . . that's all anybody'll talk about," she sing-songed.

Lucas came in the front door with a bag over his shoulder and a cup of coffee in his hand. "Hey, Chloe, I thought that was your car out there," he said, smiling and stopping just a few inches from me. "Morning, Marge."

"Hey, Lucas, how's your day going?" I asked, turning from Marge slightly to look at him, which meant looking up at him. Fudge, this guy was tall; it surprised me almost every time I was around him. "I see you got your scrubs washed in time for work today."

"I'm barely here on time; I overslept. You wore me out yesterday." He groaned, rotating his shoulders a bit.

"Me!" I exclaimed, massaging his left shoulder. "You're the one that wanted to keep going; I was good after twenty minutes. Especially once I found that sweet spot."

"Yeah, but admit it. You loved it."

"Oh, yeah. Totally worth the soreness today. But next time we should stretch afterward."

"Agreed. By the way, you left this in the back of my truck yesterday," he said, pulling my bikini top out of the bag on his shoulder.

"Oh, thanks, that was thoughtful. I wondered where that went."

Marge's head exploded in a cloud of Jean Naté confetti. "What the . . . But when did . . . Now wait just a—"

The two of us grinned at each other, perfectly aware of what we'd just said and how it sounded.

"See you tonight?" I asked, and he gave me a slow nod.

"Wouldn't miss it," he murmured, his voice low and full of promise. "You headed home now?"

"Mm-hmm." I nodded also, just as slowly. I pursed my lips.

He licked his. Marge sighed dreamily, and I had to cough to cover up a laugh. "Walk me to my car?"

"I thought you'd never ask." Setting his bag and coffee on the front desk, he guided me out the front door with his hand in the small of my back. Not pushing, just the warmth of his skin telling me which way to go.

"See ya, Marge," I called over my shoulder, then rested my head on his bicep for good measure. We could hear her sputtering halfway out into the parking lot. "I think we just made her day," I cackled, collapsing against the side of the clinic.

"I don't know how you kept it together. I thought for sure I was going to lose it when you started in with the sweet spot."

"Well, that's typically when everyone loses it," I quipped, and he groaned. We took a moment to compose ourselves, and then started to walk over to my car.

"So, tonight?"

"What about tonight?" I asked, wiping a tear from my eye, still chuckling a bit.

"Pretty sure you just insinuated back there that we had plans for tonight."

"I did?"

"You said, and I quote, *'see you tonight,'*" he said. "In a very Marilyn Monroe voice too, which was a nice touch, by the way," he said.

"Oh, yeah, I guess I did," I mused. "Well, we don't really have to do anything. It was mainly for effect, just to mess with her a bit."

"While I always love an opportunity to mess with Marge, I'd hate to make us liars. What time should I come over?"

"Come over?"

"You said it, sister. Now you plan it," he replied, pointing at me. "It'll be hard to top paddleboarding, but try."

There was that twinkle again. You'd think a guy that twinkles as much as he does wouldn't get to me, but boy . . . this guy's twinkle had some voodoo magic.

"I can't promise anything as elaborate as paddleboarding, but how about dinner? Should be a nice night; we could grill and sit out on the patio?"

"Done. Six thirty?"

"Done."

And with that, a plan was made. And he was keeping his promise: those nights and weekends were getting filled.

Speaking of getting filled . . .

*No one was speaking of getting filled!*

Officially, that day I stacked dog treats, made thirty phone calls to animal shelters within a hundred-mile radius, letting them know we'd be open soon and to call us with anything they felt they couldn't handle, and color coded the dog bones. I also signed up two more veterinarians in Carmel and Salinas for our spaying/neutering program where we offered potential adoptive families the opportunity for that service for free.

Unofficially? I daydreamed about a certain vet with ice-blue eyes. The daydream also featured those eyes staring up at me as he trailed wet kisses across my tummy, around my navel, and . . . no.

No, I told myself repeatedly. The word *rebound* kept, well, rebounding through my head. Rebounds never lasted. They weren't meant to last—they were supposed to be the in-between guy, the transitional guy, the one you lost your mind with after a particularly bad breakup, the guy who went down on you in the kitchen while you made him dinner and . . .

Fudge. Now I couldn't get that image out of my head.

But on the surface? I was cool, calm, and collected. Like the cucumber I was currently peeling to make crudités. Just a simple platter with radishes, heirloom pear tomatoes, red carrots I'd found at the farmer's market, and some orange peppers I'd cut into matchsticks. And homemade buttermilk ranch dip. Made from buttermilk I'd gone to a local dairy to get.

What? Just because it was a last-minute invitation doesn't mean a guest should feel any less welcome . . .

I could hear my mother's voice in the back of my head, imprinting her rules of entertaining and forever being a good hostess. Always smiling, always easy, incapable of letting anyone know that the turkey came out of the oven and fell on the floor. If no one saw it, serve it. If the soufflé falls apart? Pretend it's exactly the way it was supposed to happen. And if a hot ginger vet puts his face between your thighs and licks you until you come? Well, dear, just scream into a dish towel, because you've got guests in the other room.

Oh my. Where was this all coming from? Delayed reaction to seeing him in his bathing suit? Because, wow.

I arranged the cukes on the platter, clustering them next to the tomatoes. Due to my mother's training, I knew how to cook, and I knew how to put together a beautifully thought-out table. And as it got closer to six thirty and the impending ginger kryptonite, this vegetable platter was the only thing keeping me from running to the bedroom and grinding on my hand for a few minutes.

What? Beauty queens get themselves off all the time. Believe me.

But the only thing I set myself to grinding was the pepper mill. Which I did, to the tune of "Come Fly with Me." The house was equipped with stereophonic sound, hi-fi to the max, and the complete vinyl works of the Rat Pack. So while I handled my cucumber, I let Ol' Blue Eyes romance me a little. To be clear, the Blue Eyes I was referring to was Frank . . . Oh, you know who I meant.

I swayed a little as I finished the platter, feeling my skirt swoosh around my knees. Maybe it was the influence of the house, but I'd been compelled to buy a very 1960s-looking dress in town the other day. Kelly green, it had little straps and a fitted bodice, empire waist with a full flaring skirt. Too much for a dinner that was only happening because I was messing with Marge? Maybe, but it made me feel pretty. I'd piled my blond hair into a bun on top of my head, but a few pieces had escaped as I twirled with my cucumber. I hadn't quite decided on shoes, and was still pondering this when the doorbell rang. Barefoot, I danced to the door.

I peeked out at him through the colored glass, and I could just make out his features. Again I was reminded how very tall he was. Better go with the heels. Heels? This is Lucas—what was I making a big deal about? Taking a deep breath, I opened the door.

I took another deep breath almost immediately, because the only thing better on him than scrubs was a pair of comfortable-looking jeans and a navy blue sweater. Casual but probably cashmere, with the tiniest hint of white at the top where his undershirt showed through. I followed the column of his throat to his Adam's apple: perfection; to his jaw: perfection; and then his lips—holy fudge: perfection. Just a few inches above were those eyes, set off by the navy in his sweater. Messy red hair, ruffled by the ever-present coastal breeze, completed the ad for Banana Republic that was currently being shot on my front porch.

In his hands? Not roses. No, he brought something unique, something unexpected. Dahlias. Deep red, almost burgundy, dinner-plate sized with velvety soft petals.

"Hey there, Rebound, you look pretty," he said, his eyes taking me in. "These are for you."

I was in so much trouble.

Following me inside, he stopped just before stepping down into the sunken living room. Marveling at the decor once more, he turned in a circle to take it all in. The leather couches, the scoop-back chairs, the built-in entertainment center complete with record player. Where Frank was now crooning "Summer Wind."

"I still can't get over this place; what a great vibe!" He turned in another circle, shaking his head. "*Vibe*. See? I'm already channeling the lingo, chickie baby." He chuckled, snapping his fingers. "I feel like Bob Hope might stop by at any second."

"He's down on the golf course with Bing, but he'll be along for cocktails," I said with a laugh, and started for the kitchen. "Speaking of, can this chickie baby get you something to drink?"

He followed, and I could feel his eyes all over me. Did I swish my skirt a little more than was necessary? Oh my, yes.

"What do you think Frank and company would have to drink?" he asked, and I looked over my shoulder at him. His eyes were on my behind. And when caught? Didn't even have the decency to blush. Naughty boy.

"Probably martinis, although I heard a rumor that Dean Martin rarely drank. It was part of his image, though, so whenever you'd see him on stage with a scotch? It was usually—"

"Tea. I heard that too. Iced tea, to keep up appearances," he finished for me, and I nodded.

"Appearances are important," I said, picking up the platter and then spinning to head back into the living room, where the tiki bar was. When I turned, he was right behind me.

"Well, hello," I said, my carrots now pressing into his tummy.

"Hello," he answered, reaching out to take the platter from my hands. "I'll get that." He looked down at the vegetables, then back up at me. "This looks impressive."

"Just a little something before dinner," I said, scooting him into the living room. Where the bar was—I needed a drink. He set down the tray and selected a pepper while I started to mix up two martinis. "Vodka or gin?"

"Vodka please," he answered, crunching down on the pepper. I added booze and ice into a shaker, shook for thirty seconds, then poured into two martini glasses.

"Olive? Onion? Lemon?" I asked. I'd stocked the bar. Well prepared.

"Lemon's good, thanks," he replied, and I nodded as I used a tiny paring knife to peel back a sliver of lemon. I added a twist to my own glass, then handed him his.

"Cheers," I said, clinking his glass. We sipped, and our eyes met over the rim of the glasses. No one said anything, except for Frank, who was now crooning about strangers, and them being in the night. Heavy.

The silence stretched out, and finally he said, "Well, we sure are fancy tonight, aren't we?"

"I know!" I said with a laugh, and it was easy again. "After that amazing day yesterday, I wanted to do something nice for you."

"The dress is nice," he said, letting his eyes roam once more.

"Thanks. I've been so busy lately there hasn't been a lot of opportunity to dress up, you know?" I gulped my martini. "Not that this is an occasion to dress up; that's not what I mean. I mean, it's just dinner, nothing special, just two people, having dinner, at home . . . I'm going to stop talking now, okay?"

He simply said, "So show me around your pad."

"Pad?"

"It was fifty-fifty between that and digs."

"Pad it is; I'll give you the tour," I said gratefully, leading him into the less formal family room. "It's really my dad's pad; it's been in his family for years. Thank goodness my mom didn't get it in the divorce."

"Your parents are divorced?" he asked, following me into the dining room, where I flipped on the lights so he could fully appreciate the kitsch.

"Yeah, they're both back in San Diego. They fought like it was their job. Better for everyone that they're divorced—although they had a huge fight over this house, lemme tell ya." I grimaced.

"She wanted it?"

"Oh good lord, yes, which never made much sense to me. We only came up here now and then, and all my mother talked about was how much she wanted to redo it. Maybe she wanted it just so that he couldn't have it—wouldn't surprise me."

"Are you guys close?" he asked, admiring the miles of orange Formica.

"My mother and I? Hmm, tough to say right now," I admitted, opening the screen door onto the patio. "It's complicated."

"Sorry, didn't mean to bring up a sore subject."

"Nah, its okay. She was furious that . . . we called off my, the wedding, and she hates what I'm doing up here. Wow, not really complicated at all." I sighed, sipping my martini. Not complicated except for my tripping over my pronouns. I needed to be more careful.

I flicked on the Christmas lights that were strewn through the trees out back, and suddenly it was like being in a fairyland. I loved to sit out here, especially at nighttime; it was one of my favorite spaces in the house. Brick patterned patio floor, giant hedges that offered some privacy, and a view that went all the way to the coast on clear days.

"Why would she hate what you're doing up here? Everything I've heard about Our Gang sounds pretty terrific," he asked, his voice confused.

"Yes. You know that and I know that, and everyone else knows that. But when someone says those things to her, what she actually hears is 'Our Gang, that place where my daughter is throwing her life away to pick up dog doodoo and raise a bunch of vicious mutts.' She can't understand how the same girl who won a crown and a sash by throwing a fire baton could also want to do this. Not when there are social committees to chair, and a golf grip to master," I finished, realizing I hadn't taken a breath that entire time.

"Wow," Lucas said.

"Yeah," I said, drinking the rest of my martini and then rattling the ice in my glass. "Another?"

"I think I kind of have to, after that," he said with a chuckle, draining his glass. "Fire batons? Damn."

I shook off the melancholy, took the glass from him, and nodded toward the gas grill. "You go get that fired up, I'll make the drinks, and then we'll get dinner going. I need to eat something, or I'll get sloppy drunk and you'll end up having to put me to bed."

I started across the patio, then turned back to him just as he was opening his mouth. "Shush," I warned, then my dress and I flounced over to the bar. Where I mixed two more martinis with a twist . . .

We made dinner together, Lucas in charge of grilling the skewers of steak and onion, while I tossed cherry tomatoes in a hot pan with some olive oil, fresh garlic, and lots of parsley and thyme. I boiled fingerling potatoes in a brine of water and salt, then steamed them for a few minutes in their skins, making them perfectly tender inside. I then tossed them with a little brown butter and cracked pepper. With the kabobs, it was a perfect meal to eat outdoors, under the fairy lights.

I'd wisely switched to ice water after my second cocktail, and I could see a two-drink maximum was going to have to be the new standard around Lucas—especially when he was wearing navy blue. It was almost impossible to stop myself from crawling across the table, curling into his lap, and licking his face. Maybe I *should* have made the time to grind a bit earlier—it might have taken the edge off.

Once dinner was over and we'd switched over to espresso (made with the ancient espresso maker my grandfather had in the kitchen since it was built), we just sat and talked for hours—the kind of hours you can afford when you have zero cares in the world and no responsibilities. We had those cares, yet we still stayed up talking well into the evening.

We moved inside when the night air got chilly, and I was curled up on what I'm sure in its day was called a davenport, across from Lucas, who was sitting on the floor in front of the fireplace, which was crackling away comfortably. Ella and Louie were on the record player now, singing "You Can't Take That Away from Me."

And speaking of records, for the record, no redhead should ever sit in front of a fire. Because it's just not fair to the fire. Honestly, the way the firelight caught his hair, throwing flashes of burnt orange and whiskey honey around the room, it was just . . . not fair.

As I was ruminating on this, my phone rang. Surprised, considering it was well after nine, I looked at the phone and saw that it was Lou.

"Hey, Lou, what's shaking?" I asked, laughing when I realized I was speaking in Rat Pack. Lucas just shook his head, snapped his fingers, and pointed at me. Ring a ding.

"Hey, Chloe, you ready to get your first dog?"

"Huh?" I asked gracefully.

"Got a call about a dog they picked up in Salinas. Looks like it might have been a bait dog, lots of old scars."

"Okay," I said, clutching the phone.

"They're gonna hold him for you to pick up tomorrow morning; I'll email you the details. Okay?"

"Okay," I repeated, eyes wide.

"Easy, princess—you'll be fine."

"But we're not ready yet, there's still so much to be done and—"

"You've got the pens ready, right?"

"Yes."

"And food and water?"

"Well, yes."

"Then you'll be fine," he said, his voice kind. "You can't always wait until everything's perfect—sometimes it happens when it's not supposed to. You roll with it, right?"

"Right," I whispered, looking at Lucas, who was by now on the couch next to me.

"I'll call you in the morning, and don't worry so much. You're going on your first freedom ride! Enjoy it!"

"I will, Lou, and thanks for calling. I've got this, no problem."

"I know. I'll talk to you tomorrow. Oh, and Chloe?"

"Yeah?"

"Don't wear your tiara—that dog's already gonna be spooked enough as it is."

"You're pretty funny for an old hippie," I cracked, and he hung up the phone laughing.

"What's going on?" Lucas asked.

I sat back against the couch. "I'm getting my first dog tomorrow—I have to pick him up in Salinas."

"That's great! Congratulations!" he said. "Want me to go with you?"

I did. I really did. But I needed to do this on my own. So I shook my head and politely declined.

"Well, if you change your mind, just call me. I'm taking the late shift tomorrow night, so my morning's free. You let me know."

"Thanks, but I'll be okay. I'll be fine." I nodded my head vigorously.

"Well, then, I'll let you get some sleep for your big day."

He helped me bring the cups into the kitchen, then I walked him to the door. He lingered a bit in the open doorway. "So listen, tonight. I had a really good time."

"As good as paddleboarding?" I asked, smiling up at him.

"Different kind of good time." He nodded, and leaned down. I held my breath. But all he did was place a gentle kiss on my forehead. "Good luck tomorrow. You call me if you decide you need some help, promise?" he whispered.

I could only nod. Because his lips on my forehead were, in fact, enough to make me breathless.

"Night, Chloe."

Then he was off the porch and into his truck, starting the ignition. As his taillights splashed across the back of my convertible, I realized . . . Fudge—I can't pick up a pit bull in a convertible!

"Hey, Lucas, wait! I need your truck tomorrow!" I called out, running after him.

Ah, well, you couldn't do *everything* alone.

# chapter nine

Lucas picked me up bright and early, with coffee and donuts from Red's: every kind of chocolate donut they made, apparently. He'd brought me chocolate glazed, devil's food, chocolate cream filled, and even half a dozen chocolate donut holes.

"There were originally a dozen, but they were rather demanding," he said with a sheepish grin.

"The donut holes were demanding?"

"That I eat them, yes."

"Well, donut holes'll do that from time to time." I snorted and took the bag from him.

"Based on the pudding and the Pop-Tarts, chocolate seemed like the way to go," he said, side-eyeing me as he spoke.

"Safe bet," I answered, cramming one into my mouth. "Niiiiice."

We drove along, heading inland toward Salinas. My knee was swinging back and forth, my hand was tapping on my thigh as I chain-ate donut holes one right after the other.

"Nervous?" he asked.

"A little," I admitted. "Is that weird?"

"Not even a little," he assured.

"It's just . . . I don't know, it's like my first day on a job. Up until now, it's just been painting and fixing and filing and planning. But now?"

"Now it's real," he said, answering my unasked question.

"Exactly. Now it's real." I popped in another donut hole, chewed, then said, "What if I suck?"

"I sincerely doubt that." He laughed, handing me his coffee. "Here, add another sugar, will you?"

"Seriously, though, what if I'm not good at this?" I asked, adding his sugar, then stirring. "What if it's too much? What if—"

"What if you get bitten? What if you let the wrong dog out at the wrong time, and you're chasing the runaway with a flashlight at midnight? What if your favorite gets adopted?" He merged onto the highway, then looked at me briefly. "Those are all things that'll happen—I can guarantee it."

"Is this my 'get ready for greatness' speech? Because it's starting out a little strange," I said, handing back his coffee. "Here you go."

"Thanks." He sipped, then set it in the cup holder. "My point is, all of those what-ifs are out there, but so are these: What if you get to throw tennis balls for two hours one day, and that's your job? What if you get to be there when one of these females has a litter of pups? What if you meet the dog of your dreams?" He smiled, and reached out to steady my knee, which was still tap-tap-tapping away. "What if you fall in love with this new life? And it all starts with getting this first dog?" He pointed to the sign that said Salinas.

"You're good," I allowed, sipping my coffee.

"I've been told."

"Shush."

We arrived at the local animal shelter to a riot of yips and barks. After checking us in, a female tech led us back to a hallway lined with rows and rows of cages. All full of beautiful animals that just needed a chance. I gulped down the lump that had immediately risen in the back of my throat as I took in all those wagging tails, those hopeful eyes, those "play with me" paws.

This is why I worked with therapy dogs. I'd never worked on the shelter side; it had always been too tough for me to handle. To see all these gorgeous animals that just needed a home, when I knew what happened to most of these dogs . . .

"Oh my God," I murmured, my breath catching as I realized how many of them were pit bulls. Lucas' hand was on my shoulder, soothing me, grounding me. We continued along the hallway and came to the last pen.

Huddled in the corner, facing away from us, was the guy we were here to get. Rescued from a fighting ring awhile back, he was scheduled to be put down because he'd simply run out of time. He hadn't been adopted.

"He's super sweet once you get to know him, but a little shy at first," the woman who was showing us around said. She opened the gate, and at the noise, he turned around. The first thing I saw were the saddest golden eyes I'd ever seen. Rising to his feet, he stood a little unsteadily. He seemed to be favoring his right side, and as he turned to walk toward us, I noticed the scarring on his left flank. It made sense why he was unsteady, and my blood began to boil at what he'd obviously been through.

Muzzled, he chuffed out a warning when he saw Lucas.

"Might want to hang back a bit," the tech said, nodding to Lucas. "Many of these guys come out of rings, which are mostly run by men, so he's standoffish with males."

"I don't blame him," I murmured, sinking down to my knees at the front of the cage. He approached, head down, but curious.

I didn't look at him too closely, letting him come to me, allowing the dog to get used to my scent.

"You good, Chloe?" Lucas asked, and I smiled, especially when I felt the dog sniffing at my hair. I resisted the urge to pet him, knowing that right now I just needed him calm enough for me to get a sense of what he was like. After a moment, I looked at the dog now sitting next to me. Head, wide and regal. Chest, barreled and strong. Beautifully brindled with brown and white, his tail thumping against the floor. His golden eyes weren't so sad now; they were inquisitive.

"You wanna come hang with me, mister?" I asked, reaching out with my hand, fingers curled in like a paw, for him to sniff. He sniffed, then he licked through the muzzle, and my eyes filled with tears. I looked up at Lucas, who was nodding.

Standing slowly, I took hold of his leash. Curious, with tail wagging, he walked with me out of the cage. Stalling a bit when he saw Lucas, he steered clear but remained at my heel, still limping but tail up. And wagging.

As I signed the paperwork, the woman behind the desk pointed to it and said, "The guys on the night crew gave him that name, but he hasn't had it very long. You could change it if you wanted."

Lucas leaned over my shoulder to read the paper, and we both saw it at the same time.

"Oh my God," I breathed.

Lucas clapped me on the back with a laugh. "That's fantastic, chickie baby."

I looked down at the dog. "Come on, Sammy Davis Jr. I've got some records by your boys at home." Chuckling, I headed out to the truck with the dog in tow.

• • •

Lucas wanted to do a thorough exam before bringing him to the ranch, so we stopped by the clinic on the way home. He'd called ahead, and when we pulled in, Miguel, one of the wonderful vet techs I'd gotten to know, was waiting outside for us.

"Hey guys, heard you've got a new boy for us to take a look at!" he called out. I gestured toward the back of the truck.

"He's in the back; I'll get him."

I hopped out and ran around to the back, ignoring the amused looks Lucas and Miguel shot at each other. I wanted to do this; this was my job now. Lucas had put the cab on the truck so the dog wouldn't be whipped by the wind on the highway, instead resting comfortably inside his large pet carrier. I climbed up into the back of the truck, talking to him the entire time.

"Hey boy, how ya doin'? Have a good ride back here?" I asked, slowly and quietly unlocking the gate, not wanting to startle him. He'd gotten a bit skittish when we had to lift him into the truck, and I was hoping he'd jump down on his own. Not wanting to further injure the leg he was limping on, I'd asked Miguel to bring out the PetStep, a kind of portable step stool for dogs for instances exactly like this.

Once it was in position, I reached in and got hold of his leash, gently tugging him forward. Once he understood what I wanted him to do he came willingly, albeit a little slowly. Once more, he stalled when he saw the two men, but after sniffing the air for a moment, he came down the steps one at a time. And when he'd reached the asphalt, that tail was wagging again.

"Well, look at you!" I was amazed at the resilience of this dog. "Come on, Sammy Davis Jr. Let's get you checked out so I can get you home. I've got a bucket of tennis balls with your name on it."

Marge took one look at the dog when we came in and put

her hand on her heart. "Well bless my soul, look at this pretty boy!" she squealed, leaning over the counter to see him as we went back to the exam rooms. While she cooed, I took a moment to compliment her on the very festive hot pink vest paired with a pair of lemon-colored slacks. I say slacks because they just couldn't rightly be referred to as pants. They were from a decidedly slacks-type era.

"Lucas, honey, I'll tell your dad you two are here," she said, then reached into her pocket. "And here, Chloe, see if he wants one of these."

"Thanks, Marge," I said, pocketing the treat and following Lucas down the hall. Inside the exam room, Sammy picked a corner and huddled into it, keeping his bad side toward the wall. Protecting it? Poor guy. He whined just once, then laid down with his head on his paws, watching us carefully.

"Hey there, big guy, no one's gonna hurt you. We just want to get you feeling better, okay?" I said softly, crouching down on the floor next to him. Once more, reaching out with my fingers curled inward, I let him sniff me and was rewarded with a head bump. I smoothed my hand across the top of his head, delighted he was letting me pet him already. I kept my strokes long, smooth, and gentle as I moved down across his body.

"Hey buddy, think I could take a look at you?" Lucas asked, bending down next to me.

The dog let out a low growl and backed farther into the corner.

"He doesn't seem to like men too much." I sighed.

"I can't blame him for that. He seems to like you, though," he said, patting me on the shoulder.

"Want me to try to get him on his side?"

"Normally I'd get a tech for that, but he seems comfortable with you. Let's keep the muzzle on for now, though."

"You're in charge," I replied as I encouraged Sammy to roll over onto his good side, exposing the side he'd been keeping hidden.

"I disagree. You are very much in charge here," Lucas said.

His face darkened as we took in the extent of the dog's injuries. It was clear that this dog had seen some action. Old scars ran the length of his flank, some still healing, some old and gnarly, healed over horribly. His fur was patchy here and there, where it no longer even grew.

"Oh," was all I could manage. Other than that, I kept quiet as Lucas gave him a quick once-over. It certainly would have been easier up on the table, but Lucas seemed content on the floor. His hands were sure and able, with no quick or unnecessary motions.

Sammy thumped his tail every now and again, encouraging me to keep up my constant head-to-tail petting. He was so trusting, when he had every right not to be.

"Okay," Lucas said, slowly standing up and making some notes on a chart. "I'd like to keep him here overnight, if that's okay with you. I need to clean out those wounds, and under the circumstances, I think sedation is going to be the best way to go. Then I can give him a thorough examination, make sure everything else is okay. Sound good to you?"

"Sure, whatever we need to do. I want to get this boy running again," I said, smiling down into those golden eyes. Sammy seemed better already.

Lucas nodded, then extended a hand down to help me. Just as he pulled me up, I noticed Marge's face peeking through the window on the exam room door. I rolled my eyes at her, and Lucas turned to see who I was rolling them at. She just smiled at us, making no effort to hide the fact that she was peeking.

Lucas turned back to me with a look I was beginning to

know well. "I really can't resist," he said, backing me against the wall, grinning the entire way.

"What are you up to?" I asked, looking up at him as my back met the wall, just next to the door. I could see Marge trying vainly to peer inside, and as I lost sight of her, I realized she was now out of range. All she could likely see was the navy blue scrubs, the owner of which now caged me in with his arms. "You're evil, you know that? You're giving her way to much to think about."

He laughed, and leaned a bit closer. "She's bored; she needs things to think about."

The closer he got, the more Sammy Davis Jr. was not having it. Wriggling across the floor, he deposited himself on my feet, laying across them and chuffing out another warning to Lucas.

"Ha! See, he knows what you're up to." I giggled, leaning down to pat Sammy lightly on the head. "Now, fix up my dog so I can take him home."

"Yes, ma'am," he answered, then looked at the door's window. "Coast is clear; want to head back up front? Sammy can stay here."

"Are there any tiny angels out there packing tiny arrows?" I asked, and he made a show of looking again.

"Not that I can see, but there is a Labrador packing quite a large . . . anyway."

I patted Sammy one final time and was rewarded with a tiny lick, and then we headed to the ranch.

Since we'd ridden together, Lucas had to drive me home before heading back in to start his shift at the clinic. As he pulled into the driveway, he looked over at me. "I'll call you later, let you know how he's doing."

"Think he can come home tomorrow?"

"I'm sure he can. I just want to make sure he's good to go," he assured me. He looked like he was going to say something else, but then didn't. He started once more, but still said nothing.

"Something on your mind, Lucas?" I asked, wrinkling my brow.

"Yes, actually." He shut off the ignition and turned toward me.

And just like that, the mood shifted. I was aware of everything. His salty/woodsy scent. The way his eyes were deepening almost to indigo. The way his arm now draped casually across the back of the seats, putting his forearm within licking distance.

Luckily, before any licking could occur, my phone rang. "Hold that thought," I said, then looked at my phone. Fudge. "It's my mother." Shaking my head, I turned back to him. "I gotta take this. Call me later?"

"Deal," he said, and I jumped out of the car with a wave.

I'd started to answer the phone when he called, "Hey Chloe!"

"Yeah?"

"You did great today." He grinned, and drove away.

I could hear my mother in the background. "Hello? Hello Chloe, are you there?"

"Hi, Mother," I said into the phone, grinning as he drove away.

"Who are you smiling at?" she asked.

"You can tell that I'm smiling?" I was astonished.

"The same way I know that you're slouching."

"You're four hundred and fifty miles away. How in the world can you tell I'm slouching?"

"Your voice changes; it always has. Spine straight, please," my mother said crisply. "Now, who was that young man you were talking to?"

I literally looked all around, expecting her to come out from behind a bush. "How did you—never mind. What's up, Mother?"

"Can't I call just to talk to my own daughter?" she asked.

I stifled a groan and looked skyward for support. The only thing that told me was that it looked like rain. Sigh. "Of course you can. How are you?"

"Wonderful. Thank you for asking."

No one said a word. Usually, I'd try to fill a silence. Not anymore.

"So how are the gang dogs, dear?"

"Not gang dogs, Mom: Our Gang. You know very well what the name of this place is; it wouldn't kill you to say it right every now and again."

"Fine. Our Gang. Does anyone have rabies yet?" she asked, her tone icy.

I groaned. "Honestly, Mother."

"You sound like a hippopotamus, Chloe. Why are you groaning? Have you been eating too much dairy? You know what that does to your system—"

"Mother."

She just continued, "—and what it does to your insides."

"Mother. Hey. Mother."

"No one wants a gassy girlfriend—"

"Mother!" I yelled, finally breaking through. No slouching now, I was fully at attention and pacing. "I wasn't groaning because of dairy, for God's sake, I was groaning because . . . Oh, forget it. What did you need?"

"What did *I* need?" she asked, her tone even cooler now that I'd snapped at her.

"Yes, you called *me*, remember? I've got things to do because we just picked up our first dog today, and—"

"We? Who is we?" she asked, changing to search mode. Now

she was out for intel. "Is that that young man I just heard you talking to?"

Damn, she was good. "The young man you're referring to is Dr. Lucas Campbell. And there is no 'we'; he was just helping me out."

"*Dr.* Lucas Campbell, a doctor? I'm impressed. How did you meet him?"

"He's a vet, Mother."

"He was in the army?" she asked.

"Vet as in veterinarian."

"Oh."

"His family's animal hospital is one of the local supporters for Our Gang," I told her, dashing her hopes of a cardiothoracic surgeon son-in-law. "He went with me to pick up my first rescue dog this morning. A beautiful pit bull named Sammy Davis Jr.— isn't that a funny name?"

"Well, I'm glad to hear you've got a man around to help you, other than that Lou character. But I hope you're being careful when you're out crawling the streets, Chloe. You never know who could be out there, just looking for a pretty girl like you to—"

I laughed. "I'm pretty sure the meanest street in Monterey is the one without a Starbucks. Although there's a strip mall without a Pilates studio that's looking a little ragged," I joked.

She sighed. "Chloe, Chloe, Chloe." I could tell she was shaking her head. "What are you doing up there?" she asked quietly.

"I'm not getting into this again," I said, trying like hell to keep my voice calm. My mother could irritate me faster than anyone on the planet, but a raised voice from me meant she won. When I was Chloe with the Program, I rarely questioned her. Chloe Who Crawls the Mean Streets of Monterey, however, questioned her frequently.

I admit, I'd been the one to let her manage things in my life longer than was probably healthy. It wasn't her fault that her tiara princess had course-corrected and "rebelled," but it *was* her fault if she refused to see that I wasn't coming home anytime soon. And it was *my* fault if I continued to allow her to affect me so. It was a balancing act—one that we were both learning.

"I saw Charles at the club yesterday," she said. "He brought a woman there—a date. We barely spoke, though he usually asks questions about you. He's moving on."

"That's good. He *should* move on. That's what I'm trying to do too—and your mentioning Charles every time we talk isn't helping," I said, feeling anger heat my cheeks. "I'd love it if you never mentioned him again, okay?"

Silence. Well, partial silence. Remember, her eye rolls are audible.

"Fine," she allowed after a moment.

"Fine," I agreed.

More silence.

"Did I tell you Molly Adams is getting married? To a congressman, can you believe it! I ran into her mother at the market the other day."

I listened for another few minutes until I begged off the phone and paced around the house, thinking about my mother being happy there was a man around to help me. Pffft. I was grateful to Lucas, of course; he was a huge help. But the way my mother said it, it was like I couldn't do a thing without needing some help. Pffft.

Pffft.

As I was pffffting, I looked out the front window, my gaze settling on my car. A gift from my parents when I graduated high school, I'd driven it ever since. Sporty, fun, fast, and a little preppy—I loved that car.

But it wasn't right for me anymore. I couldn't have picked up

Sammy Davis Jr. this morning without Lucas and his truck. As it was, I couldn't even haul more than two industrial-size bags of Dog Chow. The car was perfect for San Diego Chloe. But Monterey Chloe needed something different.

Grabbing my keys and my purse, I jumped into the car, dropped the top, and headed down the hill for my last joy ride.

"You did what?" Lucas said, when I came sailing in through the front door of the clinic that afternoon.

"I bought a new car! Come see, come see!" I pulled him through the waiting area by the hand. "Hiya, Marge!"

"Hiya, sugar!" she called back, smiling big when she saw me holding Lucas' hand. I dropped it quickly, holding the door open for him instead.

"I don't understand. Why did you get something new?" he asked, his face curious.

"The convertible wasn't practical anymore—not with what I'm doing now. And I didn't want to have to call you every time I needed to go get a dog. Not that I don't appreciate it, but I needed something bigger. Something more in line with my new life here, more outdoorsy," I explained, practically skipping through the parking lot.

He couldn't help but laugh at my excitement, and followed me through the cars toward the back. "You went by yourself?" he asked.

I shrugged. "Sure, why not?"

"I would have gone with you, you know."

"Why would I need you to go with me?" I asked, then did my best Ta-Da Pose. "Ta-da!" I sang out, pointing to my new car.

"That's why," he sighed, looking at what I'd bought.

A 1989 Suburban. Blue with white paneling. It was a thousand feet long, a thousand feet wide, had actual carpet on the floor, and smelled liked pine.

"Oh, Chloe," he said, his mouth quirking up at the edges as he struggled not to laugh.

"What? It's great! Wait until you see how it handles," I said, tugging at the driver's-side door, which tended to stick a little.

"So what did you pay for this car?"

"Nothing! I got a great deal on my trade-in and—"

"You traded in your convertible?" He was no longer laughing. "Can I please see the paperwork?"

"Hey, I handled it, it's no big deal. I looked online at the trade-in value before went in, on that Carrie Blue Book site? And this car was priced at almost exactly what my car was worth! And the best part is, I even talked the guy into giving me free car washes for the entire year. I was all wheely dealy," I said proudly, climbing into my new car. I slammed the door shut, and then rolled down the window. "Look, manual windows! How cool is that!"

"Very cool. Did you happen to notice it's leaking under the engine?"

"The guy said it did that sometimes, but was perfectly normal for a car this old. What color is it?"

"Green."

"Oh, yeah, he said if it did that, to just bring it back; they'll top something off."

"Chloe, you really should have taken someone with you," he said, shaking his head. "This is a piece of shit. They saw a pretty girl with a nice BMW, and they totally took advantage of you. We need to go back and get this straightened out. You can't keep this car."

"Like hell I can't!" I climbed out of the car. He was taking away my buzz and I was started to get pissed. "I know what you think: stupid, pretty Chloe can't handle her own problems. But I got this, okay? I'm not taking the car back."

"I'm not trying to start a fight here. Of course you can take care of your own problems. But have you ever done *this* before? Bought a car?"

"No," I allowed, the spike of anger giving way as quickly as it came.

"Chlo, I took my dad with me the first time I bought a car. Hell, I took him with me the first *three* cars. It's kind of a big deal, and you want to make sure you're not getting, well, taken advantage of," he said softly, tapping on the hood of the car. A bit of rust fell onto the asphalt.

Ah, fudge, what had I done? I'd been excited to get this car, but I did have a funny feeling afterward that maybe I'd acted too impulsively. And now that funny feeling was back in the pit of my stomach.

"I just wanted to take care of it on my own, you know?" I asked, turning toward him. He wasn't laughing, he wasn't mad, he wasn't making fun of me. "That's all."

And then the tears came. Oh, for God's sake. Between the emotions of picking up the dog this morning, the conversation with my mother, the excitement over getting the car, and now this . . .

"Hey, c'mere," he murmured, and just like that I was in his arms.

And now *that* affected me. I buried my face in his chest, feeling the tears spill over.

"*So* stupid," I sniffled. I nuzzled into his shirt, not caring that I was in the middle of the parking lot, just needing to be held. Was that so terrible? I couldn't admit earlier that I needed someone's help, but I could totally and completely admit that in this moment, in this space, I needed to be in someone's arms.

His arms, specifically. "Oh, God, I totally just sold my car for this beast didn't I?" I laugh-cried, clutching his back.

He said nothing, which was wise. He merely pulled me closer, rocking me as I cried. When there was a tear stain the shape and size of Florida on his shirt, I finally pulled back. Clutching his arms, I blinked up at him. "What in the world am I going to do?"

"We're going to go back there first thing tomorrow morning and get this worked out. Don't worry about it," he said, wiping away a lingering tear.

"Are you sure? What if they don't take it back?"

"They will. We'll work it out."

"Sorry about your shirt," I said, brushing at the wet spot.

"No problem. At least you managed to cry in the shape of a giant dick."

"That's Florida!" I cried out, no longer brushing but slapping.

"No, it's not," he insisted, holding my hands to stop the slapping.

I stopped and gazed up at him. "I'm so embarrassed. It's just been a weird day."

"Want to talk about it?" he asked, and I looked down at our held-together hands.

"Not really," I whispered, and let go. "Sorry for busting in on your day like this."

"Are you kidding? This was way more exciting than what I have planned next. I've got an owner who thinks her Chihuahua is depressed."

"Does she want to buy him a car?" I joked.

He smiled, then changed the subject to a happier one. "Sammy's doing well, by the way. He's still under sedation, but you should be able to pick him up tomorrow." As I started to clap my hands, he said, "*After* we get this car sorted out."

"Thank you, Lucas," I said. "I really appreciate this."

"You've certainly made it interesting around here," he said, his voice soft.

"Interesting good?"

"Hell, yeah, chickie baby," he replied, his face lighting up.

I laughed, but he laughed even harder when I tried to roll up my stuck window. Ah, well—it was a nice day.

# chapter ten

"No, no, you can't put that there. You need to unload those around back in the shed."

"You got it, Chloe."

"Chloe, the Mitchells' home visit went great! Can we approve them?"

"Do it! Let's get Rocky outta here and on his freedom ride!"

"Got those flyers back from the printer, Chloe, you want them in the office?"

"Yeah, set them on my desk, would you?"

I blew the hair from my eyes, wishing I'd grabbed a headband this morning. Although, to be fair, when that alarm went off at 5 A.M., I hadn't been thinking too clearly.

Might have had something to do with all that wine last night.

More likely, it had something to do with all that vomit last night. Not my own, thank you. Doggie vomit. Which you tend to step in when one of your charges sneaks a giant bag of Doritos, and then yaks it all up.

I blew my hair once more, mentally promising myself I'd

grab a headband when I got back to the house for lunch. Right now, I had more pressing things to deal with.

"Hey there, cutie pies, how we doing today, hmm?" I cooed, leaning over the whelping box and counting puppies. Still six, and that was good. First litter delivered at Our Gang, which brought our in-house total to twenty-seven. Twenty-seven . . . wow.

We'd been officially open for business for a few weeks now, with the grand opening party tomorrow. And Our Gang was booming busy! We popped our doggie cherry with the wonderful and talented Sammy Davis Jr., and just kept on going. This latest population expansion was a surprise, the result of a stray we'd picked up that was pregnant and due any minute. She'd delivered two weeks ago, and my team had celebrated with an impromptu party and cherry Coke as a stand-in for champagne. Speaking of which . . .

"Hey, Jenny! Did you get beverages ordered for the grand opening?"

"Of course; you gave me that list weeks ago," she called back, reminding me once again that I worked with the best. "How're they doing?" she asked, appearing around the corner of the barn.

"They look great, very wriggly." I laughed as I was professionally nuzzled by one of the puppies determined to climb inside the neck of my shirt. They were just beginning to open their eyes, and their collective adorableness was off the charts.

"You want me to change out the bedspread?" she asked, and I nodded. Jenny was a veterinary student, volunteering her time in exchange for extra credit in her program. Bright and cheery, she added a bounce to everyone's step. Especially Tommy, a local guy who went to the local community college and helped us out nights and weekends.

Nights and weekends. Well.

Since Our Gang officially became open for business, Lucas and his father had thrown the full weight of their animal hospital toward helping us get on our feet. They donated their time and services to any dog that came in, making sure they were healthy and doing any spaying or neutering for free. They also continued to spread the word in the community, and we'd already had three adoptions.

And Lucas? My nights and weekends were still spoken for.

We were spending a lot of time together. We'd fallen into this easy pattern of having dinner together, either on the patio at my place or on the deck of his, which had a killer view of the bay. We'd told each other stories about our exes, almost exorcising our collective demons. It had been many weeks since I'd walked out on my wedding, longer still for Lucas. We were divinely attracted to each other—and yet.

We had never moved beyond friendship, although I thought about that almost-kiss in the barn all the time.

We had never moved beyond friendship, although if I leaned across him to grab something off the kitchen counter and accidentally-on-purpose brushed my breasts across the back of his hand, his breath would catch and he'd clench his fists as if stopping himself from touching me.

We had never moved beyond friendship, although if he was helping me with my jacket on those chilly evenings out on the patio and accidentally (pretty sure also on purpose) pressed his body against my back while straightening out my sleeves, breathing magical puffs of salty, woodsy-scented Lucas air all around my head and pretty sure also nuzzling against my ear, sending a shockwave of sizzling heat straight to my bloodstream, enough so that I pressed back against him, feeling his warm body connecting to every part of my now very overheated body . . . wait, what?

Still just friendship. Rebounds without benefits.

Why weren't we taking this relationship to the next level? A question with several answers.

Part of it was that he was getting ready to leave for another tour with Vets Without Borders. In a matter of weeks he'd be in Belize, and I'd be here. Okay, something to consider.

Part of it was the fact that in the beginning, I'd been adamant that this was friendship alone, because I needed time and space to process my breakup with Charles. Though I hadn't regretted that decision once, I also didn't want to jump willy-nilly from one relationship to the next. I almost wished I'd met some delicious and dumb guy that I could be all whammy bammy with, getting the rebounding done with someone I didn't care about, and could then leave behind for someone pretty much like . . .

Oh, hell. Someone *exactly* like Lucas Campbell. Because there'd be no halfway, no "just for the sexing" with him. Hell, no. We'd be all in, 100 percent. I could fall for this guy—and he was leaving. I'd miss the fudge out of him. Speaking of which . . .

"Jenny, I've got to run into town. Carousel Candies is holding ten pounds of fudge under my name for the party tomorrow." I set the puppy down reluctantly.

"Make sure I get to help taste test," she said.

"Done!" On my way to my new truck, I signed off on two deliveries and took a call from a bakery that specialized in all-natural dog treats and was donating the tasty biscuits for the grand opening.

Hopping into my truck, I said another silent thanks to Lucas, who'd wrangled the car dealership into something much better. When we'd walked in they immediately knew who he was; the benefit of a small community. Within a couple of hours, my original contract had been torn up and I was back on the streets with a not-so-old Land Rover Discovery, with a custom cage in the back for transporting my four-legged residents. A car I truly loved and that fit my new lifestyle, which now included a rack on the top for my new kayak—something else Lucas had introduced me to.

As I was driving, I got a call from my cousin Clark, who was on his way down to Monterey with his fiancée for the grand opening, and to look at the puppies.

"Babies need a dog, Clark," I heard her instructing him the last time we were on the phone. And with the new litter, it was perfect timing.

"What time do you think you'll get in?" I asked, glad that Lucas had installed a new stereo system with Bluetooth.

"Looks like we're due in around five, is that okay?"

"Perfect, cocktail hour." I pulled into the parking lot by the candy store. "What's Vivian drinking these days?"

"If you've got sparkling water, she's fine with that."

"She's fine with root beer too!" the woman in question chimed in.

"Vivian, we've discussed this. Too much sugar can make the baby—"

"Oh, can it, Clark. A soda every so often isn't going to make the baby anything. How's it hanging, Chloe?"

I smothered a laugh. "It's hanging great, Viv; I'll be glad to see you. And I'll get your root beer."

"See, Clark, all you have to do is ask. People will do anything for a pregnant woman."

"I realize that, but you shouldn't be so presumptuous as to think that Chloe will just drop everything to run out and get you—"

"She offered!"

I pressed end; they no longer even knew I was there. Once

they got going, they tended to tune everyone else out. It'd be a fun weekend, they were my first houseguests. On impulse, I called Lucas.

"Hey, Rebound, how's your day?" he answered, and I chuckled.

"You want to come over for dinner tonight? Although I should warn you, it won't be just us."

"I love an invitation that comes with a warning. What's up?"

"Clark and Vivian are coming for the opening, and to check out the new litter."

"Sounds like fun. What time?"

"Whenever—they're getting in around five."

"Cocktail hour. Perfect. Need me to pick anything up?"

"Nope, I'm heading into town to get the fudge for tomorrow, and I'll grab what I need at the store while I'm there."

"I should be finishing up here around four thirty, so I'll head over then. Sound good?"

"Sounds good," I agreed. I hung up, wondering if he was wearing his navy blue scrubs. Mmm. I rolled down the window to get some air. Must be the weather heating up . . .

The day got away from me, as it often did when there was so much going on. I'd managed to grab a quick shower after heading back into the house from the barn, something that was always necessary after spending time with my critters. Dogs tended to smell like corn chips, and while I enjoyed a good Frito like everyone else, I didn't want to smell like one.

As I stood in the bathroom after my five-minute shower, I looked at the bottles cluttering the counter: styling gel, pomade, thermal protectant, mousse, plumping serum; to say nothing of the teasing combs, round brushes (one inch, one and a half inch, one and three quarter inch, two and a half inch), flat irons, curling irons, and even a dusty old set of hot rollers. None of which had been touched since I'd moved to Monterey.

And let's talk Caboodles. I had several, filled with every color eye shadow imaginable, false eyelashes, lipstick, lip gloss, lip plumping gel, lip liner, and enough blush to supply an entire dance team for the next two years. Hardly any of it touched since I came here.

I needed to get rid of all of it; it was just taking up space. When you've got a bunch of dogs to feed and walk and play with, your beauty routine gets whittled down to the basics. Good shampoo and conditioner, some sunscreen, and maybe a pinkish lip balm. Where it used to take me at least ninety minutes from stepping out of the shower to stepping into the car with Charles, now I could manage in twenty, if I hurried.

And I *was* hurrying. It was almost five o'clock, and I'd just finished toweling off my hair when I heard—

"Chloe? Hey, you here?"

"Lucas?"

"Yeah, where are you?"

"Back here, getting—"

Lucas appeared in the doorway of the bedroom, holding a bottle of wine and wearing an astonished expression.

"—dressed! Hey!" I scrambled for my towel.

"Oh, boy." Lucas backed out of the door. Standing just outside in the hallway, he called, "Sorry!"

"Really! What the *fudge,* Lucas?"

"The front door was open, so I just—wow. So sorry."

"If you wanted a peep show, you could have just asked," I chided, hurrying into a bra and panties.

"Would that have worked?" he asked, and I poked my head around the doorframe.

"Might have," I teased, and grinned when his eyebrows went up. "Now you'll never know." I disappeared and headed into my closet to grab some clothes.

"Peep show now; I'm officially requesting," he said as I pulled on a sundress.

"Too late, that window has closed, that door has been shut," I said, going to the door again and stretching one bare leg around the corner. "Besides, you just saw everything, right? Now there's no mystery."

"I saw nothing, I promise. It was like a fleshy blur and then a towel."

"Fleshy blur—you sure know how to flatter a girl," I scolded, and heard him groan.

"Does this help?" he asked. Seconds later his own leg, with his jeans rolled up to his knee, came around the corner.

"Nice." I laughed, and thank goodness the next thing around the corner was his face. "Very nice." His eyes twinkled down at me, an easy smile on his lips.

"When I said fleshy blur, I meant it in the best possible way."

"I totally believe you."

"Seriously, Chlo, I didn't see anything. Which is a good thing."

"I literally have nothing to say to that." I frowned, reaching out and pinching his cheek. His hair was spiky and still a bit damp, from the shower, maybe? Didn't matter, this kryptonite was pinging.

"It's a good thing, because *had* I seen anything, your dinner party might have been wrecked."

"Wrecked?"

"Wrecked. Because who knows might have happened. Your cousin could have walked in on something very different than what he was expecting." His eyes flashed fire, and I had a sudden vision of being turned the other way in this very doorjamb, the slip of a sundress I was wearing being thrown up, and a very sexy veterinarian thrusting into me from behind.

"Fudge," I breathed, my face suddenly flaming.

He chuckled. "Mm-hmm, exactly what I was thinking."

*Oh!*

This could go two ways.

I could make a joke, back away, and let things go on as they had been. Great friends, unresolved tension.

Or, I could lean in and finish that kiss in the barn.

I . . . leaned.

He leaned.

"Chloe? We're here!" Clark called.

Damn! I'd forgotten there was a third option.

"And where's the bathroom? This pregnant lady needs to pee like a racehorse!"

"That's charming, Vivian. We just got here."

"Oh, shush, Clark, she doesn't care about— Seriously, Chloe, where's the bathroom?"

I turned my lean-in to a lean-on, and pressed my forehead against the column of his throat. "They're here."

"It would seem," he murmured, running his hand down my spine. Fuuuuudge.

My nose filled with his earthy scent, I tilted my head up to look at him. We smiled, and I went out to greet my terribly ill-timed guests.

It was a fun night—great food, great music, new friends, and family. We started with a cocktail hour that consisted of three mai tais and a very icy root beer. Lucas had found an old tiki bar recipe book, and we'd been re-creating some of the tasty cocktails from that era. So far our favorites had been the Beach-comber and the Painkiller—although the mai tais were pretty damn tasty.

Watching Viv and Clark together was something else; I've never seen anyone flirt and bicker simultaneously so well. With the level of adoration between those two, their bickering was clearly foreplay. Vivian only had eyes for Clark, while he thought she hung the moon. Viv talked a good game, but she was so smitten with my cousin it was funny to see.

Lucas and Clark had immediately clicked, and the two were inside the house now, scooping ice cream for everyone.

Vivian and I were sitting on the back patio under the stars, enjoying some coffee to Dean Martin's "All of Me."

"Explain yourself this very second," Viv said, putting her feet up on the seat between us and leaning back in her chair.

"Explain what exactly?" I asked, curious.

"Explain how *you* are not hitting *that*?" She pointed through the sliding glass door at Lucas, coming out of the kitchen holding two bowls.

"Oh my God," I moaned, praying that he didn't hear her. He didn't seem to, although Clark took one look at Viv and raised his eyebrow.

"What are you up to?" he questioned, setting down a bowl of ice cream in front of her.

"Why would I be up to anything?" she asked innocently, attacking her ice cream with a vengeance.

"Because you look like you're up to something," he said, sitting down next to her. "You look guilty."

"I'm just sitting here visiting with your cousin, waiting for my fiancé to bring me some ice cream," she said, blinking at him. "Whatever could I be up to?"

I snorted and took the ice cream Lucas handed to me. His

expression was equally curious, but a glare from Viv made Clark drop the subject.

"So, Lucas. You're shipping out soon I hear. Belize?" Viv asked, spooning up her mint chocolate chip.

"Yeah, I'm doing another tour with Vets Without Borders. I leave for Belize in a few weeks."

"Right after the Fourth, right?" she asked.

"Yep."

"So two weeks, not a few," Viv said, and I dropped my spoon with a clatter.

"I guess so, yeah."

Stunned, I didn't listen as they continued to talk. Wow, he'd be gone in two weeks! Two weeks from now and my nights and weekends would be decidedly Lucas free. He'd be out of the country and away from Monterey for—

"Three months? Did you know that, Chloe? Three months!"

I rolled my eyes. "Yes, Viv, I knew that." I sighed, catching Lucas' eye across the table. "Vets Without Borders does amazing work. I'm sure he'll have all kinds of stories to tell us when he gets back," I said, my voice full of pride. Three months. Wow.

"Oh, I'm sure he'll have stories," Viv said in a tone, and now I was one fixing her with a glare.

Oblivious, Clark started asking Lucas whether he'd visited Belize before, and whether he was planning on visiting the rain forests while he was there.

I took the opportunity to pinch Viv's arm. "Hey, I see what you're doing—knock it off."

"First, I can't believe you just pinched a pregnant woman. Second, I can't believe you are not hitting that! What on God's green earth is stopping you? Third, and this is the pregnancy hormones talking, if Clark says it's okay, *I'm* going to hit that if you don't!" This was all said in a stage whisper while Lucas and

Clark talked guy talk about monkeys or something. "And fourth, can I have some more ice cream?"

"Oh, for God's sake. First, I'll pinch you again if you don't keep your voice down. Second, it's complicated. Third, you hit that and I'll pinch more than your arm. Fourth, of course you can have more. Mint chocolate chip or mocha almond fudge?"

I was nothing if not a good hostess.

"First, try it. Second, nothing is so complicated; that man clearly wants you bouncing on his dick. Third, Clark would never let me, hormones or not. And frankly, he keeps me pretty damn happy, if you know what I'm saying. And fourth, mocha almond fudge, please," she finished, pushing her bowl toward me.

"Bouncing on his dick?" I whispered back, horrified.

I whispered a little too loudly, because I became suddenly aware of two sets of male eyes on me. One pair, warm and brown, looked equally horrified at my choice of words. The second pair, ice blue and dazzling, merely looked amused.

And now a pair of sea-glass green eyes, full of laughter and mischief as she waved a spoon in my direction. "I'll take two scoops of that mocha almond fudge, if you don't mind." Viv sat back against her cushions, pleased as punch.

"Coming right up," I said through gritted teeth. I dashed into the kitchen, where I promptly put my head in the freezer. And that's how Lucas found me moments later.

"Pretty sure that's how the ice cream melts," he said, startling me and causing me to knock my head on the ice trays.

"Fudge," I groaned, pulling my head out and rubbing it.

"No, thanks, I'm a mint chocolate chip man myself," he said, reaching around me and grabbing that container.

Picking up the mocha almond fudge for Viv, I looked at him balefully. "You're hilarious," I muttered, reaching for another bowl.

"And you're weird. Tonight, at least," he shot back, licking his spoon.

I'd love to be that spoon. I'd love to be that spoon right now. And if that meant rolling around in peppermint and chocolate chips and climbing into a bowl, I'd do it. Hmm, maybe he was right about the weird part.

"Sorry, guess I'm just nervous about the grand opening tomorrow." I sighed, returning the ice cream to the freezer and leaning against the fridge. "My mother's coming, did I tell you that?"

"That's great! I thought she wasn't going to be able to make it."

"She wasn't; she had some charity event this weekend. But my dad called her and told her she was being an ass." I wrinkled my brow. "Frankly? He didn't need to do that. It's going to be stressful enough tomorrow without her here judging the paper napkins and plastic knives and forks."

When I'd first invited her to the grand opening, I was pretty sure she'd find a reason not to come. And I was right: the pediatric cancer ball event was the same night and there was no way she'd miss that. It was traditionally one of her favorite events. But my father waded right in and fought the good fight, no doubt throwing around phrases like "For our daughter's sake," and "Need to be supportive," and probably more than a few of the "Marjorie, don't be an ass" variety.

The result? They were both flying up. Together. I mentally shuddered at the thought of those two sharing a commuter jet, feeling terrible for anyone that had the bad luck of being seated near them. My parents didn't fight in public. They annihilated each other with kindness. The type of kindness that made you want to slam your own head in a car door just to have an excuse to get away from it.

"Hey, I watched you personally agonize over the knives and

forks, and they're awesome. I've never felt so strongly about knives and forks. And the paper napkins? You got the best ones at the party store—the best. The party's going to be great, don't worry so much," he soothed, reaching out to rub my shoulder affectionately. "And if she gets too out of hand, I always have horse tranquilizers in my truck. That'll shut her right down."

I burst out laughing. "It may come to that," I admitted, wiping my eyes.

"I'm on it," he said, still with the rubbing. "Now come on, your ice cream is melting." He started to lead me back onto the patio. "By the way, what was that about bouncing on his dick? Whose dick are we talking about?"

When you drop ice cream on a brick patio, it's impossible to clean up without getting the hose out. And in so doing, I may have sprayed a pregnant lady accidentally. On purpose.

# chapter eleven

Marge was right about her baked beans; they were sensational. Everyone's paper plate was piled high with them, along with fruit salad, coleslaw, and a hot dog or hamburger. We went with a picnic theme: red-and-white checked tablecloths on the picnic tables, utensils in plastic cups on each table, balloons and streamers overhead in the bright sunshine. And a huge sign over the entrance gate that said Our Gang Grand Opening, in case anyone missed that we were now officially, 100 percent, open for business.

We had invited all of the volunteers and their families, owners of several of the local businesses that had already supported us, and the off-duty staff of the Campbell Veterinary Hospital. Including Marge, who when she wasn't strong-arming everyone into professing their love for her beans, was circling Lou like a beehived polyester shark. A beehive with an Our Gang pin tucked into it, which was quite sweet.

The radio was tuned to an oldies station playing classic Motown. Some people were chowing down, while others were trekking up and down the hill by the barn to see all the dogs, which were freshly bathed and smelling like baby powder. And happy to have the visitors. Between the buckets of tennis balls and the donated chew toys, the dogs were in heaven. Exactly how it should be. Happy and racing around their dog run, with Sammy Davis Jr. leading the pack.

Our first resident, he'd become a mascot of sorts. He'd almost been adopted twice, and each time, my heat beat a little faster. When another dog was chosen each time, I'd spent a little extra time with my sweet boy, assuring him he'd find a forever home.

The truth? He'd already chosen his owner, and thank goodness for that, because I couldn't bear to let him out of my sight. After the last close call I'd moved him into the house with me, and just like that, I was a dog mommy. That big pit bull grin was smiling at me right now, and I grinned back. "Go play, buddy," I said, patting him on the flank and sending him back into the tennis ball frenzy.

"Hey, Chlo, great party, but we've gotta get going if we want to make it home before dark," Clark said, walking up the hill with Viv in tow. "We'll be back as soon as you say our little guy is ready."

"Or before. In fact, I might just scoot in there now and load my pockets up with puppies when you're not looking," Viv said, trying to edge around me on the path.

I laughed. "You'd be a terrible thief, Viv. You just told me what you were planning. Now I'm patting you down before you leave." I reached out, pretending to pinch her again.

"Seriously, stop with the pinching. Clark, tell her to cut it out."

"If my cousin is pinching you, I'm pretty sure you deserve it," Clark chimed in, to her great distress.

"I'm your fiancée! That means you always have to be on my side, no matter what I do," she said, stamping her feet.

"Impossible woman," Clark murmured, reaching for her hand, and she immediately blushed. Huh.

As they made eyes at each other, I caught sight of my parents coming up the driveway, my mother's heels tottering on the gravel.

"Do you want to say hi to Aunt Marjorie first?" I asked.

"Oh, boy," Clark said under his breath. "Whoa, Aunt Marjorie with Uncle Thomas? Together? And they're not fight—too late," he said as my mother shrugged off my father's attempt to steady her on the gravel.

"Oh, we're staying. I'm not missing this." Viv's tone was light, but she reached out and squeezed my hand.

The three of us traipsed down the hill toward my parents, and I could see my dad looking for me. I could also see my mom looking around and taking note of every single thing.

I took a deep breath, then called out, "Hey, guys!"

"There she is! Hiya, kiddo!" my dad cried out, bundling me into a swing-around hug. "How've you been?"

"Hey, Dad, so good to see you," I said, muffled by his shoulder. He set me down and gave me a quick once-over.

"You look fantastic, Chloe, really fantastic," he gushed, and I just beamed. Once a daddy's girl . . .

"Hello, Chloe," my mother said, and I turned to her. She gave me a not-so-quick once-over, no doubt noting my attire. Cut-off jean shorts, sneakers, a white tank top with the Our Gang logo printed across the boobs, a ball cap, zero makeup, and my long blond hair in two messy braids.

I let her once-over, and twice over, for that matter. I was comfortable, I was happy, and for once, I was literally on my own turf.

"Hi, Mom," I chirped. "Good to see you." And part of me really meant it: I missed her. From time to time. "How was the flight?"

"Oh, you know those tiny crop dusters, so bumpy. How are you, dear?" she asked, leaning in to drop a kiss lightly on my cheek.

"Great. What a turnout, huh?" I asked, gesturing to the yard filled with friends and coworkers. Kids running everywhere, dogs barking, and Marge was even getting people to dance.

"Yes, it certainly seems like a crowd." She smiled, then looked over my shoulder. "And Clark, your mother said you might be here. How are you, darling?" she cooed, stepping past me to hug my cousin. She'd always adored him.

"Hello, Aunt Marjorie, good to see you. It's so great you could come up for Chloe's big day."

"I wouldn't have missed it for the world," she said, and I rolled my eyes behind her.

My dad caught it and winked at me, then turned to Clark. "Good to see you," he said, and they did the one-armed back slap guy hug.

"Great to see you, Thomas, long time no see. I'd love you two to meet—"

"And this must be your Vivian! Just look at you," my mother interrupted, offering her hand to Viv. "You must be ready to pop!"

"I'm only seven months, not quite ready to pop just yet," Viv corrected, shaking my mother's hand vigorously. "I've been so looking forward to meeting you; I've heard so much about you, Marge! Can I call you Marge?"

"Oh, well, I—" my mother started, when a sugary southern voice joined the conversation.

"Did I hear my name? Did someone want more of my baked beans?" Marge sidled up to the group and wrapped her arm around me. "Now, who do we have here? This tall drink of water must be your father—what a cutie pie!" she cried, reaching out and pulling my dad down to her rhinestone-encrusted bosom. He shot me a surprised but not unhappy look over her beehive.

Releasing him, she turned to my mother, who took a defensive step back. "And you must be Chloe's mother. Well, you two are just the spitting image! Look how gorgeous you are—you're just pretty enough to eat!" She reached out for a hug, but my mother quickly stuck her hand out, avoiding the beehive grapple. "Now, you just come right over here, we need to get you something to eat! You look abso-tootly famished! I've got these beans over here, an old secret family recipe, you know . . ."

And just like that, my mother was whisked away to the buffet table, and had a paper plate heaped with secret family recipe beans in her hand before I could even say a word. I looked at my father, who just watched his ex-wife being strong-armed by a woman in a seventies polyester pantsuit. Then we both burst out laughing.

We were still laughing when I felt, rather than heard, Lucas approach. He was just a little behind me, but by my side. I looked left, and there were those blue eyes twinkling down at me. "Hey," I said, bumping him with my hip.

"Hey," he replied, keeping his hips to himself. "Mr. Patterson? I'm Lucas Campbell, a friend of your daughter's," he said when there was a pause in the conversation.

Viv was beaming, literally beaming, as she watched him shake my dad's hand. So much hand shaking around here today.

"A friend of Chloe's? Are you the Lucas I hear so much about?"

"That depends very much on what you've heard, sir." Lucas laughed easily.

"Lucas who helped my daughter out of the jam with that giant Suburban?" my father asked.

"Well, sort of. She did most of the talking the second time around; you should have seen her when she got fired up." Lucas slipped an arm around my shoulder, patting me in a "way to go" kind of way. I'd take it.

"And are you also the Lucas that got her in the water and on a paddleboard?"

"She's a natural," he crowed. "When she stops looking for fins."

"I'll never stop looking for fins," I shuddered, and he grinned down at me.

The arm was still around the shoulders. Viv's smile was now stretched around her entire head.

"Can I get you anything to drink Mr. Patterson? Water, soda, beer?" Lucas asked.

"Lucas, I just got off a small plane with my ex-wife."

Lucas thought a moment. "Chloe's taught me how to make a mean martini. Straight up or on the rocks?"

"Rocks. Always rocks."

As they headed toward the house, Lucas said, "You've got a helluva bar here, Mr. Patterson. Chloe and I have been working our way through this old sixties cocktail recipe book. You ever had a zombie?"

"Have you been trying to get my daughter drunk, Lucas?" my dad asked as Lucas held the patio door open for him.

"Absolutely, Mr. Patterson. Absolutely," Lucas said with a grin.

The last thing I heard my father say before they disappeared was, "In that case, call me Thomas."

I looked at Viv and Clark and threw up my hands, shaking my head.

Viv looked me dead in the eye and said, "Hit that. Hit that now."

"Hit what? Who's hitting someone?" Clark asked.

I went to rescue my mother from Marge.

All in all, not too bad.

Eventually the party dwindled down to just a handful. We'd made two more adoption matches today; Steve and Edie went to a farmer and his wife just outside town who'd been looking for a matched set. The dogs had been abandoned when their family could no longer afford to care for them, and we'd kept them together until we found a home that would take them as a pair. As always, I felt a little lump in my throat when I saw my dogs going to their forever home. We'd also raised a pretty hefty sum through donations today, and many guests had brought things like dog beds, chew toys, cans of dog food, and still more tennis balls.

All in all? A success.

The music was still going strong, though the only ones dancing now were Marge and Lou. Wrapped around each other like pythons, the hippie and the matchmaker were something to behold. And by that, I mean it was terrifying watching them practically mount each other on the makeshift dance floor.

"No more slow songs, I told you that," I whispered to Lucas, who was trying his best not to watch the train wreck that was currently two-stepping by to the tune of "I Only Have Eyes for You."

"Come on, chickie baby, it's nice. In a somewhat gross way."

"But I liked this song! Now it's forever tainted by this memory," I moaned, turning away. And catching something I never thought I'd see again in my life. My father, leading my mother onto the dance floor.

Now, I'd been told by my mother expressly when planning

my wedding to Charles that under *no* circumstances would there be a Mother/Father dance taking place, and that if I pushed it, I'd regret it. So imagine my surprise when the two held hands and, with an appropriate amount of space in between them, began to dance.

"I don't believe it," I said, my jaw somewhere down by my feet. "I've got to get a picture of this; Clark will never believe it."

He and Vivian had left long ago, arguing over some historic lighthouse he wanted to see on the way home. As they'd headed to their car, that discussion shifted into which route to take home. I'd also seen Clark's hand disappear down the back of her skirt as they walked, and I had a feeling that if they stopped, it wasn't going to be to look at a lighthouse.

"I'm sorry my parents couldn't make it," Lucas said. "Dad had to cover a shift at the clinic, and my mom's getting over the flu. She's dying to meet you, though, and said to tell you congratulations."

"Dying to meet me? You been talking about me?" I asked, taking my eyes off my parents dancing for the first time in years to look up at Lucas. Dusk had fallen, and a warm breeze was blowing in off the ocean, carrying the faintest scent of brine, cut with the night-blooming jasmine that was just beginning to open.

"If I had, would that be so bad?" he asked.

"No," I murmured. "Not bad at all." I swayed a bit to the music, watching the couples that had now joined Marge and Lou, and my mother and father. Suddenly I wanted to be dancing in my backyard.

I looked up at Lucas, just as he started to say, "Would you—"

"Chloe, dear, your father's just informed me that there seems to have been a mistake at the hotel, and there's only one room available. So if it's all right with you, it looks like I'll be staying here."

"What?" I asked, looking around wildly and spying my father heading inside with a devilish grin. "I mean, of course you can stay with me, Mother."

She sighed dramatically. "I do hope you have enough hot water for my bath. This house always seemed to have the tiniest water heater in the free world. Though since you used paper plates, that should save on some hot water."

"There's plenty of hot water, Mother. It's practically scalding." I sighed and leaned against Lucas, who tucked me into his side.

Something that my mother's eyes didn't miss for a second. Narrowing them, she looked up at Lucas. "My, you are tall, aren't you?"

"Yes, ma'am," he answered, and I giggled into his armpit.

She gave him one more appraising glance, then called to my father, "Thomas, if you're leaving me here, you're doing it *after* you've brought in my bags. I'm not hauling them up that long driveway myself."

"Yes, Marjorie. I said I'd get your bags. Pipe down."

"One dance, and he thinks he can take that tone with me again," she said, but not without some amusement.

As she headed into the house I slumped further into Lucas' side, the day's excitement beginning to wear into exhaustion.

"Rain check on the dance?" Lucas asked.

"Oh, were you going to ask me to dance?" I said, tilting my head and giving him my best coy look.

"Just like your peep show, I guess we'll never know," he replied, catching me by the hand and spinning me out, just to spin me right back in.

I laughed. "Hey, what's with the slick moves?"

"Every ring-a-ding kid has his moves," he said in his best Sinatra.

And I realized that I'd been in almost constant contact with him all day—whether a shoulder rub, a hip check, or a spin move designed to wrap me in his arms. Those ring-a-ding moves? They worked. I stared into his eyes, wondering if enough time had passed to move forward, and frankly not caring if they had.

Then I felt a tap on my shoulder, and turned to see Lou and Marge, hands held and eyes dreamy.

"You two leaving?" Lucas asked the beaming couple, pulling me in front of him. I could feel him behind me, warm and solid and strong.

"Marge here told me about a bar in town that plays nothing but Crosby, Stills, Nash & Young. I have to check that out," Lou told him. Then he looked at me. "Princess, you kicked ass here. I'm so proud of you."

"Aw, thanks, Lou. Is this the part where I say I couldn't have done it without you?"

"Yes."

"Lou, I couldn't have done it without you," I said, meaning every word.

"Oh, go on." He blushed.

We said good night to them and the last few stragglers who were leaving, then turned back to each other.

"So," Lucas said.

"So." I didn't want him to leave just yet.

Silence.

"Want some help cleaning up?"

"I'd love it! You're in charge of bringing in the beans."

We headed to the table, and as we turned around to bring

the first load of leftovers into the house, my parents scrambled away from the window so we wouldn't catch them peeping. Subtle.

An hour later, everything had been cleaned up and there wasn't any trace of a party. Lucas had helped scrub up the few dishes, and then we made the last round of dog checks. They were all a bit amped up from the commotion today, but once the lights were off they started to quiet down for the night.

We were in the kitchen with my parents as Lucas took the last load of trash out. "You're almost out of trash bags, Chlo."

"I think there's another one in the pantry."

"Nope, we used that one last week when Sammy Davis Jr. got into the jelly beans." He told my father, "I'm a vet, and even I was grossed out by what was coming out of that dog." And with that announcement, he sailed out the door.

"He certainly seems very familiar around here," my mother remarked, stacking leftover napkins into perfect towers.

"He's a good friend," I said, feeling something pinch at me at the word *friend*.

"And nothing more?" she asked.

My father shushed her. "Marjorie, it's none of our business."

"I think I have every right to ask these questions. I'm her mother," she said, her posture, even on a bar stool, as perfect as always.

I remembered walking through our house, around and around, with a book on my head. People think that kind of thing only happened in old movies, but it happened in my dining room. *"Poise, Chloe. You must have poise and grace. You can always tell a lady by her posture."*

"Besides, if she told me anything, I wouldn't have to *ask* these questions," she finished, giving me a pointed look.

"And why do you think that is, Mother? Why do you think I don't tell you anything?" I asked, slouching on my own stool. Her eyebrow went up, but I didn't.

Point: Chloe.

"I'm sure I don't know. Unless there's some reason you don't want to share things with me? Maybe not so sure of your choices anymore, dear?"

"You have *got* to be kidding me. Are you really sitting there with the balls to say that—"

"Oh, yes, of course, it *was* St. Bart's where the Tuppermans spent their winter, not Saint Lucia. How right you are," she cut in.

I did a triple take. What the—

Ah—Lucas had come back into the kitchen. *Dirty laundry must never be aired in front of company. Always keep the pretty white frilly things in front.*

Point: Mother.

But I was so tired of frilly white things. They were her specialty, not mine. My father was silent at the end of the counter; he'd heard it all before. Lucas stood in the entryway, looking extremely uncomfortable; my mother's attempt to change the subject was more awkward than if we'd just kept on talking.

She looked at me expectantly. And I'd had it.

My line should have been: "Yes, I heard they enjoyed St. Bart's immensely."

What I actually said was, "Oh, Mother, blow it out your ditty bag."

You could hear a pin drop. Or a slight breeze blowing through a punctured ditty bag.

After that, all you heard was the scraping of a bar stool and two pairs of male feet making for the front door. One called, "See you in the morning, kiddo!" The other said, "Nice to meet you, Mrs. Patterson!" A door slam, tires peeling out, and then true silence.

Finally, "I must say, Chloe, I really don't appreciate you speaking to me in such a rude way, especially in front of your new boyfriend."

"He's not my boyfriend, Mother." I sighed, leaning onto the counter with my head in my hands.

"You sure about that?"

"You think I don't know whether I have a boyfriend or not?"

"Well, I don't know. I don't understand *anything* you're doing anymore. But I must say, a small town veterinarian is hardly who I would have picked out for you."

"Pick someone *out* for me? He's not an outfit, Mother," I snapped, lifting my head up and staring at her. She was totally unaware of how she sounded, how she was affecting everyone and everything. "And if he *were* my boyfriend, which he is not, I would be incredibly lucky. And what the hell's wrong with a veterinarian? If he were a gas station attendant, he'd still be an amazing man who makes me laugh and makes me giddy and makes me *happy*, for god's sake! Why would that make you so *un*happy?"

"I just wanted so much more for you, Chloe. How happy would you be, living here in this tiny town? And while it's certainly an admirable profession, will a veterinarian be able to provide the kind of life for you that Charles would have?" she asked, clearly still not listening to me.

"There are so many things wrong with what you just said, I don't even know where to start! First of all—and I need you to *hear* these words—I am *not* dating Lucas. Not even a little bit. But even more concerning to me is that you somehow think he's not good enough for me. Do you even *hear* some of the things you say? Because you sure as hell don't hear me." I was on the move now, hands on hips and practically in her face.

"Don't you raise your voice to me—"

"I am *not* finished! Most parents would be thrilled that their daughter was dating someone like Lucas, even just focusing on his profession, which you seem to be. He works for a family business that's been around for almost fifty years—talk about job security. But that's not glamorous enough for you. It's not as flashy as having a surgeon as a son-in-law, or a congressman or an attorney. Shouldn't the man be more important than the job? The social accolades? The benefits?"

"You say those things like they're mutually exclusive, but there's no reason you can't find everything you're looking for in one man. That's what Charles could have been," she said pointedly.

"Charles was *never* going to be that. That's what you don't seem to understand. I. Didn't. Love. Charles. Nice guy, great provider, okay sex—"

"Chloe, really—"

"But I didn't love him. Why in the world is that not enough for you?" I asked, my voice quiet now.

I stared at my mother, who was still perched on the edge of her bar stool, sitting just as tall as can be, makeup still perfect, clothes still wrinkle free though she'd been at a picnic all day, hair flawlessly swept back in her usual chignon. And blinking back at me, truly surprised that I don't seem to understand where she's coming from. Neither of us had a clue what the other one was thinking, was feeling. So where did we go from here?

I started back toward the guest room, almost blindly.

"Where are you going?" she called.

"I'm going to make sure you've got clean sheets on the bed."

I felt the bite of tears and forced them back. "And put fresh towels in your bathroom." She didn't answer, and I continued down the hallway. Wiping away a tear that had escaped, I pulled some sheets and a comfortable blanket from the linen closet and carried them into the guest room, where my father had placed her bags earlier.

He'd arranged this. He'd made this happen. He thought that if the two of us could just spend some time together, we could talk it out and begin to knock down some of the wall that been growing since the wedding.

But that wall had started to go up a long time ago, and I didn't know what it would take to bring it down. I yanked the bedspread off the bed, then angrily shook out the fitted sheet.

"Do you want some help with that?" My mother appeared in the doorway.

"Thanks, but I've got it," I said, quickly wiping away another tear that had escaped. I kept my back to her as I stretched the corners around and tried to tuck it in.

"Why don't you let me do one side? Then you won't have to keep running around the bed." She tugged on the corner, and I let her. It was easier than arguing. It was easier than running around in circles.

"You know I only want what's best for you, right?" she asked, her voice not acidic for a change.

I softened. I couldn't help it. "I know you think you do—yes," I said with a sigh.

Shaking out the top sheet, I fanned it up over the bed like a parachute. For a split second, I caught her eye underneath the canopy. She looked tired. By the time the sheet had settled, she looked composed, as usual. We pulled the sheet tight, hospital corners at the bottom. As I smoothed the sheet up toward the top, she tugged a little more on her side, pulling the sheet over just a bit. I tugged it back over to my side, making it the same on both: even.

Point: neither.

"You say you didn't love Charles," she started.

I shook my head." I didn't—"

"Let me say this, please," she asked, and I nodded. I stood on my side of the bed, blanket in hand.

"You say you didn't love Charles, and I can see now that you didn't. But, Chloe, love is not always the only thing you need to make a marriage work."

"You said that before, but how is that possible? How can that not be the most important thing?" I asked, sitting down on the bed.

"Because it's just not." She sighed, sitting down as well. "I loved your father more than anything in this world." She studied her hands, rubbing the fourth finger on her left hand absently. Not so absently? When she looked up at me again, her eyes were bright. "And it was absolutely not enough."

"Ah," I said, nodding my head once. Pieces were falling into place so quickly I could practically hear them clinking.

"We had nothing in common, Chloe—nothing. Except we were stupid in love. And were for a long time. But at a certain point, once you grow up, once you become parents, you need more than that. You need common goals, common interests, a clearly chosen path of how you're going to live your life. We didn't have that, and we grew apart. I didn't feel appreciated. Your father didn't feel appreciated. Things happen. You say things you can't take back. You *do* things you—" She stopped herself, her gaze focusing as she realized what she was saying. "Well, things happen. But by then, it was too late."

She looked at me carefully as her eyes began to close off once more. "Love isn't everything, Chloe, it just isn't. You didn't want to marry Charles, and I accept that. But moving up here, starting this new business, it's like . . . it's like I don't even know who you are anymore."

I took a deep breath, then held it, still not sure what I was going to say. I let it out in one long sigh as I stood up and began to shake out the blanket. "I know you don't understand it, but it's something I need to do right now, for me. I need something for myself. Just for me."

"And working with these . . . dogs is what you want to do?" she asked, gesturing for the other end of the blanket.

"Yeah," I said, handing it to her. "I really think it is."

She was quiet. We worked in silence, folding the blanket toward the foot of the bed. Then she said, "Remember the Feldings? They lived down at the bottom of the hill?"

"Sure, the ones that handed out toothpaste on Halloween?"

"That's because the father was an orthodontist."

"They also got egged every Halloween."

"Be that as it may, I ran into Mrs. Felding at the market the other day. Their son Stephen is going into practice with his father. He's back from Cornell, and single as can be. She asked about you and—"

"Mother. Seriously," I said, staring hard at the floor.

"Chloe. Seriously. Can't you take a joke?" When I looked up her eyes were bright, but this time with mischief.

I rolled my eyes, but allowed a grin. "I'm going to go put some water on," I said, walking past her on the way to the kitchen. "Maybe after your bath we could have some tea?"

"If you'd like," she said, her voice controlled but delighted.

"I'd like." I smiled, then pointed toward the bathroom. "Don't forget you have to jiggle the handle to get the hot to mix with the cold."

"For goodness' sake, I'd forgotten all about that. Do you have any idea how many times I tried to get your father to hire a plumber? A real one, not just that caretaker." She went on and on while she took out her bath products, and I just leaned in the doorway and listened to her.

Until she prompted me to go get the kettle on, so the teapot would have time to warm up.

# chapter twelve

The day of the Fourth of July picnic and parade was one of those picture-perfect California days. Seventy-five degrees, not a cloud in the sky, with a kicky breeze blowing in on off the coast. I spent the better part of the morning with the dogs, playing fetch with a million tennis balls and a racket. Glad my perfect backhand was finally paying off. I paid some bills, answered some emails, avoided two phone calls from my mother, and then managed to get in a quick shower.

My mother and I had spoken a few times since the grand opening party. She wasn't quite ready to give up on the idea of me moving back to San Diego, believing I'd tire of this "gang dog" thing, but things were less tense than before. And that was a very good thing. And speaking of mothers, today I was going to get to meet Lucas' mother. He'd called the morning after my parents left, wanting to make sure my head was still on, or if it had been blown out along with the ditty bag. Which he still didn't quite understand.

"So explain to me once again what a ditty bag is?" he asked.

"It's just a small bag that might hold things like paper clips or push pins, or you might take it on a camping trip to hold your toothbrush, toothpaste, and bug spray," I explained. "Or I might have had one that I kept backstage when I did pageants."

"And what might have been in that bag?" he asked, curious.

"Preparation H and butt glue."

"I can't talk to you ever again," he said, horrified.

"Oh shut up," I said, laughing, and dropped a piece of bread into the toaster.

"Are you making toast?"

"Nothing wrong with your ears," I said. "And, yes, I'm making toast."

"Late breakfast?"

"Or early lunch. Didn't really eat breakfast this morning," I replied, gazing out at the driveway, where my parents' car had been just a little while ago.

"How'd it go with your mom?" he asked, his voice careful.

"Not bad. Not bad at all, actually," I admitted, spreading Nutella on my warm toast.

"That's good, right?"

"It's very good. I think she was still hoping I was going to show up in a gown and a veil in the driveway with Charles, shouting, 'I do I do!' "

"That's not going to happen, is it?"

"Good lord, no," I said, biting into my toast. "I'd never get married in a driveway."

He paused, then laughed. "Oh, I don't know. Nothing says I love you like a little crushed gravel and an oil slick."

"Did you have a reason for calling this morning, or did you just want to make me swoon with your redneck pillow talk?"

"How do you feel about fireworks?"

"In general?"

"*Specifically. Like, we're going to the carnival in town, and you're invited.*"

"*Who is we?*"

"*Just my family. My mom and dad, and my cousin Sophia and her boyfriend, Neil, in town from San Francisco.*"

"*The whole family . . . hmm,*" I teased, trying to tamp down the little flutter in my chest. "*I suppose after the ditty bag fiasco, you owe me a little family drama.*"

"*At the risk of sounding like a douche bag, we're a little more low key than your family. The only fireworks tonight will be in the sky.*"

"*I can't really say no to that then, can I?*" I said with a laugh.

And just like that, I had plans for a holiday outing with Lucas and his family. I smiled as I quickly braided my hair, still damp from my shower. I dressed simply for the day, white linen sundress and espadrilles, and was dabbing on a little lip gloss when I heard Lucas pulling up the drive. Dashing out front, I caught sight of a different car, not the truck from the animal hospital he was usually driving.

"What's this? You've been holding out on me, Campbell," I said, admiring the Mustang convertible, all bright red and shiny.

"It's my dad's; he rarely lets it out of the garage." He hopped out and came around to my side. Dressed casually as well, he wore blue jeans, a green T-shirt, flip-flops, and a wide grin.

"How'd we get so lucky today?" I asked as he opened my door for me.

"It's the Fourth of July, it's a gorgeous day, and he knew as well as I do that this car needed to be driven around today." He grinned, placing his hand on the small of my back for just a second or two as I climbed in, but it was enough. "Especially with a beautiful woman along for the ride."

"Oh, are we picking someone else up?" I asked, making a horrible face when he shook his finger at me.

"Funny girl," he teased, and we were off to the carnival, top down. It *was* the perfect day for a convertible. In town we parked and found his parents. His mother was a lovely woman, a tiny little bit of a thing. A little round, a lot sweet, and incredibly kind. She held tightly to the leash of Abigail, their golden retriever.

"I used to work with goldens a lot when I worked with the therapy dog program in San Diego," I said, kneeling down to say hello to the beautiful dog.

"We used to have someone in town that did that, but once she passed away no one has really shown much interest in bringing the program back," she mused. "Maybe that's something you could do. Eventually. Lucas would love to help you with that, I'm sure."

"What will I love to help with?" Lucas asked, turning from the discussion he was having with his father. His eyes met mine, looking at me chatting it up with his mom, and it was like he knew this was good. This felt right. I offered him a smile, one that he met with one of his own. A secretive smile, knowing, and full of something other than "let's get a therapy dog program going."

It took my breath away. The world faded; the noises from the carnival games became just a background blur to that sweet, sexy face.

"I was just telling your friend Chloe here how she should think about starting a therapy program here in town, maybe with some of her dogs," his mom said, looking back and forth between us.

"Oh, so this is your friend Chloe I've been hearing so much about," a new voice said from behind me.

Turning around, I saw a girl. Tall, incredibly curvy, with long red hair. No smile. She began to circle me—literally circle me. As she did, I had no choice but to mimic her movements. It was like a scene right out of the *Beat It* music video.

"Sophie, would you not be so dramatic, please?" Lucas said, laughing under his breath. I gave him "a what the fudge?" look.

"Sweet face, cool it. Don't be so scary," another voice said, and I found myself staring up into the face of a very large, but very friendly guy. Linebacker type. Big grin. Vaguely familiar. Dr. and Mrs. Campbell just stood there, grinning. What was going on?

"So. Chloe," the redhead said, looking me over carefully. I wasn't going to start circling again; I stood my ground. "Are you interested in Lucas here? Like, romantically? And of course you are, because look at him."

"Oh, will you—" Lucas started.

Red held up her hand. "Answer the question."

"Are you serious?" I asked, beginning to wonder if there was a hidden camera somewhere.

"All I'm saying is, the last time my cousin fell in love, that bitch broke his heart. So forgive me if I'm a little overprotective," the redhead said, trying to stare me down.

"Cousin?" I asked as Lucas came to stand next to me, his presence warm and reassuring.

"Chloe, this is my very dramatic, very protective, very forward cousin Sophia, and her much more laid-back boyfriend, Neil. They're in town for the Fourth."

"Usually I have to work on the Fourth," the now-identified redhead Sophia chimed in, looking smug. "I'm a cellist."

"Okay," I said.

"With the San Francisco Symphony?" she said, looking like I should give a fudge.

"Okay," I repeated, leaning against Lucas a bit.

"I play with the orchestra. You know, fireworks go off over-head, symphony plays, patriotic and all that?" she said, making sure I, and anyone around, knew that she was special.

"And when I said okay, that wasn't 'okay, I don't understand,' but 'okay, I heard you and that's great and are you done talk-ing yet?'" I straightened to my full height, returning her stare. "And what I'm doing with your cousin—or rather, not doing—is frankly none of your business."

The boyfriend snorted.

"Okay, she's cool. She can stay," Sophia said, leaning over to kiss Lucas on the cheek.

"Gee, thanks, Sophia," Lucas muttered, catching her into a close hug and then passing her off to his parents as he shook Neil's hand. "Neil, this is Chloe."

"I gathered." Neil offered me his giant paw of a hand. "And don't pay any attention to her. His ex really got Soph riled up—it was all I could do to stop her from trying to kick some ass. But in truth?" He leaned in, conspiratorial style. I couldn't help it; I leaned in too. "She wouldn't hurt a fly."

"I would so," she huffed. "As long as it didn't hurt my hands."

I nodded. "For the record, Lucas and I really are just friends."

She looked at both of us for a second, hands on hips. "Mm-hmm," she hummed while shaking her head, clearly not believ-ing it for a second.

"Come on, feisty, I need funnel cakes." Neil literally picked up Sophia with one arm and began to carry her vertically down the midway towards the fried-everything stand.

Lucas' parents left as well, leaving me standing wide-eyed next to Lucas. "Tell me again how there would be no weird family dynamic tonight? I'd love to hear that one more time," I teased.

He looked embarrassed. "I had no idea she'd come on like

that," he said, holding up his hands in defense. "She's always been a bit headstrong."

"Headstrong? Your cousin just had me for dinner, and then had funnel cakes for dessert, and you call her headstrong?"

"You did great." He smiled, and I took the opportunity to jab him in the ribs.

"Hey! They've got fried Twinkies!" Neil called out, Sophia now perched lightly on his back.

"Twinkie?" Lucas asked, offering me his arm.

"I prefer chickie baby," I replied, linking my arm through his and letting him lead me toward his family. And with the smell of ocean air and sand in the air, with a touch of hot asphalt and fried dough, it was a picture-perfect Fourth of July day.

The golden day turned into a starlit night. We'd spent the day wandering the carnival, snacking and drinking cheap beer, playing carnival games, and mostly losing. But I was now the proud owner of a cotton-candy-pink teddy bear almost half my size, courtesy of Lucas. I don't know how much he ended up spending to win it for me. Determined, he spent at least twenty minutes throwing rigged baseballs at rigged milk cans until he finally came away a winner. Victorious, he presented me with a bear, and promptly begged me to please rub his now-sore shoulder.

I told him he should rub his own shoulder, which earned me a high-five from Neil, a wounded look from Lucas, and an appraising eyebrow raise from Sophia, who seemed to be slowly warming to me. Whether I was warming to her, I wasn't quite sure. But Neil was great. They were down from San Francisco to see her folks. She'd grown up in Monterey, was only a year younger than Lucas, and it was apparent that the cousins became as close as siblings, just like in my family.

I also met about a million other new people. The Campbells knew almost everyone in town, and every few minutes we stopped and chatted with another group of friends. Lucas always introduced me and told people all the wonderful things Our Gang was already doing, and planned on doing for the community overall with our eventual outreach program. I'd made several good contacts, people who I thought were genuinely interested in what we were doing and really wanted to get involved. This town? Close knit, and kind.

As the evening arrived under a cloudless sky, we wandered with everyone else toward the bandstand. The Fourth of July in Monterey concluded not just with fireworks and music, but with the crowning of Little Miss Stars and Stripes, a local pageant. My mother had kept me out of local pageants, saving me for the ones she felt could lead to bigger and better things. But the truth is, sometimes these local pageants can be the most fun. This one was loaded with sparkle and glamour, small-town pride, and just enough camp to make it fun.

Sophia huffed, "I still can't believe you were engaged to a former Little Miss Stars and Stripes. A beauty queen—that should have told you something right there."

Lucas was looking very uncomfortable.

"Was that Julie?" I asked.

As he nodded, Sophia told me, "She was a total twat."

Lucas said, "For your information, Chloe was a beauty queen. Miss Golden State, right?"

Now I was the one blushing and looking uncomfortable.

"Seriously? Miss Golden State?" she asked, and I nodded. "Well, *you* don't seem to be a twat."

"I'm oddly flattered by that," I replied, and she offered a smile.

Then someone tapped the microphone on stage, and we all turned to see a parade of cute little girls dressed up in their finest red, white, and blue dresses. As the crowd oohed and aahed, an official-looking man introduced the beginning of the annual Little Miss Stars and Stripes pageant, and asked us to please welcome the judges for this evening. The high school cheerleading coach, the owner of the local supermarket, and a former Little Miss Stars and Stripes.

"Speaking of twats," Sophie muttered under her breath, and Lucas suddenly went as still as stone beside me.

"Please welcome back to town, all the way from Hollywood, where she can currently be seen in commercials for Mattress Giant, Julie Owens!"

General applause. Hissing from Sophia. Lucas had gone mute.

Oh, boy.

"What the hell is *she* doing here?" Sophia whisper-yelled.

The announcer said, "Former Little Miss Stars and Stripes Julie Owens is back in town to help us crown our next winner. As you know, we usually have our current Little Miss crown the new winner, but Becky Whippleson is recovering after a nasty accident involving a skateboard and Vespa scooter. We wish Becky a very speedy recovery."

"So, she's back just for this?" Sophia asked.

"She came back home just for this. Isn't that wonderful, ladies and gentlemen? Leaving behind her booming career in Hollywood, she rushed back home to help us out," the announcer said, sounding more and more like a game show host by the minute.

I looked onstage to see Julie, clad in a red sequin gown and a crown, waving to the appreciative crowd. Then I chanced a look up at Lucas, still frozen but taking it all in.

"I can't believe she's here. She better not stay for the fireworks, or I'll have a bottle rocket with her name on it," Sophia said, a little louder this time.

"Tell me, Miss Owens, will you be staying for the fireworks tonight? Helping us celebrate the Fourth?" the announcer asked, and handed her the mike.

"I sure will, Mr. Wilson. I can't wait to celebrate our nation's birthday with my family, and hopefully some old friends, here in my hometown!" Julie crowed, and the crowd cheered along with her and the rest of the Little Miss minions.

"Oh, for the love of—" Lucas rolled his eyes.

"Do you want to leave?" I asked in a low voice, leaning in so the rest of his family couldn't hear.

He gave me a tight smile, then shook his head. "Nah, I'm good. Besides, I promised you fireworks."

When he tucked me tight into his side, I let him. And we watched his ex-fiancée crown Little Miss Ah, Forget It.

And then came the fireworks. But the ones in the sky were dwarfed by what I now refer to as Big Dumb Mean Julie Fudging with My Fourth of July.

If I'd left my fiancé standing at the altar, which technically I did *not* do, and then came back into town unexpectedly, I would *not* deliberately seek out said fiancé and try to explain why I did what I did *in front of his family*.

If I ever ran into Charles and the rest of the Sappington clan, I'd be gracious, keep the chitchat to a minimum, and be on my way as fast as possible to minimize the emotional damage on either side. But you're darn tootin' that the first time I see Charles, it will *not* be in public. I'll make sure it's on our own terms, with us both coming to the table to talk and yell and scream in privacy.

Not how Little Miss Mattress Giant rolls. No, she made eye contact with Lucas during the pageant, and it was all she could do to stay on the stage, practically foaming at the mouth to get to him.

After she placed a crown on the new Little Miss, she thanked the crowd, did a weird little curtsy-wave, and practically steam-rolled through the crowd to get to Lucas. He kept his arm firmly around my shoulders. For not dating, our shoulders sure seemed to be getting some play. Nevertheless, I stayed.

"Lucas!" she cried out, running through the crowd like she was auditioning for a Nicholas Sparks movie. And for the record, Julie Owens was beautiful. Tall and curvy, with long blond hair and bouncing boobs. She was your All-American California Girl. I'd been told I was the All-American California Girl. But where I got comparisons to Christie Brinkley, she'd be better compared to Pamela Anderson.

I hated her on sight. She might be the nicest person in the world, but she'd hurt him, so I hated her. And she was now hugging Lucas, with her bouncing boobies, so I hated her.

There were so many other sets of angry eyes on her I almost felt bad for the girl. But, bouncing boobies. So, yeah, no.

The incredulity continued when she flung herself, actually flung herself, into his arms, catching Lucas so off guard that he damn near fell over, recovering only at the last second. "Um," he managed, his arms full of bouncing.

"Pretty sure you meant to say *what the fuck*," Sophia said, her mouth, along with everyone else's, hanging open.

"I'm so glad to see you! I'm sorry I didn't call and let you know I was coming home, but it happened so fast, I thought I'd surprise you!" She giggled, still trying to snuggle into his arms as he began to pry off the bouncing.

"It's a surprise, all right," he muttered, finally getting her off of him. "Julie, what did you think I'd—"

"Dr. and Mrs. Campbell, good to see you! How are you?" she cooed, turning to them.

"You've *got* to be kidding me," his mother said, and I smothered a laugh. "Chloe, dear, we'll see you later, okay? Call me; we'll have lunch and talk about getting this therapy program set up." She leaned in and kissed me on the cheek, shot her son a clear warning look, and tugged her husband away.

"Good luck, son. Chloe, so glad you could join us tonight," he called out.

Which caused Julie to finally look at me. I tried to stifle the insane bubble of laughter that threatened to erupt.

"I don't think we've met," she said, tilting her head to the side and studying me carefully. "You are . . . ?"

I looked to Lucas to make the introduction, but he was too flummoxed. I couldn't blame him. "I'm Chloe Patterson." I did not offer my hand.

"I'm Julie, but you probably know that already. I saw you all watching the crowning, wasn't it fun? When they asked me to come, I just couldn't say no. I've done pageants all my life, and even though I haven't held a title or worn a crown in ages, it's just something I can never quite leave behind, you know?" she rambled.

I arched an eyebrow exactly as my mother might and said wryly, "I can imagine."

"Chloe was Miss Golden State." Sophia came next to me, slipping her arm through mine. "Sort of makes your Little Miss Crap Show look a little ridiculous, wouldn't you say?"

"Here we go," Neil said.

"Sophia, nice to see you. Slumming it in our little home-town, are we? I thought you never left San Fran?" Julie asked, her eyes narrowing.

"Slumming it? Yeah, this"—Sophia gestured to the beau-tiful bay, covered in sailboats bobbing in the moonlight, the bandstand covered in red, white, and blue bunting, the carnival midway glowing with thousands of twinkling lights—"is really slumming it."

Julie shrugged her shoulders, dismissing her. Dismissing ev-eryone, in fact, stepping back to Lucas and gazing adoringly up at him. "I came to see *you*, silly. Think we could talk? Besides, I need a ride home."

Lucas was seriously smart—not just with books, but with actual street brains. He knew better; he'd never fall for—

"Uh. Sure. Yeah. I . . . yeah. Chlo?" Lucas said, looking over her shoulder at me.

"What! I mean—wait, what?" I asked, trying to cross my arms. I couldn't actually manage it, because I was holding an enormous pink teddy bear.

"C'mere a minute," he asked, backing away from his family a bit.

I did, leaving Sophia and Julie discussing which part of Julie's ass Sophia should kick, and how far Julie could shove a cello bow up Sophia's nose. I was betting on Sophia. We headed a little ways away, to the edge of the sandy beach. I could feel the grains spilling into my sandals as I sank a bit. Chilly. I shivered—not totally because of the chilly sand.

"Chloe, how pissed would you be if I took her home?"

Loads. Tons. Truckfuls of pissed.

But we were just friends, right? So trucks full or not, I couldn't really tell him 'No, don't go.' Could I?

He looked into my eyes, his so full of . . . something. And as I looked up at him, the fireworks began. Big, and bright, loud and sparkly, over the ocean and over our heads. But he didn't look away, just looked into my eyes. Did he want me to tell him, 'No, don't go'?

*No, don't go,* I thought. But I said, "I can't answer that, Lucas."

"I think you just did."

"I just don't want you to get hurt," I replied.

"What?" he asked, leaning down to hear me over the high school band, now playing "Yankee Doodle Dandy" as loud as it was off-key.

"I said, I just don't want you to get hurt!" I yelled, putting my mouth right next to his ear.

"I won't!" he yelled back, our faces right next to each other now, the space between us filled with tension, a sudden sense of urgency, and John Philip Sousa.

"Do you want—I mean, are you sure about that?" I stammered, trying to say what I wanted to know without actually tipping my hand.

*Stay with me.*

His gaze settled on my lips. Which I licked.

"Maybe I should—"

*Say it! Yes, say it!* I thought.

"Lucas! Come on!" I heard from behind me.

And as the cymbals crashed, he made his decision. "Call you tomorrow?" he asked, and I nodded. He kissed my cheek, which burned like icy fire, and then he was gone. With Little Miss Mattress Giant. And I was still on the beach, holding a pink bear, with cold feet, whispering, *No, don't go.*

When the last starbursts had left the sky, I realized now *I* was the one without a ride home. Sophia and Neil were kind enough to drive me home, and during the ride I got to hear all about how often Lucas and Julie used to fight and break up, only to make up again. I also had to listen to Sophia plot the demise of Julie, if indeed she was back to stay. And I further had to listen to Sophia tell me how much she now liked me, and felt like I would be a great choice for her cousin. If, in fact, he was still available.

Neil tried to keep the conversation away from Sophia's plotting ways. He asked questions about Our Gang, and mentioned that they had some friends in San Francisco who were getting married and were thinking about adopting a shelter dog. I told him that when they were ready, I'd be glad to have them come down and meet my dogs.

When they dropped me off and it was just me and the quiet mountains, I was glad to be alone.

Alone. This is what I'd wanted, right? To be on my own, doing it my way, just like Frank said. Tied to no one, answering only to myself, depending on no one. Just me and Sammy Davis Jr. I got ready for bed alone, I turned out the lights alone, I plodded in circles alone, restless. Not ready to end this day. Alone.

I was still alone on the back patio, Sinatra on the hi-fi, hastily made mai tai in hand, a little teary and a little bleary, when I got a text from Lucas.

> If you're awake, can you
> come to the front door?

I stood in the doorway, hiding my lower half behind the door, as my lower half was currently clad in nothing but panties and air. He was standing on the porch leaning against the post, looking weary and beautiful. His eyes seemed bluer than normal, perhaps due to the contrasting red that lingered there. Caused by whiskey, or tears?

"Hi," he said, sounding exhausted.

"What are you doing here, Lucas?" I asked, resting my temple against the door.

"Can I come in?"

"I'm not wearing pants."

"I'll risk it," he replied, the left corner of his mouth lifting. I opened the door further, and his eyes roamed over my choice of pajamas. "Is that my—"

"Shirt, yes, it is." I shrugged, attempting nonchalance. "You left it here one day after we were out kayaking, and I never got it back to you."

It would be hard to get it back to him, since I'd been sleeping in it most nights since. An old chambray work shirt, it was soft and broken in, smelling of salt and sun and . . . oh, hell . . . Lucas. If I cared to examine what it meant, that I chose to surround myself with his scent every night, one might draw a conclusion that I was unwilling to face quite yet. Especially since that conclusion left me on a beach, without a ride home, while he went off with his ex.

But, yeah, it was just a shirt.

He let his eyes linger on my bare legs.

"Can I come in?" he asked when his eyes finally met mine again.

"Sure," I replied, holding the door open.

He heard the Sinatra and let "That Old Black Magic" pull him out to the patio, where he knew I'd been.

"Cocktails? This late?"

"Couldn't sleep; I figured one of these should do the trick."

I held up my tiki tumbler, then took another long pull. "So?" I tried to keep the bitterness out of my voice, but it wasn't hard to tell that I carried a grudge from earlier. He'd hurt me.

"I'm sorry I left you tonight. That was a bad idea."

"Bad because you left me? Or bad because you left me and went off with her?"

"Is there a difference?"

"There is." I sighed, settling back into my patio chair, crossing my legs. Once more, his eyes flickered to my skin. Once more, I observed this, and filed it away.

"So, what happened?" I asked, hating myself for wanting to know. But I did. Something was beginning to simmer, deep and low and barely there, but beginning to peek out around the sad. Anger? Jealousy? Fear?

"In a nutshell, she told me she wants to come home. It seems that Mattress Giant doesn't pay too well."

"She's only been there a little while; it takes time to build an acting career. Is she taking classes? Does she have an agent? She shouldn't give up so easily; she needs to be patient," I rambled, convincing no one that my concern for her career was the only reason that I thought she should stay far, far away.

"Julie isn't really known for her patience."

"Tons of my old pageant friends went to LA and tried their hand at acting. She should stick it out awhile longer. She should . . ." My voice trailed off, because Lucas was just shaking his head.

"I was surprised to see her tonight. I can't deny that it messed with my head a bit. I haven't seen her since our wedding day. Christ, how weird does that sound?"

"Not that weird," I managed.

"I saw her that morning, though I wasn't supposed to. I was

already at the church and she came to get pictures taken. Everyone was trying to keep us apart—you know, groom not supposed to be see the bride?" he asked, his eyes flitting up to mine.

"Mm-hmm." My mother hadn't budged on Charles not seeing me before the wedding. What's funny is, I'd had no opinion on it whatsoever.

"Anyway, I was there already, and stepped outside to get some air. And there she was, walking up the front steps of the church with her friends. Dressed in this ridiculously poofy white dress." He chuckled, everything he must have been feeling in that moment written all over his face. "She was on her cell phone, and she was laughing. I stayed in the shadows just around the corner, and I remember thinking, she's going to be my wife by the end of this day. Thirty minutes later, I was sitting in a coat closet reading a note from her that she was leaving. She was already gone by the time I got it. And I thought, why did she even bother putting on the poofy dress?" He looked at me, like I might have an answer.

I couldn't say anything.

"Anyway, she wouldn't return my calls, she wouldn't see me—she needed some time. But she was out of town and down the coast within days. We finally talked a week later, when she apologized. She kept going on and on about how it wasn't working for her, and she didn't want to stay in Monterey her whole life. I couldn't even hear anything she was saying."

"Lucas," I whispered.

He shook his head. "No, it's okay. Really, it's okay. It's funny, because now, I look back and see it. We broke up all the time, even back in high school. And she lied. A lot. About all kinds of things. Big lies, tiny lies, always with the lying. But, Jesus, who puts on a dress when she knows she's not getting married?"

"Maybe she was still planning on going through with it. Maybe it hit her all at once."

He shrugged. "Maybe it doesn't matter anymore."

"Maybe she wants you back."

"She's not moving back to Monterey." Lucas went toward the bar, where there was still a blender full of mai tais.

"She's not?" I asked, examining my toes, trying very hard to keep my voice level.

"I told her to move back if she really wanted to. This will always be her hometown. She's got good friends here, and all her family. She'll always have a home here, and a circle waiting to welcome her back." He paused to sip his cocktail. "But I told her that if she moved back home for me, that it would be a *very* bad idea."

"Oh?" I squeaked, my voice rising through the pergola rafters and out to the stars.

"Yeah. Bad, bad, bad idea," he repeated. I finally chanced a look up at him. His blue eyes burned with an emotion I couldn't name. "It doesn't matter if she wants me back, because the thing is . . . I don't want her. I haven't for a while now."

"Oh," I breathed.

"But like I said, it did mess with my head a little." Then he let loose one of those lethal grins.

"That's understandable," I admitted, taking another swig of my cocktail, and just like that, the bad tension left the room. The tingly tension was still very much here, though.

"Speaking of messing with my head, how strong did you make these?" he asked, taking another sip and raising an eyebrow.

"I just dumped stuff in; didn't bother measuring."

I lifted my drink in salute to the new song on the turntable, "Witchcraft." "Mmm, I love this song," I said with a sigh.

The song made me brave. That, and the mai tais. Curious about something, I stood up. "So she messed with your head. Did she mess with anything else?" Wow, head rush.

"Chloe?" he asked, a curious expression on his face. "Are you asking me if I messed around with my ex tonight?"

"I don't know. Yes. No. Shut up. Did you? Don't tell me. Well?"

I had an entire conversation by myself while trying to walk across the patio for another drink. Turns out, I didn't need another. Because standing up had led me to the conclusion that I was a little tipsy. Listing a bit to the left, I looked around for Lucas, who was standing at the other end of the bar, his tiki tumbler frozen in midair.

"Oh, forget it, you cute veterinarian, with your bedroom eyes and your sexy freckles and your hot . . . kryptonite hair." The words spewed out, words that would come back to haunt me. But right now, in the moonlight, with that damn Sinatra playing, I had no recourse but to move forward. And I literally did, moving right on over toward Lucas and taking one more sip of mai tai before setting it down on the bar.

"Since I only understood about half of what you just said, I'll just go ahead and tell you no."

"No?" I asked, tripping over my own foot, and thanking goodness for a bar stool that I could grab on to.

"No," he repeated, a slow grin creeping across his face. "Cute veterinarian?"

"Beside the point," I waved my hand in impatience. "So, nothing happened?"

He shook his head. "Bedroom eyes?"

"Shush," I said, closing my eyes. When I opened them, he stood before me.

"I brought you something," he whispered, and from behind

his back, he produced two sparklers. "I promised you fireworks, didn't I?"

"You did." I smiled. "Light 'em up."

Striking a match against the bar, he lit both sparklers, then handed me one. And as we swooped and swirled and wrote our names in the sky, sparks flew. I began to hum along to the song, adding a word or two here and there, and before I knew it, Lucas had spun me into his arms, dipping me old school.

"What are you doing?" I laughed breathlessly, horizontal to the floor, our sparklers raining down on our suddenly intertwined limbs.

"I couldn't help it. Starry night. Sparklers. Incredibly strong cocktails," he murmured, our faces so very close together. "It's witchcraft."

"It's not just the witchcraft, Lucas," I whispered, sliding my hands up his arms, so strong and holding me so very tightly. Lightly, so lightly, I brushed my fingertips along his neck, his skin still warm from our day in the sun. His nose bumped against mine, and I could feel his little puff of breath. Twisting my fingers into his silky hair, I blinked slowly, dreamily. And then he kissed me.

Soft. So soft. And sweet as can be. His lips brushed across mine just once, and I was hooked. Ruined for all other lips. He kissed me a second time, and my eyes fluttered open, wanting to see him. Surrounded by fairy lights, I felt suspended in midair. I was all toe curl and finger twirl. Which tucked deeper into his hair, as my tongue swept out to taste him. Mmm. Coconut rum and ginger vet. I let out the tiniest of sighs and felt his fingers dig into my hips, holding me impossibly tighter. I arched my back, just enough to get closer to him, and a sizzle ran through me as his tongue met my own.

"You taste divine," I whispered against his mouth, and felt it curve into a grin. He swept kisses along my jaw, up my cheek, and then disappeared somewhere underneath my ear, and just behind. I squealed a little, but the good kind, where it's almost tickling but incredible at the same time. I dropped my head back as he continued a path down my neck, still dipping me, mind you, and I laughed hazily at the fairy lights above. The tiki bar and all its colorful umbrellas. The pink teddy bear on the chair.

Which he won for me. And now he was kissing me, and I was loving it. And I would seriously let him love me all over this patio . . . if I didn't get my head together. But holy fudge, those lips . . .

I let myself indulge for one or two more seconds . . . or three or ten . . . and then I brought his face back to mine. Because I couldn't think clearly when the man had his lips on my neck. Oh, yeah.

Oh . . . no.

Did I want to be doing this? Now? Right after he saw his ex? After his head was admittedly messed with, not just by Little Miss Crap Show but by my extra-strong witchcraft? This felt good, oh boy did it feel good, but I wanted more than good. Selfishly? I wanted my own night. My own evening, separate from everyone and anyone, past or present. And preferably not sponsored by Mattress Giant.

With the strength of a thousand nuns, I placed one more chaste kiss on those impossibly sinful lips, and pushed him away. Just slightly, but enough for him to know our dancing dip was coming to a close. At least for now.

"Chlo?"

"It's late."

"But the kissing," he murmured, sweeping another line of perfect tiny kisses across the hollow of my throat. Which I cleared.

"You've had a long day; we've both had a long day. We should . . . Jesus, you look good in moonlight . . . Oh my God, I can't believe I just said that," I mumbled, feeling my cheeks heat. And my tummy burble. Oh boy, too many mai tais. "I think we'd better call it a night." I started for the door, but he caught my hand.

"What just happened here?"

"You kissed me."

"*You* kissed *me*."

"No way, mister, you kissed me first. I kissed you back."

"You let me dip you. You knew a kiss was coming," he said, arching an eyebrow.

"I admit, I had a feeling." I smiled, touching my fingertips to my lips, still able to feel it. Fudge, I could feel it in my toes. "But no more—not tonight." I hurried him through the house, toward the front door.

" 'Not tonight'? What did you think was going to happen here?" He looked amused.

"I know what *could* have happened, very easily. But not when I'm already in my panties."

"We can take care of that real quick," he said, now waggling his eyebrows back and forth like a villain.

"Out," I said with a laugh.

"Girls are weird," he said as I pushed on his back.

"We totally are. You're okay to drive home?"

"Sure, I only had a few sips. Are you seriously kicking me out?"

"It had nothing to do with the kissing."

"I should hope not. That was some damn fine kissing."

"Agreed." I nodded. "It's just a lot to process, all in one night."

"What do you mean?" he asked, looking at me carefully.

"I mean, we had this amazing day with your family. You won

me a bear. You gave me the best first kiss of my entire life. It's a lot to think about. And believe me, I'm thinking about it. And when I'm in bed in about ten minutes, I'm going to choose to remember *those* parts, and mentally skip right over the scene with your ex."

"Ahhhh," he sighed, understanding.

"Ahhh is right. I just . . . I've been thinking about you, and us, in that way, for awhile now I guess. And I want my own night." I covered my face. "Does that make any sense at all?"

"It actually does, a little bit," he replied, taking my hands away from my face and holding them in his own. "You think I came here tonight because of Julie?"

"Didn't you? A little bit?"

"I came here to see you, Chloe. That's it," he said, pulling me against his chest and wrapping his arms around me. "My head was messed up tonight, sure. But not that messed up."

"It was a great day, Lucas. Thank you," I whispered into his shirt. I might have to steal this one from him, too. Finally, I pulled out of his arms and pushed him toward the front steps.

He stopped in the driveway and turned around. "The best first kiss of your life?" he asked, his eyes all a-twinkle.

"Oh, yeah," I said with a grin, and he took one step forward. "Uh-uh, no more."

"Just *one* more?"

"Turn. It. Around," I insisted, stepping back inside. "Call me tomorrow?" I asked, peeking around the door as I closed it.

"You can count on it."

# chapter thirteen

The next day was a blur. When Lucas finally left the night before, the memory of that kiss, and those lovely kisses that followed, lingered on my lips like a ghost of something incredible. There was more passion, more promise in that kiss than I had ever experienced in my entire relationship with Charles. And I couldn't get it out of my mind.

Of course part of me wished that I'd asked him to stay, and I'm pretty sure he would have. But he also seemed to understand why I'd stopped him, why I needed to make sure that when this finally happened, we were both in the clear. Just Lucas and Chloe, rather than Lucas and Chloe and Julie.

I kept myself busy, and not just with daydreams of a ginger vet with lips to die for. I played with the dogs, I organized invoices, I ordered some new supplies, I kept busy. And I daydreamed. Oh boy, did I daydream.

Lucas was pulling a double shift at the hospital, but he'd texted and asked if he could come by after work. Who was I to say no to that?

The day went on like so many do, unremarkable. I focused

on things like making sure there was a bottle of wine in the fridge, that there were tiny umbrellas stocked behind the tiki bar in case we wanted to try our hand at a new cocktail, that his favorite kind of tortilla chips were in the pantry. That any unruly hair south of the Mason-Dixon line had been dealt with.

Then late in the day, after dinner, I got a strange call from a frantic woman on the Our Gang line. Her thick accent coupled with her crying made it difficult to understand what she was saying at first, but it soon became clear what she was reporting. She'd seen one of the Our Gang flyers in town. She needed help, but had been too afraid to reach out before. She knew a guy who was involved in dog fighting, but until she'd visited the site herself, and actually saw the condition of the dogs and where they were being kept, she hadn't felt moved to action. Until now. She gave me an address, several times, of a compound on the outskirts of town where she said they were keeping fight dogs, pit bulls. The guy who was in charge of the dogs was headed out of town for a few days, and the dogs would be alone. Unprotected.

I instantly hung up the phone, got in the car, and headed out.

I should have known better than to go pick up a dog alone on an anonymous tip, but the woman sounded so desperate on the phone that I didn't want to waste any time.

*Call Lucas. Don't be a fool; call Lucas.*

But I didn't. And when I walked into that shed and saw those dogs, I knew I was in way over my head.

I counted eleven dogs, all mixed breeds and pit bulls. Chained to boxes or posts, with no food and barely any water. And the smell. I had to cover my nose against the filth they were living in. And *not* living in—because although I tried my best not to see it, there were two that hadn't made it.

The fighting ring was built into the wall in the back. Built high, with—oh my God—seats all around. People would watch as these dogs fought, sometimes to the death.

First thing I did? I called the police. The next thing I did? I called Lou, who told me to wait in the car and he'd call animal control. I was on my way back outside to wait until the authorities arrived . . . but then I heard it. The dogs were so riled up, barking so loud, that I almost didn't . . . but there it was again. A whimper.

I moved toward the ring, closer and closer, my feet moving without my brain because I knew I shouldn't be there, knew I should wait for help, knew that I wasn't ready for something like this . . . and there it was.

Lying on his side, torn, shredded, was a blue-gray pit. Breathing shallow, blood . . . so much blood. Eyes mostly rolled back, but still aware.

Without knowing what I was doing or a thought to the consequences, I climbed over the plywood railing, landing next to the dog. He was in such bad shape that he didn't even flinch, which meant he needed help fast.

Tearing my sweatshirt off, I wrapped him as best I could, and struggled to lift him. As he whimpered once more I began to talk to him, and to myself. "Okay, buddy, let's get you some help, okay? Come on, sweet boy, let's get you out of here."

He weighed at least fifty pounds, and as carefully as I tried to balance him in my arms, he slipped a few times, making me readjust my carry. He whimpered each time, and it was taking everything I had not to lose it.

I kept talking to him as I moved through the warehouse, not seeing the blood trickle down onto my legs or seep into my tank top, not seeing the other dogs that were still barking and pulling at their chains. I kept my eyes on the eyes staring back at me.

I was undoubtedly hurting him—didn't they always say when someone is really hurt, don't move him? But I couldn't help it; I couldn't leave him there. I needed to do something, anything.

I could hear the sirens approaching as I made it out to my car. I knew the other dogs would be okay, and I'd be at animal control the very next morning lobbying for every single one of them—the ones that were still alive—and I'd bring all of them back to my ranch.

But right now I had this guy in my arms, and I was going to take care of him myself. Not even bothering with the cage, I managed to get the SUV's front passenger door open and pull a blanket from the backseat. Setting him down carefully, still wrapped in my sweatshirt, I made him as comfortable as I could, and then I drove like a bat out of hell for the Campbell Veterinary Hospital.

Five minutes before we got there, he stopped whimpering. One minute before I pulled in, he stopped breathing. Screeching into the parking lot, I pounded on my horn, taking up the two emergency spots by the entrance. Miguel saw me through the glass door and immediately ran out to help.

"Get Lucas! Right now!" I yelled, running around to the passenger side.

"Do you need some help with—"

"Just get him!" I leaned across the dog, who still wasn't breathing. I tried shaking his collar, to get a reaction—nothing. Just limp. "Come on, come on, sweet boy, we're *here*."

I picked him up like he weighed nothing and ran into the waiting room, searching, looking for . . . there he was, coming out of the back room with Miguel hot on his heels. His face went white when he saw me, wild, covered in blood and shit and now tears, because he wasn't fucking *breathing* anymore!

"Chloe, what happened to you—"

"Lucas, you need to do something, you need to do something! I can't, he can't, you need to do something, he's not—" I rambled, tripping over my words as I held the dog close.

"Miguel, tell them to set up in the OR and clear exam one. And tell my father to meet us in there," Lucas directed, guiding me toward the exam room. He slipped his hands under the dog's head, cradling him as he took him from me and laid him on the table.

"He was . . . there was this compound . . . outside of town . . . and I got this call and . . . so many dogs . . . and then I heard . . . in a ring . . . and he was crying, and I got him . . . I got him out . . . but then he . . . he stopped—"

"Honey, I need you to breathe, okay? You did so well, but I need to listen to this guy now, okay? Shhh, Chlo, shhh. You did great," Lucas said, his voice soothing, moving swiftly around the table, talking fast now to Miguel. My sticky hands clenched open and closed as I watched Lucas begin to do CPR, listening to his chest, trying to clean off some of the blood. Bite marks, gash marks, all along his flank, the side of his mouth was torn, and . . .

Marge was pushing me down into a chair, handing me a Dixie cup as I watched them wheeling the dog down the hall, Lucas and Miguel and his father. They disappeared behind a swinging door into a room where there was a stainless steel table and some bright lights and instruments and . . .

I threw up all over my shoes.

"Oh, sugar," Marge murmured, and handed me a towel. I wiped off my mouth, and she held me against her. And we waited.


Blunt-force trauma to the head. Heavy blood loss and internal hemorrhaging. Multisystem failure. Dead.

I stayed until they finished working him over. I stayed while Lucas and his father filled out a report to file with animal control. I stayed while Lucas finished up the last little bit of his shift—and then I stayed the hell away from my SUV. Even walking by it with Lucas guiding me through the parking lot, I saw the crazy parking job, the bloodstained blanket on the passenger side, and I let his hand in the small of my back tell me where to go. His truck. My house.

He kept up a steady stream of words for a while, words like *you did all you could,* and *you did so much more than most, blah blah blah.* About halfway up the hill, he stopped talking and let the silence soothe.

I'd cried myself out; now I just felt numb. I plodded up the walkway, Lucas behind me, then beside me as he unlocked the door and held it open. I went straight to the bar, poured myself a long shot of something brown, and knocked it straight back. It burned, it *really* burned, but after the second shot my fingers and toes started to tingle, then warm. Lucas stood on the other side of the bar, just watching.

"You did great tonight, Chloe. You know that?"

"I don't want to talk about it," I mumbled, looking down, noticing for the first time how disgusting I was. I was covered in . . . stuff. "Jesus, look at me. You too." His scrubs were also covered in . . . stuff.

"Comes with the territory," he said quietly, looking me in the eyes.

"Yeah, well, I don't like this territory." Tears welled up again.

"You should get cleaned up," he said. He was right.

"So should you."

"I've got clean clothes in the truck. I'm fine."

"Good, then you can put them on after you take a shower.

Guest bath, down the hall. Towels in the closet." I pointed, and shuffled down the hall to my room.

Satisfied he was doing as I asked, I headed into my bathroom and closed the door. Stripping down, I wrapped everything in an old towel and set it outside the door. I was throwing everything away, including my shoes. Everything.

Turning the water as hot as it would go, I stepped under the spray and steeped for what seemed like hours. My muscles were bunched and tightened; I was tense and felt stretched out like a rubber band. I just let the heat pound down all around me, looking until the water was no longer stained pink. Then I scrubbed until I was squeaky clean.

I climbed out and wrapped myself in my soft robe, shoving my wet hair back. I felt better because I was cleaner, but I still felt ready to come out of my skin. I paced in a circle in my bathroom. I thought about Lucas' face when I came into the clinic.

Before the clinician kicked in, he'd been terrified. Because he thought I was hurt? I thought about how I must have looked, half covered in blood, half out of my mind. He was worried about *me*, about what might have happened to *me*.

And then watching him, his tender care for the dog, the purpose of every action, the utter command he had of the situation. He was incredible. And, he was leaving. In a little over a day. For twelve weeks.

Hot tears came again, running down my cheeks. My nights and weekends were leaving. And who was I kidding? My days too.

I paced faster, wrapping my arms around myself, then swinging them wildly. I was antsy, I was angry, I was frustrated, I was empty, I was . . . aching. Literally aching. I needed. I wanted.

I left my room, went down the hall, heard the water still running in the guest bath, and opened the door without thought. I could see his shape through the glass door, foggy and fuzzy but there, just on the other side of the glass and steam.

Had I taken even half a moment to stop and think about what I was about to do, I would have stopped. I would have backed away, put on my pajamas, made some coffee, and been waiting with toast when he came out.

I slipped out of my robe, opened the glass door, and moved in behind him.

"Chloe," he said. It came out rough and low and heated. He was facing away from me, his head tilted down, arms stretching out to press against the wall.

I reached out with one hand, brushing lightly with my fingertips, and ran it along his spine. His back was strong and muscled, muscles that shifted under his skin as I touched him. Freckles on his shoulders, a tiny scar on his left side just above his narrow waist. I kissed it, and he groaned. "Chloe," he repeated, his hands now curling into fists as his entire body thrummed with tension.

"Yes," I replied. He turned slowly, water dripping down through his gorgeous hair, his eyes burning as they traveled over my naked body. I didn't flinch under his gaze; his stare made me bold, and I arched my back and let him look.

"You don't need to do this," he said, looking for any sign of me backing away or changing my mind.

"You're wrong," I murmured, stepping into the spray, stepping into him, pressing my chest against his and burying my hands in the back of his head. "I absolutely need to do this."

As my lips neared his, I met his eyes, his gaze heating me through and telling me that yes, this was absolutely the *best* idea ever. I knew I could sneak a kiss, pretend to be confused because of the emotions of the evening, and he'd let me get away with it. I knew this would complicate things; I knew this would make it impossible to go back to what we had before. But I didn't want what we had before. I wanted, hell, I *needed* more. I instinctively ran in the opposite direction, and brought his mouth to mine.

Soft, incredibly soft lips brushed against mine once, twice, and then again. I sighed into his mouth as his hands settled on my hips. I could kiss this man for a year. He stepped between my legs, pushing me toward the back of the shower, and I moaned against his lips, feeling the length of his body pressing into mine as I twisted to feel more of him, needing as many points of contact as I could get.

I delighted in the feel of lips on mine, his mouth teasing at my own as my hands roamed in his hair. "Do you have any idea," I said as our kiss broke and he tilted my head back to press his mouth against my neck, "how much I love your hair? I never told you, but gingers make me crazy." I groaned as he sucked at the skin below my ear. "The second I saw you, I thought, this is the sexiest man I have ever seen." I pressed wet kisses against his collarbone.

He ran his hands up and down my back. "The first time I saw you, at that restaurant, I knew I wanted to see you naked. As soon as possible."

"And here I am," I murmured, stepping back so he could take a good look. "Naked."

His eyes smoldered as his gaze swept across my body. "Chloe," he whispered. "You're perfection."

I purred, I actually purred, dragging my hands down his torso, over the defined muscles in his chest, the tiny little hairs that gathered there. Letting my gaze follow my hands, I decided to sneak a peek as well. "Mmm, and you're—holy sweet fuck, are you *kidding* me?"

Here's the thing about an enormous penis. They don't just

live in romance novels. They don't just live on famous actors, although John Hamm and Michael Fassbender need to admit a certain ginger vet into their Big Cock Club. They're real. And they're out there. Right here, even, in my guest shower.

For every peanut, there is an **eggplant**. For every Charles, there is a **Lucas**. And since I'd had one, I feel I deserved the **other**.

My *"Holy sweet fuck, are you* kidding *me?"* still ricocheted off the tiles, bouncing off his shocked face.

"Pardon me?" he finally said, his hands frozen on my hips, his lips still halfway down my neck.

"Sorry. Actually, *not* sorry. Actually, congratulations." I pointed down. "This is kind of amazing."

He threw his head back and laughed out loud. "My dick is amazing?"

"Oh, please, like you don't know. You're bigger than a breadbox!"

"Baby's arm."

"Huh?"

"Bigger than a baby's arm, that's the phrase."

"That's gross! What does that have to do with a—stop laughing at me!"

He didn't stop laughing, but he did start kissing my neck again. Which normally would have been enough to make me surrender to the sizzle running wild through my veins, but I literally couldn't take my eyes off it . . . er . . . him.

"I don't even think that'll fit," I said.

"Oh, it'll fit," he murmured, then pulled away. "Wait—are we . . . talking about . . . fitting?"

"If you think we can. Seriously, Lucas—you're *huge*."

"Seriously, Chloe, you're awesome. Will you walk around behind me with a megaphone from now on?"

"Quiet, you," I said, bringing him back to my mouth for another searing kiss. Every single thought went out of my head, which was filled up instantly with Lucas. Here. Now. Hot and heavy and wanting.

I focused on this moment, this gorgeous man and his delightful tongue that was thrusting inside my mouth, mating with mine and making my breath come even more quickly.

My mouth opened wider, trying to bring as much of him inside me as I could. My urgency was matched by his own, his hands pressing into my skin, strong and sure, each finger on a different part of my spine, nails embedded, fiery and wicked strong. I broke the kiss just so I could breathe, only to be sucked back down in another wave of need, stronger than the last.

"Need you, need to see you," he murmured into my hair, picking me up roughly and setting me down on the ledge at the end of the shower, knocking shampoo bottles left and right. Dropping to his knees on the tile, he kissed a path down my collarbone, down the center of my torso, hands now reaching out, surrounding me, cupping my breasts and kneading my wet skin. His mouth closed around my nipple, sucking hard and fast, his tongue rolling in a way that made me alternately slap at the wall and push deeper into his mouth.

"Lucas. Oh. Lucas. Oh. Lucas," I chanted, my hips beginning to roll in concert with his tongue. He released my breast to bring another punishing kiss to my mouth, still tasting of coconut rum, passion running wild now. He pulled my hair to bring my face up, looking deep into my eyes. His face was full of lust. Longing. Lust. Frustration. Lots of lust.

"What are you thinking about?" I asked, my voice throaty, filled with that same lust.

"You really want to know?"

I placed my feet on either side of him, using my knees to

cage him in and coax him further into me. "Tell me. What are you thinking about right now?"

Lucas stared hard at me, then knelt on the shower floor. He kissed my tummy, let his tongue trace a circle around my belly button. Hands once more touched my skin, his knuckles trailing up the backs of my legs. I leaned forward on the ledge, mimicking his movements with my own hands, tracing little patterns across his cheekbones, pausing to touch the indent above his upper lip, stealing a kiss on my fingertips as his mouth chased me a bit. I let him catch my thumb between his teeth, nipping at me as I let out a soft gasp. Even the air was frantic, charged with the excitement you feel at the very beginning of something. You don't know quite what it is yet, what it might turn into. But you're aware of the epic.

"You want to know what I'm thinking? Right this very second?" he asked as I put both hands on the back of his neck once more, trying to pull him back into my orbit.

"Uh-huh," I murmured, watching as his hands moved farther up my legs, dancing across the tops of my knees.

"It's a little bit dirty," he replied, leaning down to press one wet kiss against my left kneecap.

"I've never really had the dirty," I admitted, my mind flashing to missionary after missionary with Charles. I blushed a bit under Lucas' stare, but held it. I was done with timid. I wanted to try tiger.

He pulled me even farther down on the ledge, toward where he was kneeling. "Still want to know," he asked, wrapping one of my legs around him, "what I'm thinking about?" He wrapped the other leg around him, his hands moving even higher, digging into my thighs.

"I think so?"

"You think?" he asked, raising an eyebrow. He leaned up

again, nuzzling at my neck, just below my ear. His tongue darted out just the tiniest bit to lick at the skin below.

I shivered in the very best of ways and nodded yes. What his mouth was doing to my ear might be illegal. And I wanted it.

"What I'm thinking about right now is the same thing I've been thinking about since you showed up in this town, blushing in that mirror over the bar." He moved to my left ear, his right fingertips now tickling the inside of my thigh. "How you look spread out for me, naked and pink."

I gasped, and he bit the side of my neck hard enough to leave a mark. He continued, now scraping his teeth lightly down towards my collarbone. "I'm thinking about your tits, how gorgeous they are, and how they'll look when I'm fucking them."

He buried his face in my skin, sweeping kisses across my breasts once more. His fingertips teased and taunted my nipples, which stiffened at his touch. "But, Miss Thinks She Wants It Dirty, what I'm dying to know"—he reached down below, grasping the inside of my thigh and pushing it open wider, higher around his waist—"is what your pussy will taste like the second before you come."

Lucas totally brought the dirty.

He pushed me back against the wall and settled between my knees, scooping his hands under my bottom and pulling me to the very edge of the ledge. Instinctively, I closed my knees. Instinctively, he spread them wide. I gasped as he licked his lips. I gasped as he blew the tiniest puff of breath across my naked skin.

"Look at you," he said, his voice husky and thick. And I gasped when that honey tongue licked my skin, and gasped again when a deep groan came from the back of his throat.

He nuzzled into the crease at the top of my thigh, licking the skin there and teasing me with little sweeps of his tongue, flicks and flutters. I could feel his nose prodding at me, inhaling me deep as I tangled my hands in his hair, holding him exactly where I wanted him. I moaned when his hands teased me apart, opening me further to him. One finger, then two, dipped down and gently eased inside, then began thrusting. My back nearly bowed in half, the assault of sensation running wild through my body. No one, *no* one, had ever played my body the way he was, and he was just getting started.

His lips surrounded me, kissing and licking, my cries bouncing off the wet tile, water still raining down on his back, as he buried his face in between my thighs. I ran my hands down that very back, leaning over him, arching, finally leaning back again against the wall, my fingers tucked into that hair, holding him. I shivered and moaned. I shook and groaned. Words began to pour forth from my mouth, words that I'd never said out loud before; detailed, wicked words. Then he finally pressed his tongue exactly where I needed him to.

"Fuuuuccckkk," I groaned, eyes closing against the terribly wonderful pressure building within.

"There's my dirty girl," he whispered—and sucked my clit into his mouth. My eyes shot open, every muscle in my body tensing. With his fingers thrusting inside, and a mouthful of me, I came so hard that I shook, my hands still in his hair, my mouth open in a silent scream. And when color came back into the world, he did it again, his free hand anchoring my hip as I thrashed and crashed and came apart.

But he wasn't done with me. Before I could gasp thanks for the awesome, he wrapped my legs around his waist, stood with me, turned, and sat down on the ledge I'd just been perched on. Leaning in, he kissed me deep, and I shivered at the naughty that was all over his mouth. "So now I know," he whispered into my ear, his voice gravelly and deep and full of wicked.

"You know what?" I sighed, boneless and punchy from the sizzle still coursing through my veins.

"What you taste like a second before you come." He nipped at my ear and I squealed, nuzzling further into his neck.

"That was beyond," I murmured into his skin. "Insane. Ridiculous," taking the opportunity to give some tiny kisses of my own. "Ring a ding ding," I purred as I continued to kiss along the side of his neck, his collarbone, down across his shoulder. He shifted as I rose up a bit higher on my knees, resting my hands behind his neck as he wrapped his hands around my hips. Which brought his Something Enormous in direct contact with my Still Tingling.

"Still think you'll fit?" I asked.

"Hmm?" His voice was somewhat muffled by my left breast, which he was currently torturing with his tongue. If you defined the word as meaning exquisite and earth shattering.

"*This*," I repeated, bouncing down a bit to illuminate. "Now that I'm all warmed up?"

"You sure about that?" he asked, raising his head to look at me. And something else was rising once more. Not that it had ever really—

"Mm-hmm," I nodded, sliding against him, feeling how hard he was against my soft. And just like that, he picked me up, holding me close to his chest, legs still wrapped around, and we were out of the shower. Grabbing his bag off the counter, he carried me down the hall to my room, leaving big, wet footprints on the floor.

"Be careful! Don't slip—ahhh!" I squealed, as he took a corner too quickly and bumped off the wall like a pinball.

"Oh, Christ, Chloe, do that again," he groaned, hustling down the hallway.

"This?" I laughed, bouncing again.

"I need to be inside you. Now," he growled as we tangled around each other, very close and slippery.

Tossing me onto the bed, he searched his bag, coming up with a package of condoms.

"Prepared, aren't you?" I asked, quirking an eyebrow at him.

"Chickie baby, I'm like a Boy Scout," he said, grabbing one. Then grabbing a second one.

I squealed once more when he pulled me down on the bed, bringing me back into his lap and settling me on his thighs. I watched, eyes wide, as he tore the packet open and rolled on the condom. If it was possible for my eyes to widen further, they did. It really was an impressive sight. I looked up, smiled at his sweet face, and then leaned in and kissed him. And once more, every sense I had was filled with him.

I saw golden skin and glacier-blue eyes. I heard the rumble in the back of his throat as his tongue tangled with mine. I felt the heat of his skin, the strong muscles in his shoulders and arms. I smelled the salt and the woods and the surf inherent in his California DNA. And I tasted? Me. Mixed with mai tai.

"Go slow, okay?" I breathed as I raised my hips. I could feel him as he pressed himself just barely inside.

"Spread your legs a little more—just like that," he murmured, his hands now on my hips. Our eyes met as he pushed up, and I sank down. Slow. Sweet. Solid.

And oh my, did he fit.

Once he was seated fully inside my body, I let my weight go, closing my eyes and sinking further onto my knees, feeling the sweet burn of being filled so completely. *Ohhh.*

When I opened them once more, his face was gloriously tense. His jaw was tight, his cheeks flushed, his eyes wild. I cupped his face gently as he leaned into my palm.

"It's good, right?" he sighed, arching his back slightly and gaining somehow one more scrap of space.

"Mm-hmm," I said, rocking slowly backward just once and gasping at the sensation. He was big, full, and thick, and exactly what I needed.

"Please do that again," he asked, and a small smile crept over my face. Doing as I was told, I rocked forward, the movement creating a delightful friction where our bodies were connected, and just above. His hands still held my hips, twisting my body just enough to make it more than good.

"You feel unreal." He groaned as I tilted my head back, rocking a little faster this time. He thrust up as I rocked, and if it was even possible, he hardened even more.

"*This* feels unreal," I said, shaking a little at the sensation of having him inside me, thick and beautiful. "This whole thing feels unreal."

"Chloe," he whispered, and my name on his lips, while he was inside my body, was the sexiest thing I'd ever heard. His eyes searched mine, primal, wanting, needing . . .

"Lucas," I whispered back. And then he was moving, and I was grinding, and he was circling his hips in a way that was nudging something new inside, and it made me a little crazy. He kissed me, hard, and pressed my hips back a bit. I looked down, and could see him sinking into me again and again, and just like that . . . I came. Again.

I fell forward onto him, into him, weightless, useless, I was so wracked with sweet, beautiful bliss. His hands grew more rough on my hips, taking what he needed, using my body for his pleasure, and oh my God, was that a fantastic thing to witness. I watched as his eyes grew hazy with lust. His thrusting became more pronounced, his groans deeper and more guttural, and with every muscle and tendon in his body tense, he came. "Fuck. Fuck. Fuck," he said, his voice almost a whisper as he exhaled, collapsing into me as I held him to my breast. I clutched at him, running my fingers through his hair and sighing.

He fell backward onto the bed and I went with him, giggling and laughing, laying atop him, feeling his body under mine as our breathing slowed and steadied. He kissed me once more, slow and deep. Sweet. Breaking the kiss, we stared at each other a bit, eyes searching.

And then he tilted his head to one side and gave me that killer half grin. "We should totally have pancakes for dinner."

I looked at the bedside clock. "It's after midnight, Lucas. We're way past dinner."

"Then we should totally have midnight snack pancakes."

"You don't know how to make pancakes," I pointed out.

"You're really not getting it, are you?"

"Am I supposed to make *you* pancakes?"

"That's a great idea!" he said, mock surprise on his face as he ran his hand smoothly over my bottom, then gave it a little spank.

"Oh!"

"I knew you were a dirty girl," he laughed.

Pancakes. Not the worst idea.


At 2:17 A.M., I attempted to make pancakes. At 2:19 A.M., I banished Lucas to an orange leatherette bar stool at the other end of the island because he was handsy, and I went through five eggs trying to get just one in the bowl without shells everywhere. So pointing my whisk, away we went to the safe side of the kitchen where I could cook and he could watch. And watch he did. I could feel his eyes on me now as I poured batter into neat little rounds on the griddle. I snuck a peek or two myself. Clad in those broken-down jeans and his T-shirt, no shoes, no socks, Lucas looked rumpled. Sexy. And well ridden. And I should know.

We'd had the sex. And it was amazing. But already I was beginning to wonder what this meant. Where was this going? What would happen to the easy, breezy way we had with each other now? And what was going to happen when he left the country, in like, hours?

"What's on your mind?" he asked, breaking me from my stupor.

"Hmm?" I looked at him, confused.

"You just went somewhere. Where'd you go?"

"Sorry, just thinking. Will you pour some orange juice?"

"Am I allowed to leave my chair?" he asked, and I grinned at him.

"If you can behave, then yes. Only for juice, though. Then it's back to your post." I flipped the first round of pancakes over on the griddle, then took the opportunity to watch *him* as he moved with a quiet grace around the kitchen. He knew that the metallic tumblers in the far cupboard would keep the orange juice icy cold all through the meal, knew the orange juice was in the door of the fridge instead of the back—he was well acquainted with my kitchen.

And not just the kitchen. As I watched him open the carton, those long elegant fingers reminded me of everything he'd done to my body only minutes before. How careful and strong and sure they were, whether coaxing toe-curling orgasms from me, or tenderly sweeping a piece of hair back from my face so he could sneak a kiss.

Back on his stool, orange juice poured, his eyes returned to me once more. I deflected. "How many?" I asked, pointing to the griddle.

"As many as I'm allowed to have," he said seriously, and I looked over my shoulder at him. He already held his knife and fork in hand. "And if they taste as good as they look, I may have to eat yours too."

"No way, mister, I'm starving." I flipped the pancakes onto two plates, then covered said pancakes with butter and syrup. "Start with these, and if you're still hungry I'll make you more."

"Oh, I'll still be hungry," he murmured, getting that same look on his face he had earlier. I crossed to him, setting his plate down before him and neatly sidestepping his roaming hands. I needed a few moments to process what we'd just done. I'd take those moments while filling myself up with pancakes.

"So good in my mouth," he said around a mouthful, beaming.

I couldn't help but giggle. "My mom's recipe. She didn't make them as much as I got older; too much sugar, you know. But when I was little, every Sunday morning she'd make pancakes. Then I got hips, and oatmeal and fruit became my breakfast." I stabbed up a gooey forkful, dripping with butter and syrup.

"Wait, what do hips have to do with pancakes?" he asked, really not understanding at all.

"Pageant girl, remember? Everything was about caloric intake. How many were coming in, and how many was I burning off," I explained, giving my hip a squeeze, something I couldn't have done even two months ago. "I've gained at least ten pounds since I've moved up here, thanks in part to the pudding hoard in there."

"That's crazy," he said, shaking his head.

"You've seen the pudding."

"No I mean, the whole girls-not-having-hips thing. You're *supposed* to have hips. That's all there is to it. Otherwise, what would we boys have to hang on to?" he said, winking at me over his pancake.

"So it's an evolutionary thing? Hips exist solely for your hands?" I asked, remembering exactly the way he'd done just that, holding my hips, pushing and pulling me back and forth on top of him. I blushed at the very recent memory.

"I'm a doctor, Chloe. I know what I'm talking about," he said very seriously.

"So I should defer to you on this one, should I?" I laughed, getting up to make some more pancakes.

"You should. All my patients do."

"Well, if the poodles trust you, I suppose I should too." I grabbed the mixing bowl and gave it another whisk as he chased one last bite around his plate. And as I watched him, I realized that this, *this* very thing, was what I wanted to do for the foreseeable future. Walk around my kitchen in one of his shirts, bare beneath, cooking for him while he watched me do it. Talk about poodles and hips and all manner of things. I was struck by the simplicity of it all; how easy and how perfect it was. And I smiled at him. "You want some more?"

"If it's not too much trouble," he said.

"Lucas?"

"Yep?"

"You gave me three orgasms in less than thirty minutes. Pretty sure that justifies a few more pancakes, don't you think?"

His face was pure male satisfaction, with a hint of mischief. "Are you having any more?"

"Three was pretty fantastic," I chuckled, ladling a few more circles on the griddle. Warm hands suddenly slipped around my waist from behind, pulling me snugly back against him. His hands found my shirt buttons and started unbuttoning them one at a time.

"Hey, I can't be naked and cook you pancakes," I protested, slapping at his hands. If by protested you mean using the least amount of energy to remove those gorgeous hands from my still humming body, then protest I did.

"You sure about that?" he whispered all hot and bothered in my ear.

"I'm gonna burn your pancakes," I warned.

"I'm gonna watch you burn my pancakes," he warned back, now sweeping my hair up and kissing my shoulders.

"I'm gonna hit you with this whisk," I threatened.

"I'm gonna bend you over this counter."

Pancakes were burned. An orange Formica counter was defiled.

"**A**m I hurting you?"

"Depends. Can you feel me breathing?"

"I think so."

"Then I'm good."

"I'd say you were more than good."

"Well, of course you'd say it. You're still inside me."

"Dirty girl."

"I'm not, though. Seriously, this is so unlike me."

"Apparently not."

"According to my track record, it is *very* unlike me. Official Chloe never gets to have sex in the kitchen."

"Well, I don't know who this official Chloe is, but I'm enjoying the shit out of *un*official Chloe." Lucas punctuated this sentence with a kiss in the middle of my back. I was facedown on the counter, my shirt up around my shoulders. He had, in fact, bent me over the counter. And he had made it so very good. He was slumped across me, resting most of his weight on me, and I felt covered, cuddly, and content.

"Midnight-snack pancakes are my new favorite meal," he murmured from somewhere just above my bum.

"Quarter-to-three pancakes, if you want to get technical," I giggled, stretching my arms over my head and lengthening my spine.

"Isn't that a song?"

"There's a song called quarter-to-three pancakes?"

"Quarter to three," he sang under this breath, "There's no one in the place, except, you and me . . ." He placed a kiss in exactly the small of my back. ". . . and pancakes . . ."

"Oh, man." I laughed, harder still when he bit me on the bottom. Quarter to three, what a long day this had been. Wait, it was tomorrow already. Which meant that he was leaving . . . Fudge. He was leaving for Belize the next day. For three months.

And that's why we'd decided not to start anything. Well, there goes that bright idea. I moved a bit, just enough that he got the hint and stood up, pulling me with him. I hastened to pull my shirt down, my skin still flushed with the excitement he'd coaxed forth.

He sensed the change, and caught my hand. "Hey."

"Hey," I answered, resisting the pull for a second. But one look at that messy hair and I fell against his chest. There was no frenzy, no frantic now. I rested my head on him as he leaned against the counter, running his hands up and down my spine. I listened to him breathing, and even though it seemed blasphemous in the face of what had just happened, all I could think about was how I used to fall asleep to Charles' sounds. First deep sighs as he settled in. Then tiny quick breaths as he found the best spot on the pillow. Then finally the slow, lingering exhales as he'd begin to nod off. And when I knew he was asleep, that's when I'd nod off.

It's funny that when something is over, it's not just the big occasions, like anniversaries and birthdays, that bring up emotions. It's also the little things. The shows recorded on the DVR that he loved to binge watch. It's the sandwiches cut in triangles, never in half. It's the breathing patterns you know so well you can tell the instant they begin to dream.

When I'd started this new life in Monterey, one of the things I'd looked forward to most of all was being patternless. For the first time in my life, I *could* be patternless. Untethered. No one would know when I came and went, no one would know or critique what I ate for breakfast. No one would know if I peed with the bathroom door open or closed. The answer is closed, by the way.

The thing is, Lucas *did* know. He knew when I came and went, he knew what time I usually woke up because of the dogs. He knew what I liked for breakfast, he knew where the backup chocolate pudding hoard was stashed, he knew what it meant when Dino was on the hi-fi instead of Sinatra (that I was extra tired), and he knew that I always peed with the door closed. Because my God . . . who would pee with the door open?

I might have come here patternless, but I had set down roots almost immediately. I could see myself living here forever. Without knowing I was doing it, I'd tethered myself to the one man in town who knew what it was like to have his heart broken by the woman he loved. Though we'd joked about rebounding, that's not what had happened.

I might love this particular tether. And he was leaving in less then twenty-four hours. And he'd be gone for twelve weeks. Which in the grand scheme of things? Was nothing. One grain of sand in the huge hourglass in the sky. But as the woman currently wrapped around this big piece of wonderful, I *wanted* these new patterns. I wanted to learn whether he wanted his love every night before sleep, or if he was the kind of guy who'd wake up needing me. Did he shower in the morning, or after work? But . . . maybe it wasn't such a good idea to talk about this right before his trip.

After all, we'd just gotten out of long-term relationships. And everyone says that your rebound is the guy you mess around with, have a great time with, before meeting the next *real* relationship. Could two rebounds cancel each other out? Or would they be double disaster?

I cuddled up to Lucas, his warm arms wrapped solidly around me, and we breathed together. And before I knew it, the rhythmic rise and fall of his chest lulled me out of my head and into a slow, drowsy peace.

"Should I go?" he asked, his voice low and molasses thick.

"You better not," I warned, burrowing deeper into his arms. And those arms picked me up, and carried me to bed.

He tugged the sheets back with me still clinging to him, pressing my nose into his shoulder, inhaling deeply. "You smell amazing, you know that?"

"I'm surprised, considering I didn't get to finish my shower." He chuckled, trying to set me down, but I didn't want to let him go. He gave in, slipping under the covers with me and turning the light off. I craved him, craved his scent and his touch, and I continued to run my hands along his skin, dancing kiss after kiss along his shoulder as I wrapped myself around him once more. Had it really been so long that I'd been without contact like this? Was I just skin drunk?

Nah. I was Lucas drunk. He was the perfect cocktail.

I yawned, and it almost took my head off. "I'm so tired, but I kind of don't want to close my eyes."

He pressed a kiss to my forehead. "You thinking about tomorrow?"

"Yes." I laid my head on his chest, listening to his heartbeat. It was literally like a lullaby. "I forgot to tell you—on the news, I saw something terrible about Belize."

"You did?"

"Yes. It sank."

"Oh, really?"

"Yeah. I'm surprised you didn't know that."

"Chloe?"

"Hmm?"

"Belize isn't an island."

"It broke off first and then it sank."

"You're right. I *am* surprised I didn't catch that on the news."

"I guess you better stay stateside, then." I sighed, snaking my leg over his.

"Can't do that."

"I know."

We both sighed.

But it was naked sighing, so there's that.

There's something to be said for being the little spoon. You're tucked in, you're cozy, you're warm and content. Someone is wrapped around you all night, not protecting you, necessarily, but if a zombie were to come in through the window, the chances are the big spoon gets it first, right?

Charles always liked to *be* spooned, but he didn't like to be the spooner. Lucas was a great spooner. When I woke up the next morning, I had one giant hand nestled against my belly, the other curled around my shoulder and casually wrapped around one lucky breast. I'd slept like a rock and woke up with a smile on my face. My body felt rested, yet sore in a way it hadn't in a long time. Or really, never had been. Not quite this way.

I turned in his arms, snuggling into his warm chest, and let my eyes linger on the face I knew so well: the dip above his lip, the long, dark lashes that no boy should ever get to have, the sprinkling of freckles across his nose, that thoroughly messed-up hair. He rocked the bed head, that's for sure. I blushed slightly as I remembered how those silky strands felt between my fingertips as he pushed into me that first time.

*"Oh, it'll fit," he murmured.*

I bit my lip, a pumpkin grin spreading across my face. Cautiously, I reached out to touch his face. His sleeping gave me the courage to drink him in, explore every contour and nuance of his face without getting caught doing so. I feathered my fingertips across his cheekbone, down to his strong jaw, showing the beginning of a light beard. I ghosted across his eyebrows, his closed eyelids, taking in the palest of lavender veins. His eyes moved under my fingers; was he dreaming? What was he dreaming about? I'd love to know.

I ran my fingers across his sweet lips, lips that I now knew were capable of kissing me like no one else ever had. No one had even come close. Also very capable at the dirty talk, something I'd had no idea I'd respond to. Oh, my, I responded.

*"There's my dirty girl," he whispered.*

I blushed once more thinking about those lips all over my skin, his soft sighs and quiet groans as he urged me on, telling me what he liked and what he loved about my body.

I listened to his heartbeat again.

*Tha-wump. Tha-wump. Tha-wump.*

As I listened, my brain got involved and changed it to:

*Re-bound. Re-bound. Re-bound.*

Ugh. I thought about what we'd said last night about the sex changing things, meaning the friendship. Which was more important? Neither us could afford to get hurt again. But this now meant too much to be just a rebound thing. There was no way he could ever be just some transitional guy.

And there was another factor here. I needed to come clean with him.

I'd been less than honest about the canceling of my wedding. I'd let him think, for too long maybe, that Charles and I had to come to that decision mutually. Lucas went through hell because of what Julie did to him. I didn't want him finding out somewhere, way down the line, that I'd essentially done the same thing to Charles. Different circumstances, yes. Different outcomes, for sure yes. Charles was more about the wedding and the formality of it all than the actual marriage. But Lucas was an all-in kind of guy, and his breakup had wrecked him. So he needed to know from me how I'd really arrived in Monterey. It was time to own this.

I was still musing and muddling this over when his heartbeat sped up, and his breathing lightened. He was waking up. Just as I pasted a smile on, he opened his eyes.

"Hi," I whispered.

He grinned. "Hey there, chickie baby," he whispered back, wrapping his arms around me and cuddling me close. Warm. Sleep rumpled. Divine. "How'd you sleep?"

"Like a rock. You?"

"Pretty good, even through the snoring." He smirked, and I dug into his calves with my toes.

"I don't snore," I protested.

"Says everyone who snores." He laughed, flipping me over and kissing the exact center of my tummy before kissing a path on up to my neck. "You snore, Chlo."

I pushed on his shoulders, weakly. Because why would anyone stop this? "Shush."

"Funny, that's what I was saying about four thirty this morning."

"Really, shush." I laughed, wrapping my arms around his neck as he continued to kiss on me. Goose bumps broke out across my skin and my heart fluttered, so full this morning. Then he nudged his way between my legs and nudged against me, making not just my heart flutter.

I bit down on my lip, my body wanting to stop the words I needed to say. But before this went further, it was going to go from playful to primal in no time. I needed to say some things.

"Lucas," I said, trying to pull him up toward me.

"Mmm?" he replied, his lips tickling and sweet.

"We need to talk about a few things, before you leave tomorrow."

"You want to talk"—he pressed against me with a very specific part of his anatomy—"now?"

"Oh, boy . . . ohhh, yes . . . Wait—yes, we need to talk," I said, leaning up on my elbows so I could see him. I traced a hand across his face, running my thumb over his lips. "And then hopefully we can go right back to this right here," I said, lifting my hips slightly and bumping him right back.

"Talk fast, woman," he said, rolling off of me and resting his head on his elbow. His other hand, however, continued to roam.

Now I had the floor, and I didn't know where to start. Was I making too big of a deal of this? Should I just rip off the Band-Aid?

"Last night was . . . wow. I don't even have words for last night."

"You said some words last night," he murmured, his hand dipping just below the sheet and cupping my breast. My toes pointed. Literally. Reflex. He did it again, and the same thing happened. So much so that the sheets rustled. Lucas looked down toward the bottom of the bed, and touched me once more. Toe point. The scientist in him was delighted. Boob. Toe. Boob. Toe.

"This is an interesting phenomenon," he mused.

Meanwhile, I was coming out of my skin. "Could you—and I promise I will never say these words again—*please* stop touching me? It's hard to think straight when you do that."

He was a scientist, yes, but a boy first, so he touched me once more, then moved his hand safely above the sheets. "Best behavior, I promise."

"Anyway, so, yeah. Last night, amazing. And I'm hoping, I mean, when you get back from Belize, that there'll be more nights like that?"

"Um. Yeah," he said, grinning so big I thought his head was going to split.

*Band-Aid. Pull off the Band-Aid so you can get back to the boobs and toes.*

"I left Charles the morning of our wedding," I said in a rush, instantly feeling better for saying it. Looking down at my hands, I continued. "I had this sudden moment of clarity, and I panicked at the thought of getting married to someone I wasn't in love with, not truly crazy-in-love with, and I panicked and I ran. He never made it to the church, he was still on the golf course with his groomsmen when I ran, but I did in fact run."

I chanced a look up, saw that his smile had dimmed, and pressed on. "And then when I met you, I realized, holy fudge, we have so much in common, but holy fudge, Julie just did almost the same thing to you that I did to Charles, and there was no way I could tell you what I'd done. And it was all so new and fresh and raw, and I was just figuring out what I wanted to do up here, and if I could truly stay and live here, and then you and I started spending so much time together, and holy fudge, Lucas, you're the best, and we were spending so much time together and then my mom and dad were here, and I was so afraid something was going to come up about the wedding and you'd find out that way, and I knew it would be better coming from me and—"

"Better coming from you?" he asked, his voice quiet. The smile had twisted into a grimace.

"Yes. That I should be the one to tell you that I—"

"Left a guy at the altar," he finished, his voice rough.

"Not technically, but . . . yeah. Yeah, I did." I sighed, ashamed that I'd kept this from him for so long.

"So rather than tell me this, something that probably had a fairly logical explanation—I mean, people do break up all the time. I should know, right? But rather than tell me the truth, you let me go on about Julie and what she'd done to me?"

He kicked the covers off and rolled to his side of the bed, climbing out. Stabbing his legs into his jeans, he turned back to face me, anger blazing in his eyes. "I must look like such a fool to you."

"What? No—God no, Lucas," I said, shocked. I moved across the bed, kneeling up and reaching out to him. But he stood just out of arm's reach. "It's nothing like that. I—I—You're—"

He stared at me, hard. He seemed to be weighing something. "I gotta go," he said, eyes cold.

"What? No way! You have to stay; we have to talk about this," I cried, jumping off the bed and grabbing his arm before he could walk away.

"There's really nothing to talk about. You lied to me. I can't go through that again. I can't get involved with a girl who's lied to me since the beginning. I've gone down that road before."

"You think I'm the same as Julie?" I asked, horrified.

"Right now? I think you might be *exactly* the same as Julie—and I can't get suckered into that again."

He turned and left.

# chapter fourteen

The worst day ever was also the longest day ever, creeping by like frozen molasses. I spent the morning shoveling dog shit. I spent the better part of the afternoon on the phone with the local ASPCA, making sure that the dogs that were rescued from the ring yesterday were transferred to me once they were given the immediate medical care they needed and fully checked out. I'd need to call Lou in on this one too. I'd never handled this many dogs at once, and especially dogs that'd been bred for only one reason. Would they be able to be socialized? Would they be able to trust?

It didn't matter. Whether or not they were ultimately adoptable, they'd come here and not be on chains, not be in the cold, not be expected to fight and snarl and shred . . . They would only be expected to chase balls and gobble treats. That, I could promise every one of them.

By lunchtime, there was no call from Lucas. I gave him the space he clearly wanted. Whether it would be a forever kind of space . . . well . . . I wasn't thinking about that yet. I *couldn't* think about that. I went back over our conversation this morning, remembering the pain in his eyes when he realized that I'd lied to him.

And when I thought back, there were plenty of times when I could have told him the truth. I could have told him why I walked away from my wedding, and how it was a different situation from the one with Julie. He would have understood—of course he could have understood that. Oh, I had played this one very very wrong.

So for now, I waited. He'd said he *might* call, but I was choosing not to remember the *might*. Because if I thought about him leaving tomorrow without seeing me again and talking to me again, I'd lose my mind.

The early afternoon became late afternoon. I'd eaten a quick lunch, perhaps lingering in the doorway to my bedroom for two or twenty minutes. The bed was still messed up, pillows on the floor, comforter twisted into a ball at the bottom, and a very large dent in the middle where two entwined bodies had left their impression. The room smelled like sex. Weird and gross? No, naughty and naughty . . .

Fudge.

Dusk fell, and I still hadn't heard from Lucas. Should I call him? Should I bother him while he's probably packing and saying good-bye to his family?

I sat at the counter, chain-eating pudding for dinner. After the pudding, I paced. Sammy Davis Jr. paced with me for a while, but eventually he realized Mommy was nutso and went back to his bed by the fireplace.

By ten o'clock I'd finally had enough of the silence, and I grabbed my phone. Before I could dial, it rang in my hand. It was Lucas.

"Hey!" I said, a bit too enthusiastically.

"Hey," he answered back. His voice was curt. Chilly. My skin broke out into goose bumps.

"How was your day?" I asked. *This man was inside you less than twenty-four hours ago, and you're asking him how his day was?*

"Productive. Got everything packed up, signed off on things at the clinic—which is the reason I called."

"Oh?" I asked. Now he needed a reason for calling?

"I wanted to give you a heads-up about the fighting ring you discovered. It looks like charges of animal cruelty are being filed against the property owners. Since I'm leaving in the morning, the police came down today to ask me some questions, take some pictures, stuff like that. I didn't want you to be surprised when they call you too."

"Sure, okay," I said. Then a thought occurred to me. "I'm not in trouble for trespassing or something, am I?"

"No, you totally did the right thing in calling them. But promise me next time you wait for the authorities to get there before you go barging into some barn filled with fighting dogs. You were very lucky last night."

"I'll say," I replied softly. "I knew I should have waited, but—"

"I'd probably have done the same thing, but wait for the cavalry next time, okay?"

"I will," I agreed. "So . . . I know you said your dad was driving you to the airport in the morning, but . . ." My voice trailed off, hopeful. *Interrupt me! Ask me to take you to the airport!*

"But what?" he asked. He knew what I was *but whating*, but he wasn't going to let me off the hook.

My heart settled somewhere very low. Dark side of the duodenum low. "So, I guess I won't see you before you leave," I managed.

"The day just got away from me." His voice sounded careful, cautious.

"Twelve weeks. That's a long time."

"Chloe," he said. But then he said no more.

Usually, any silence between us was comfortable. This silence was heavy and dark, and I didn't like it one bit.

"Can I call you?" I finally asked. "While you're down there?"

"Not sure how great the cell reception is down there."

"Didn't you get an international plan?" I asked.

"Yeah, I did." Translation: he didn't want me to call him. "Listen, I've still got some stuff to do before bed, so I just wanted to make sure you knew they'd be contacting you about the dogs, okay?"

"Yeah," I said, gripping the phone hard. "Lucas, I'm so sorry that—"

"Chloe, just don't—okay? I can't get into all this. Not before I go," he said, sounding so tired. "I'm sure I'll see you when I get back."

Oh my God. This was so very bad. "Yeah, okay, Lucas. Be careful down there, okay?"

"Will do. You too. I mean it about waiting for the cavalry next time, Chloe."

"Sure," I said, my throat all lumpy.

"Bye," he said, and that was it.

Ten minutes later I was still pacing around my living room, trying to decide whether I should call him back, when my phone rang. "Thank God," I muttered, racing to pick it up.

But it wasn't Lucas. It was Charles.

"Hello?" I asked, stunned. We hadn't spoken in weeks, other than a quick phone call about sending back some gifts.

"Hi, Chloe, how are you?" he asked.

"Uh, I'm good. You?"

"Good—great, actually. How are things up north? Your mom told me about the ranch you started up there—a charity for stray dogs?"

"Kind of. I run a rescue shelter for abandoned pit bulls."

"Ah. Interesting."

"Did you need something?" I asked. It was almost eleven o'clock. Why were we making small talk; what was going on? Weird.

"I do need something, actually: your signature."

"On what?"

"Your name is still on my life insurance, and we need to get that switched over."

"No way. I'll just kill you and retire."

There was silence, then he laughed. And just like that, we moved into normal. As normal as you could be with an ex-fiancé.

"Sure, I'll sign whatever you want. Just email it and I'll turn it around."

"Notarize it, please."

"Fancy," I said. "So who's your new beneficiary?"

"My new fiancée, actually. I'm getting married in six weeks."

"What? Wow!" I sat down in surprise. "Who's the lucky girl? Anyone I know?"

"Becky Von Stuffling."

"I've never met her, but I'm sure she's lovely."

"She *is* lovely, and quite fun." His voice sounded light. Hopeful. Intoxicated. "And a little bit twisted."

"Twisted? Heavens, not that." I laughed. "Is this the part where I say I'm happy for you?"

"Only if you really are."

I flashed on all the good times I'd had with Charles; we used to laugh a lot. He was stuffy and pretentious, without a doubt. But he was a kind, decent man, and he deserved someone better suited for him. "I *am* happy for you, Charles. Very happy."

"I was really angry with you, Chloe."

"I know," I whispered, my eyes filling with tears. I did what I had to do for myself, but I did leave a pretty big mess behind me. "I'm so sorry for what I did to you."

"At the time it didn't make any sense to me, but now I see that it was for the best. As mad and embarrassed as I was, it really was the best thing," he said softly.

I nodded, even though he couldn't see me. "Send me whatever you need to, and I'll get it right back to you." I sniffled a little. "And congratulations, Charles."

"Thanks. Bye."

I said good-bye and hung up. In a way, it felt like the last piece of the puzzle had fallen into place. He had finally moved on, and it was all truly over.

I was now the opposite of the woman I very nearly became: the kind of woman who would marry a man she wasn't entirely sure she was in love with, just for the security, for the good life. For the *supposed* good life.

I'd created my own good life, up on this ranch with a bunch of crazy dogs. And, Sinatra connection fully acknowledged, I did it my way. And I'd made my own bed before I chose to share it with someone new. Except I had hurt that someone—the last person I wanted to hurt.

I looked at the phone, then looked away. I picked up the phone, then put it down. I scrolled through to find his name . . .

then turned it off. He was getting on a plane in a few hours. The last thing he needed was me crashing through right now.

I went to bed, curled up in the sheets that still smelled like us, and tossed and turned all night.

At 5 A.M., I finally got up, threw on some clothes, got in my car, and headed for Monterey Regional Airport.

I was crashing through.

# chapter fifteen

I had zero plan. I had no idea what I was going to do or what I was going to say. All I knew was that I was barreling toward the tiny Monterey airport wearing Lucas' shirt, old jeans, and a nervous grin.

I slalomed through the few cars that were out at this hour, driving way too fast through the morning fog. I didn't know what airline, I didn't know where he was connecting through; all I knew was that he was on some six thirty flight that I was bound and determined to . . . to what?

Hell, I'd figure that part out when I got there. When I saw him—the only person I'd thought about since I got off the phone with my past the night. And after being able to finally, amicably part with my past, I knew that I wanted only one person for my future.

I pulled into short-term parking, grabbed a ticket, and ran for the main terminal. I pushed through a throng of travelers, and spied a familiar face.

"Dr. Campbell!" I cried out, breathing heavily. The chocolate pudding hoard was beginning to take its toll; my cardio was crap. I ran on, pushing through the stitch of pudding in my side. "Dr. Campbell!"

"Chloe?" he called back. "What are you doing here?"

"Lucas . . . Is he . . . still here? I need . . . I need . . . Crap, I need to start jogging . . . again . . . Lucas?"

"He just went through security," Lucas's dad said, looking confused. "Are you okay?"

Dammit! I looked toward the space beyond the huge security line, but didn't see him. Dammit again. "Yeah," I said, still searching. "I just wanted to see him before he left, and tell him—"

There! Right there, a redhead above all the others! Six foot three, remember?

"Lucas!" I shouted, and took off in a sprint. Barreling toward security, I saw him look around, as confused as his father.

"Chloe?"

I didn't care that he'd already gone through security and was still holding his shoes; I just ran. I didn't even see the other passengers. I also didn't see the TSA agent coming for me as True Love attempted to trump Homeland Security.

For the record, it does not.

Suddenly a scanning wand was waving in front of my face. "Just where do you think you're going?" an irritated voice asked. The TSA agent, a rather large woman, was standing there with one hand holding her wand, the other hand on her can of . . . ah, shit . . . mace.

"Sorry, so sorry, I was just trying to get . . . his! His attention!" I jumped up and down again, pointing to Lucas on the other side of the glass partition. I could see him, he could see me, but there was an entire line of people, the X-ray machine, and the TSA staff between us. "Sorry, I just have to tell him that I . . . That I . . ."

The agent frowned at me. "Ma'am, do you have an airline ticket?"

"No, I'm not going anywhere. I just need to tell him—"

"Ma'am, then you can't be down here," she said, starting to turn me around. Her walkie-talkie went off, and she said into it, "I've got it. She just wants to talk to some dude who already went through. Nope, it's under control." She looked back at me. "Ma'am, do you have any idea what you did?"

"Yes, I cut ahead of some people in line. I know it was rude of me—"

"You cut ahead of some people in line at an *airport*. You came running at the security entrance, screaming your head off, at an *airport*. You looked like you were going to try to crash through a federal security checkpoint *at an airport*," she said, her tone getting more and more serious. "It wasn't rude—it was incredibly stupid."

"Oh my God," I moaned.

Lucas, standing there with a "what the fudge" look on his face, called, "Are you okay?"

"I think so?" I called back, then turned to the TSA agent. I snuck a quick peek at her name tag. Standing tall, shoulders squared, one foot posed slightly in front of the other, I gave her my best smile. "Monica—can I call you Monica?"

"Where is this going?" she asked, looking at me like I was a little crazy.

I couldn't blame her, but pressed on. "Monica, I'd like to thank you for your service to our fine country. It makes my heart proud to see such a strong female protecting our airports, here in the great state of California and around our nation. As a former Miss Golden State, and a lifetime resident of California, I've had the great privilege of visiting all parts of our beautiful state, often by air travel. And every time I have, I'm always so grateful for the tireless work that you, and all of your highly trained and competent coworkers, do every day to keep us safe. So, thanks for the warning, and let's keep California and America flying high," I finished, beaming at her.

Several of the other TSA agents had leaned in to listen as well, and I shared my winning smile with them all.

"Sweetie, you feeling okay?" she asked, patting me on the shoulder.

"Truth?" I asked, still smiling.

"Oh, I think you'd better."

"See that guy, the redheaded dude?" I pointed.

"Louis?"

"Well, Lucas, but yes."

"Uh-huh?"

"I finally slept with him two nights ago, and I really messed things up, and I just adore him and he's leaving for Belize for twelve weeks, and I told him something that really hurt him, and I just can't let him leave without telling him something else: that I actually lo— And, well . . . that's when you stopped me with your wand."

"Uh-huh." She nodded, looking me over carefully, then said into her walkie-talkie that she was escorting someone to check-point C.

I looked at her warily. "Is that bad? Is checkpoint C where you take—"

"Just walk with me, sweetie," she said, rolling her eyes.

We approached the glass wall, Lucas following on his side, still looking confused, and we walked along the edge until we came to the baggage claim area—where people could walk out, but not in.

There was another agent sitting there, and she stood up when we walked over.

"Stephanie, why don't you take your break," my agent said. "I've got this for a while."

The other agent nodded and ambled off.

Settling herself behind the podium, Monica spotted Lucas waiting on the other side, backpack in hand, looking very worried.

"Hey, Louis! C'mere! Your girl wants to talk to you," she shouted, waving him over.

When he arrived, she said, "Okay, Louis, this girl wants to talk to you bad enough she almost committed a federal crime to do it. Although now that I get a look at you, I can almost understand," she said, appraising him. Turning to me, she said, "What's your name, sweetie?"

"Chloe. Chloe Patterson."

"Uh-huh. I'll remember that. Okay, Chloe Patterson. Hit it."

I started to walk forward, and she raised her hand. "Don't make me get my mace out. Without a boarding pass, you can't go past this line." She pointed to the red line on the linoleum floor.

"Chloe, what the hell's going on?" Lucas asked.

I walked up to the line, keeping my toes just on it, and when my TSA agent nodded, I took a deep breath.

"I'm so sorry to do this right before your trip. And I'm so sorry to have been such an idiot the other morning, after we . . . well . . . after that amazing night."

"Chloe, I—"

"No no, let me say this."

"Let her say this, Louis," Monica said.

We both looked sideways at her, then I pressed on. "I don't want to be your rebound."

"Oh, you've got to be kidding—"

"Louis!" she yelled, and he held up his hands.

"The other night was incredible, and I want every night to

be like that. You're sweet and kind and wonderful and funny and you let me eat pudding. Which I need to stop doing, because I almost couldn't run through this airport."

He just stood there, jaw clenching. But he was listening, so I rushed forward.

"And I don't care that you're leaving for twelve weeks, but I want to be here waiting for you when you come back. And I don't want you meeting any pretty young veterinarians down there just because I didn't tell you what I should have told you before."

I looked at my TSA agent for courage, and she nodded.

I took a deep breath and looked into those gorgeous blue eyes. "I don't want to be your rebound. I just want to be yours. And I'm so, so sorry for not telling you sooner about the way that I left Charles. I should have and it was stupid of me not to. I lied to you and I hate that I hurt you, when that's the last thing you deserve. Because you—" My breath caught, and my throat got tight. "You're it for me." Then I crunched my eyes closed, because I couldn't bear to look at him anymore. Because if he didn't want me to be his . . .

"Chloe," he said, and I opened one eye.

"I . . ." I held my breath. "Can't."

I opened the other eye, not entirely sure what he'd just said.

"I just can't do this." He shook his head. "I appreciate you coming down here, really I do. But I just can't have another woman lying to me again. I'm sorry."

And as they called his flight, final boarding, he gave me a thin *sorry* smile, and ran for his plane.

"But, I came to the airport," I said, mostly to myself.

"What did you lie to him about?" Monica asked.

"Just one thing, but it was a big thing." I sighed, wrapping my arms around myself. I can't believe he was leaving. I thought for sure if I poured my heart out, he'd . . . he'd . . .

"You thought if you came down here and spilled your guts and apologized, he'd sweep you off your feet and kiss you stupid?"

"Something like that," I admitted, not seeing even a flash of red hair in the crowd. He was well and truly gone.

"You've been watching too many romantic comedies," Monica said. "Come back in twelve weeks. Maybe he'll have cooled down by then."

"Thanks," I said, turning to leave.

"And Chloe Patterson?" she called, and I looked over my shoulder. "You ever try something like this again, and I'm going to redline you. You don't want that, believe me."

I nodded, my head feeling like it weighed a thousand pounds, and headed back toward the ticketing area. Where Dr. Campbell senior was waiting for me.

"Well, that was embarrassing," he offered.

"You saw that?" I asked.

"Chloe, it's a small regional airport. Everyone saw it."

"Great," I croaked, shaking my head. What a mess.

"Just give it some time," he said kindly. "Things like this have a way of working out." He started walking me out of the terminal. "By the way, I got a call about those dogs from the other night. Looks like we'll be able to place them all with you by the middle of next week . . ."

I let him lead me out to the parking lot, numb.

"I can't believe someone would bring a pit bull to a dog park. That's just asking for trouble," the woman said, sounding outraged.

"I know, how irresponsible! I'm amazed that dog hasn't tried to maul any of the other dogs. I've been keeping my Pekingese close to me, in case anything happens."

"That's a good idea. Those dogs are so vicious, I'm just wait-ing for that one to—"

"Ladies?" I said. "The dog you're talking about is my dog, and yes, he's a pit bull. If you can believe it, his last owner left him chained outside to a tree, with no food and hardly any water, for days at a time. Yet unbelievably, he still loves humans, no matter how horrendously they've treated him. And Sammy Davis Jr.— that's his name, by the way—has never once even nipped at another dog, even when they're climbing all over him like that Chihuahua's doing right now."

The two ladies were clad head to toe in Lululemon, their hair in perfect ponytails, makeup flawless, nails shiny, not an ounce of chocolate pudding anywhere on their thighs or tummies.

I wanted to tell them to shut their stupid faces. I wanted to tell them that there's no such thing a bad dog, only bad owners. I wanted to tell them to stop talking about things they knew nothing about.

What I said was, "I'd love for you to meet him; he's the sweet-est guy. Would that be okay? I'll hold the leash; no pressure."

Because that was how you changed a heart and a mind. In-dividual experiences. Common sense. Common ground. And that big pageant smile never failed to do the trick.

They looked at each other, then looked at me unenthusiasti-cally. "Um, sure. But he's not going to, like, rip my little Bobo to shreds, is he?" one of them asked, arching a perfectly manicured brow.

"No, ma'am, I can promise you your Bobo will be just fine."

They looked at each other once more, then nervously nod-ded at me.

"Sammy Davis Jr.!" I called out, and my own slice of golden-eyed, brindled gorgeous looked up from a spirited game of "can't catch me" with two huskies. He came bounding across the sand, tongue hanging out, doggie grin spread wide across his face.

"Good boy," I said, letting him lick my hand. "Sit." He obeyed instantly, calm even though he'd been racing through the surf seconds ago. He gazed up at me, jowls falling back from his face, creating an even wider grin that never failed to make me laugh out loud. "Sweet boy, I've got some new friends for you to meet."

I spoke in a low tone to him, as I always did. He was incredibly smart, always in tune with me, and eager to please.

The two women were cringing back slightly, but one looked more interested than the other did. She'd be the one I'd win over first.

"Do you want to pet him?" I asked, smiling again.

"Yeah, sure. I guess," she mumbled, reaching out with a tentative hand. Sammy Davis leaned in to sniff, as dogs do, and she jerked back a bit.

"It's always good to let any strange dog smell you first, before you pet them. That's it, perfect," I coaxed, as she reached out again. This time she held still as he gave her another sniff, nuzzling into her palm.

"He loves to have his ears scratched," I said, and as he lowered his head for her, she reached around and began to pet his head, eventually scratching his ears a bit. His tail thumped contentedly on the sand as he watched his friends run and play on the beach.

This was our favorite dog run, a place Sammy and I came at least once a week. We always changed up the time and day, to make sure we interacted with as many new people and dogs as we could. It was good for him, it was good for me, and it was great for everyone else to see this beautiful dog playing with everyone else and their dogs.

Sammy Davis Jr. had become the unofficial mascot of Our

Gang, and my best friend. He spent every night in the house with me and several other dogs that rotated from the barn into the house to continue their socialization skills.

Three months after opening its gate, Our Gang had successfully placed 90 percent of the original gang, with new dogs coming in every week. We'd had three more litters of pups from moms who came to us already pregnant, and placed every single one of them with new families. Only a handful of the dogs still had trouble with kids and other small dogs, something that was just a fact of life when animals were mistreated so horrendously in their earlier lives. But instead of being euthanized, or worse, left out on the street, they'd live out the rest of their lives on a ranch in Monterey. There are worse places to reside.

Clark and Viv had come down to adopt their puppy, and were only days away from their own delivery. They knew what they were having, but it was "mum's the word" until he or she arrived. They'd adopted a lovely dog, pure gray-blue with smoky blue eyes. They named him Lancelot—something about a knight? No matter, they were smitten, and that dog rode home in the front seat of a giant 1950s convertible, looking very regal.

And speaking of mum's the word, my mother, in a twist of fate I could never have predicted, had fallen head-over-heels in love with an old black and white dog named Sally. Missing an ear and walking with a limp, she'd come to us as a stray, almost starved to death. But a kinder soul I'd never met. She helped to wrangle the younger dogs, she sat patiently with the sick ones that came to us, and she was always the first one into the yard each day, and the last one back in the barn after herding in any stragglers for the night.

When my mother was visiting one weekend, I'd put her to work helping me clean out the stalls in the barn. Initially, she'd regarded everything with an upturned nose and a when-will-this-be-over attitude. But after about an hour, every time I turned around, I noticed that Sally was right next to my mother, and my mother seemed to be sneaking her something from her Talbots-inspired overalls. I finally caught her with some leftover turkey bacon, and suggested that she take Sally on a walk around the property, that she needed some exercise on that bad leg.

My mother came back an hour later, enraptured, and told me that no one was allowed to adopt Sally. Because she was taking her home with her the following day. Later on that afternoon, with Sally and Sammy Davis Jr. asleep by the fireplace, my mother and I had a traditional English tea, with tiny cucumber sandwiches, clotted cream, and about a barrel full of tears. She talked, I talked, and she told me she was . . . proud of me.

She also told me that if Lucas and I ever got married, we should elope.

Lucas.

Sigh.

Bad kind of sigh.

I hadn't heard from him the entire time he was in Belize. I kept a few tabs on him through the news service that was Marge. He was due home sometime next week, but I didn't know when I'd see him, *if* I'd see him. I'd sent him a few emails but none were replied to. I'd tried everything I knew to do, and it was still radio silence. When he'd said "I can't," he really meant it. I had to respect that.

"How long since you've had him?"

"Eleven weeks—it was eleven weeks ago." I sighed sadly.

"Pardon me?"

"Sorry, what?" I asked, coming back from Planet Lucas to the dog park, where the two women were staring at me as though I'd grown a third eyeball.

"I asked, how long you've had him? Sammy Davis Jr.?" one

of the women asked, still kneeling down and petting my very contented dog.

"Oh! Sorry, daydreaming a little. I got Sammy when—" And I launched into my tale.

Twenty minutes later I was standing on the water's edge, letting the waves tickle my toes as Sammy splashed and played. I'd given out two business cards for Our Gang. One of the women was still a little standoffish, but the other seemed genuinely interested in coming by and seeing the dogs we had up for adoption, having been won over by my sweet boy.

"You did great today, buddy," I murmured as he nudged at my knees, threading between them and looking up at me, grinning. "You ready for your ball?" As he watched eagerly, I tossed it up in the air a few times, then threw it out into the water.

But instead of chasing the ball, he craned his head around behind me, sniffing the wind. His tail began to thump wildly, banging against the back of my legs.

I turned to see what he was looking at. People. Dogs. More dogs. But he was still sniffing something. Before I could catch him, he took off like a shot toward the fence, aiming for the gate where everyone came in and out.

"Crazy dog," I said, chuckling as I made my way back up to where he was barking happily. "Sammy, what are you—"

I stopped short. Because there, on the other side of the fence, was my daydream. Deeply tanned, dressed casually in jeans and a black T-shirt, Lucas was pushing through the gate to greet Sammy Davis Jr., who was bouncing and jumping with happiness. He bent down to greet the dog, and when he stood up again I was struck again with how gorgeous this man was. Long and lean and breathing sex—eleven weeks in my imagination had not done him justice. It was all I could do not to literally run down the beach and throw myself into his arms, romance-novel style.

But I'd tried that before, done the grand gesture at the airport, and knew how that ended up. So I approached, but with caution. "What are you doing—"

I was cut off by his mouth covering mine in a slow, wet, burning, and churning kiss. He finally pulled back, hands clutching at my hips. Finishing my earlier question, "—here?" prompted him to kiss me again. Harder. Longer. Deeper. Tonguier.

This time, I managed to break the kiss and looked up into his face. "What's happening here?"

"I came home early."

"I'm getting that, but why are you—"

"I spent eleven weeks working twenty-hour days, because unless I was busy or sleeping, I was thinking about you. And even when I was sleeping I didn't catch a break, because I'd dream about you."

"Dreaming about me?"

"Yeah. Mostly naked." He nodded, sliding his hands a little higher, just under the edge of my T-shirt. "Although once you were wearing a snowsuit while trying to paddleboard in the middle of the ocean. That was one of the weirder ones."

"Okay, just wait a minute. You leave for eleven weeks without a phone call, without an email, after I humiliated myself in an airport—and now you show up and make out with me, without one shred of explanation?"

"I needed some space. I took some space." He tilted my chin up to place one single soft kiss on my lips. "And I don't want space anymore. I want you."

*Oh!*

"I had a whole speech planned out, saying how sorry I was that I didn't call you back while I was gone, that I know you're nothing like Julie and I was a real shit to say that before I left, that I missed you like crazy. But when I saw you, I just wanted to kiss you. So I did. Thanks for not slugging me, by the way."

"I was too surprised to slug you. Plus, the kissing was nice," I said, fighting the urge to bury my hands in his hair and do it again. Talk first. More kissing, after?

"It *was* nice," he repeated, and the look in his eyes had me clenching my hands into fists to stop them from pulling his face down to mine.

"But what about what I did to Charles? And not telling you?" I asked.

"Are you ever going to lie to me again?" he asked, his eyes searching.

"Big ones like that? No. Little white ones about things like how much pudding I really have hidden away? I can't promise that."

"Good enough for me."

"Are you sure? Really? Because—"

I was cut off once more by his amazing mouth. Why the *hell* was I trying to talk him out of this? I gave my hands the All Clear and they sank deep into his hair, pulling him into me, holding him, loving him. When we finally came up for air, he tucked me into his chest and I burrowed in, surrounded by Lucas. "I'm so glad you're home."

"I missed my girl," he murmured, his hands wide on the small of my back to capture as much skin as he could.

"To be clear, that's me, right?"

"Only you, chickie baby," he said with a chuckle. And then he kissed me again.

"*I've tried so, not to give in . . .*"

"Boy, I'll say."

"Oh, shush," I said.

An hour later, with a record on the turntable and Sammy Davis Jr. occupied on the patio, I lay naked on top of an equally naked Lucas, breathing heavily and unable to wipe the grin from my face.

*"I've said to myself, this affair never will go so well . . ."*

"Have you been listening to this since we met?" Lucas asked. "Is that why you didn't kiss me in the barn that day? Fucking Troublemaker Sinatra. You totally should have kissed me in the barn. Think how much longer we could have been doing . . . oh man, do that again."

"I would if you'd just shush already."

*"So why should I try to resist, when darling I know so well . . ."*

"No way, chickie baby. No way I could have resisted you another second."

"Let's be clear: it was *me* who attacked *you*. In the shower. With the naked."

"Are we playing Clue?"

"You really want to talk about board games right now?"

"No. Not when I'd rather . . ."

"Mmm, Lucas . . ."

*"I've got you under my skin . . ."*


An indeterminate time later . . .

"I want to tell you something," I said.

"Is it a list of all the things you've been thinking of doing to me for the last eleven weeks?"

"Um, no."

"Oh."

"Wait, do *you* have a list?"

"Oh, I've got a list." He laughed, moving his hands down to

my bottom, grabbing a handful and squeezing. Which made me squeeze some other parts that might still be wrapping around some of *his* parts, and oh my. He groaned, his breath warming the hollow of my throat, his teeth nipping lightly now at the tops of my breasts.

"Hey, I wanted to tell you something!" I protested, sitting up a little. Which was not a smart thing to do, because as soon as my breasts were on full view again, his eyes widened. And something else hardened further. My eyes crossed a little bit. He was still inside me, you see. And oh, my.

"Tell me whatever you want; just keep bouncing on my dick like that." He sighed, thrusting up ever so slightly.

"I love you," I said simply. Watching his face.

He froze. Midthrust. Such control. "I really wish I hadn't said something as crass as 'keep bouncing on my dick' right before you said that."

"Well, if you *had* known what I was going to say, what would you have said?" I asked, nervously chewing at my bottom lip.

A slow smile began to spread across his face. "I love you first."

I shook my head. "You love me second. I said it first."

"But you just gave me a time travel option. In which case *I* would have said it first, instead of the dick bouncing."

"Yes, but I *technically* said it first."

"What if I told you that when I said 'keep bouncing on my dick,' it was really code for 'I love you?'"

I grinned. "If that's the case, then you're gonna love what 'let me sit on your face' is really code for."

"Jesus Christ, Chloe."

"Ring a ding ding." I laughed.

"I love you. I love you. I love you," he told me.

So I bounced, right into my own happy ending.

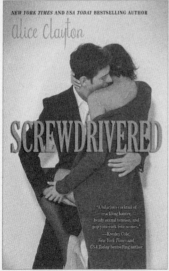